W9-BKA-521

The Inhabited World

The Inhabited World

David Long

Houghton Mifflin Company

BOSTON • NEW YORK • 2006

Library of Congress Cataloging-in-Publication Data
Long, David, date.
   The inhabited world / David Long.
         p. cm.
   ISBN-13: 978-0-618-54335-9
   ISBN-10: 0-618-54335-X
   1. Puget Sound Region (Wash.) — Fiction. 2. Suicide victims — Fiction. 3. Home ownership — Fiction. 4. Haunted houses — Fiction. 5. Single women — Fiction. I. Title.
   PS3562.O4924I54 2006
   813'.54 — dc22   2005020061

Book design by Melissa Lotfy
Typeface is Fairfield

Printed in the United States of America

QUM 10 9 8 7 6 5 4 3 2 1

"I heard a fly buzz," reprinted by permission of the publishers and Trustees of Amherst College from *The Poems of Emily Dickinson,* Thomas H. Johnson, ed. Cambridge, Mass.: Belknap Press of Harvard University Press, copyright © 1951, 1955, 1979, 1983 by the President and Fellows of Harvard College.

Montana and Jackson

A great calm stole over him. Great calm is an exaggeration.
He felt better. The end of a life is always vivifying.

— SAMUEL BECKETT, *Malone Dies*

The Inhabited World

Evan Patrick Molloy

WHEN HE LOOKS at his hand, he sees the hand he remembers—ropy branching veins, a ridge of waxy skin on the inside of the wrist where he fumbled a glowing iron rod at his father's forge one afternoon in 1966. When he looks at his legs in their rumpled khakis or their attenuated shadows crossing the ground, when he looks in a mirror, it's his own long angular face he sees, palpable enough, a three-day beard, the familiar blue-gray eyes with lush black lashes (often mentioned by women: *Swear to god, Evan, if I had lashes like yours*), the same sandy hair, a decent haircut grown out, and under it the skull, walled city of the brain, miraculously intact.

Day and night, he navigates around the house and yard, seeing what there is to see, taking stock. As often as he's made this circuit, he's not sick of it; being sick of things is no longer in his repertoire—it's as if the exact site of boredom in his brain has been drilled out. When he reaches the property line, he stops. Why not keep walking, another step, shoe on gravel? But a force like gravity keeps him here—the farther he gets from the house, the weaker his resolve to leave it. And he doesn't exactly *take* steps now. It's more like he's in one spot, then another. Not so different from the way he used to move in dreams, the constant pummeling dislocations: *this, this, this*. Except now it's not jarring and requires no more effort than progressing from one frame of film to the next. Which also explains how he can sit in a chair, or for that matter stand on solid ground, yet pass through walls and floors. The answer: He *doesn't* pass through anything, just (though the mechanics of it elude him) places himself on the other side.

The year is 2002; it's a summer's day, breezy and cloudless. Shielding his eyes, Evan stands in the rutted lane that marks the far edge of this irregular lot he once owned. He looks out across the snarls of blackberry vine where the hill drops away, over the tiled roofs and chimney caps and glinting antennas. Puget Sound is slate blue, crowned in whitecaps. He watches the silent progression of tankers and container ships—Maersk, Hanjin. People at work. Gulls sail past, whisked sideways by the wind. He takes his hand from his eyes, buries it in his pocket, moves along.

The fact is, he can no more remember the gunshot than he can his birth. It was a rainy afternoon in February. Ten years ago, 1992. That's all he can say. The day itself is mostly blank, a stubborn gap in the record. It's the same for the gray weeks leading him there, a chain of minor actions and omissions, cramped thoughts, sickness. Now and then a new fact works free and bubbles up, a new image to wonder at, teasing him, telling him that what he craves to know is not altogether lost, only out of reach; more will come in due time. What's "due time" to a man in his position? When he's ready, it must mean.

What he does remember is the constant rain, water ringing in the downspout, a metallic sound that might've been hypnotic and soothing, but wasn't. Sleep had become a pool so shallow it barely covered him. He'd undress and lie down, exhausted, but wouldn't have taken more than a few dozen unencumbered breaths before it began to drain, exposing him to consciousness again. Afraid of disturbing Claudia, he'd started using a daybed downstairs in the room he called his office. Only later, after she and her daughter had left, did he methodically seal its one tall window with tinfoil and begin twisting pink paraffin plugs into his ears before bed: sounds bored into him, background noise wouldn't stay in the background. He didn't so much wake as finally admit that he'd *been* awake, hours maybe—no longer was there much of a dividing line between what he dreamed and thoughts he'd ground away at, semiconscious. He'd been given sleeping pills—they worked at first, then didn't. If he multiplied the dose, he woke late but unrefreshed, with all the ambition of a Raggedy Andy. There was another kind that messed up his inner ear, and one that wore off at four in the morning.

But now when daylight comes, Evan's waiting in an east-facing dormer or out back in the wet grass. The dread is gone. There's no more of that *Aw, Christ, what time is it—?* If the sky's clear, sunlight spills through the hemlocks and twisty madronas on the ridge. He and Claudia often walked there, the curls of papery madrona bark crackling underfoot. The flies will already be up, spits of shadow against the white shed. The first thermals will stir, the first few songbirds, the first crow. If it's socked in, he'll hear the foghorns—long blast, then short, short, rumbling his rib cage, sending flurries of gooseflesh down the insides of his arms.

He remembers the sore jaw muscles, the sore clenched muscles where his rib cage met his stomach, cramping from hours of unconscious bearing down, and the cords at the base of his skull— he could almost feel them thrumming like heavy steel cables. He remembers his temper, trivial outbursts, the heel of his hand thumping the car's steering wheel, the office door rebounding with an almost musical *whang*. He'd never been hotheaded as a kid—excitable, sure, but no knot of frustration. And his voice, so mopey and self-sick toward the end. Even at the time, though, whining, ripping into Claudia for no reason, he'd known how he sounded—it was as if part of him were listening from backstage, perplexed, wondering what his big gripe was.

He'd love to know if he had put the gun to his mouth more than once. Made a dry run. It would've been like him to do that. Or had he meant to go through with it but stalled long enough for part of him to start cajoling like a Good Samaritan, *Look, don't, OK? C'mon, lower your arm?* (Funny how he was always talking about parts of himself.) Maybe he *had* lowered his arm; maybe he'd survived that moment. But whatever he said to himself, or failed to say, he hadn't rid the house of the gun. He'd let it stay.

Ironically, he'd never owned so much as a cap pistol; after returning from the war in the Pacific, his father would have absolutely nothing to do with firearms. No, the gun had belonged to Claudia, pressed on her by her second husband, who'd worried about her when he traveled and insisted she take instruction at a firing range. She hadn't minded squeezing off rounds at the paper targets, she told Evan—anything Claudia did, she was driven to do well. But she never liked having a weapon around— felt *less* safe, if anything. Nonetheless, it had come with her to this house on Madrona Street. Evan is positive they discussed what to do with it, but clearly no decision was reached. In the meantime, the gun had been stored on a high shelf in the cellar, swaddled in a blue T-shirt inside a steel canister, with gnarled picture-frame wire wound again and again through the hasp in lieu of a padlock.

He'd love to see himself going down the stairs to the basement, the look in his eyes. He'd love to know what he'd been doing just before that, what he'd thought as he woke that morning. But there's no black box, no indestructible tape to rewind. Just memory—impaired, fluky, with a will of its own. What he does know: He's steeped in aftermath, as changed as steam is from water, as water from ice.

The Life of Riley

ONE MORNING, the first summer of this new life, Evan spotted an orange tiger cat nosing its way out of the blackberries. Not the world's sleekest cat, nor the best groomed, but its face was wide and intelligent, and it stepped along with a certain panache. Evan knelt. The cat approached, brushed its flanks against his trouser leg, one side, then the other.

He couldn't help thinking of Riley, the aging rat catcher his father used to let winter at the iron shop. Donovan Molloy, the hard-ass. Chatted up the cat as if he were an emeritus member of the crew, fed him canned salmon he got from a buddy at the fishery, overlooked the fact that Riley crapped in clean sand they needed for the forge.

Evan stroked the orange cat's nape, petting absently, removing pelletlike burs from the coat. He spoke softly—*Only a few more, be still, good, good*—until it occurred to him that, given what he understood about his situation, he shouldn't be able to touch the animal or have his voice acknowledged. He withdrew his hand. Yellow cat hairs drifted from it, settling to the dry grass.

He and the cat eyed each other. You too? each thought.

So, kind of a revelation. And ever since, when Evan hears the crows jabbering from the power lines, or notices a possum traipsing along, or stares up a hover of wasps, he has to wonder which sort they are.

He often spies the tiger cat on its rounds, keeping to the dry mulch along the house's foundation in bad weather, drowsing away summer heat in the root hollow of a cedar. He's watched it go through the motions of squatting and trying to paw dirt. Once he saw the cat's tail fatten at the sight of an all-gray cutting through a gap in the azaleas, but the gray obviously saw nothing, smelled nothing, flinched not at all when the tiger gave a warning swipe.

The power of habit, Evan thought.

But what consolation, having the orange tiger here. Riley II. A chink out of Evan's vast solitude.

Except—and this is both puzzling and strangely unsettling—it's been more than a month since he's laid eyes on the cat. Repeatedly, he's gone about the property checking the usual hideouts, calling, *Hey, Spook, hey, boy,* listening for the telltale rattle of tags. No dice. Riley's sphere of operation isn't as limited as his own: He could be blocks away, superintending god-knows-what. Still, he's never not come for so long.

What to make of it?

Maureen

EARLIER THIS YEAR, in the dregs of winter—drenching rains, wind whipping off the water—a Mayflower van bumped over the curb, backed up the gravel drive, the big flat doors swung open, and in less than five hours, the Fessendens were out. Evan expected the FOR SALE sign to be hoisted again, but instead the house stood vacant. Free newspapers landed on the porch—the rain soaked them, they dried to parchment, then were soaked again. Light came and went across the bare floors; the taps dripped.

The Fessendens had been hard on the house. The walls were pocked and dinged; the trim had a beat-up look. A few knobs and drawer pulls were gone as well as an entire ceiling fixture in one of the bedrooms, leaving only bare copper wire curling from the box overhead. The linoleum by the kitchen stove had grooves scorched into it from the night the CorningWare plates exploded on a hot burner. Ellie Fessenden was always wrapped up in some school-related business. Field trips in the van, extra-credit math puzzles, chaperone duty. Plus the kids all swam—the house always had the vague smell of bleach from towels drying on a rack in the cellar or wadded in half-open gym bags. Mack Fessenden wasn't handy with tools and was a little scattered anyway, not much on home repair. But everyone got along. They were a happy lot for the most part. Despite the wear and tear, Evan didn't bear them the slightest ill will. He soon missed the commotion, the silliness and generosity. Their absence seemed to swell and fill every inch of the place. He went room to room, inspecting, compiling his inventory of things he'd fix if he could. Then outside, the shed, the yard. Some things he'd leave as they were—the bare spot in the grass where the wiffle-ball pitcher had stood, and another for the batter. Down under the blackberry vines were innumerable wiffle balls—also golf balls, tennis balls, hard-rubber dog balls, and one hideless softball wrapped in duct tape.

In early spring, a woman appeared, a friend of the Fessendens, perhaps, or friend of a friend, someone to housesit or rent cheaply—Evan couldn't tell what the precise arrangement was or how long it was meant to last. She was in her late thirties, he guessed. Slender, fair but abundantly freckled, with a hook-nose (what Donovan Molloy would call a *real goddamn blade*). Her hair was copper red, cropped—a boy's haircut, the knobby vertebrae in her neck showing as she bent to the sink. He wondered if she'd cut it herself and watched to see whether she'd go after it again with the scissors, but instead she let it grow.

He watched as a college boy with an unmarked step van and a hand truck wrestled in the bigger items. The rest of the weekend she worked alone, setting up the bedroom, the computer table, hanging towels from the bars in the bathroom, storing the spare linens in the cedar closet upstairs. In the kitchen, she unpacked a coffee maker and toaster oven, a single skillet, a single saucepan, odd pieces of Fiestaware, a thin collection of kitchen tools, a few stainless forks and teaspoons. Starting that Monday, she was gone during daylight hours, then back at night, working around the house again. But she left some of the place virtually untouched, several boxes unopened and stacked in the room Evan used to call his office. She's only camping out here, it seems, no more rooted than a reflection on moving water.

And now it's high summer. Gauzy cloudless days, long stretches of evening to fill. Evan has come to know her reliance on coffee and iced tea, the glass of gin over ice she allows herself every few nights. Her gaze has grown familiar, at rest or constrained much of the time, but flaring into intense impatience once in a while. Her eyes are so dark they seem opaque, like plugs of walnut—strange against the fair skin, striking. She has a cordless phone on the kitchen counter, another by her bed. She can't stand still when she talks, she roams, the same way she roams when flossing her teeth, the Dr. Scholl's slapping her heels. Sometimes, talking, listening, she comes to rest on the back porch steps, forehead down on her bare knees, free hand rubbing her freckled shin. For the road, there's a mobile phone—Evan often sees her left hand at her head as she steers the car into the drive (the once-white Mercedes with its spidery leather, its manila folders and paper cups and clattering diesel). He has to marvel at the dexterous way she claps this little device shut and deposits it in the side pouch of her purse. All these new machines, the new gestures they take. He might as well be Rip Van Winkle.

When she leaves the house, she bolts the front door, letting the windows on the cool side stay open as far as the wrought-iron stops in the sash. Air leaks in under the broad eaves, eddies in the empty rooms. One of the first hot nights, he saw her haul a compact air conditioner up the stairs and install it in the dormer nearest her bed, then latch the door and turn the machine on high. But in the morning she removed it, shoved it into the hall closet. She didn't want the house sounds smothered by white noise after all, Evan thought. Needed to know what was going on around her.

The bed itself—box spring, mattress with a light India print spread—rests on the bare floorboards. There's a frayed carpet runner along one side, a reading light on a makeshift bench, strewn paperbacks—nonfiction, reportage—sometimes a glass jar with bachelor buttons or the California poppies that grow wild behind the shed. A tiny radio serving as alarm clock, no TV. Nothing on the walls. Draped on the one chair and on a wooden drying rack, stockings and half-slips left from when the weather was cooler. Evan hasn't had to cope with her bringing a man to this bed—except for the college boy and a phone installer, no male's been inside the house since the Fessendens departed. Gradually, he's come to suspect it's intentional; she could have all the lovers she wanted, he imagines—she's taking a break from men, or *a* man, that's how it seems.

As for Evan seeing her undressed: He can look or not, his choice. He could trail her into the bathroom and watch her lather in the shower or sit on the toilet or jut her chin at the mirror inspecting the taut, pale skin under her jaw. Watching her has become his prime occupation. But what pleases him, *this* Evan, is to grant her a core of privacy, and so he does, reserving for himself the sight of her partial nakedness and the faint gingery scent of a body cream she uses. The tops of her shoulders are freckled, and the freckles extend across the flat of her chest where her shirts are unbuttoned. Around the house, she wears beltless jeans, a blue cotton top with bone buttons, or, in this heat, just a rayon camisole. One night, as Evan entered the bedroom, she was hunched on the edge of the low bed, painting her toenails. He'd never witnessed this act before—Claudia had left her nails bare, hands and feet both. He watched, fascinated. When she was done, she held her feet out straight and studied them. Then began removing the polish. Evan smelled the acetone—it reminded him of model airplane glue. A little later, she returned to the bed and reapplied the polish. He watched again.

A week after her arrival, mail began to come with her name on it: *Maureen Keniston, 12 Madrona Street,* and so on. Just as it had come for Stephen and Roberta Kuhl, for Edward and Sheila DiNobilo, for various Fessendens (including the dog, Happy Fessenden). Papers began to collect on the oblong table where she picks at her suppers, the bag salads and hunks of tuna and the plastic deli tubs. She has reading glasses but they're always elsewhere—she squints at her mail, the left corner of her mouth pulled up. She taps her tooth with her little finger. Here's the utility bill, one for a credit card. Here's the envelope that holds her pay stub from the Puget Health Consortium. Wherever she was before this, the catalogs have yet to track her down.

Sometimes there's a letter on thick white paper, looping black pen marks, enough sheets to require two stamps. *Frederick Keniston, M.D., Canton, NY 13617.*

> the orchard, at least the upper piece, as far down as the cobble wall. I hate to divide it, but I really don't want the headache any longer. I know your brother will be dead set against this. Do you have any strong opinions? I just think it's time. But I want to be clear about this, I have no intention of leaving here myself. I'm afraid I'm here for the duration.
>
> I wanted to ask if there was a chance you can get away for a week later in the summer? For some reason, it's the dog days that get to me. I'd like to look forward to seeing you. And frankly, honey, to butt in a little, when we talked the other night I thought you sounded—well, I know there's been some

If words are exposed, Evan reads them; he soaks them up. The print on the back covers of books, the receipts and flyers and warranty cards, discarded pages from the computer's printer, sticky notes on the white wall of the kitchen: *Crowder's office, noon 12 Sept. Jana/755-8490.* She gets only the Sunday paper, the

Tribune—Evan reads the top halves of the sections where she leaves them, the openings of stories, but not where they continue onto the inner pages. He remembers the drag of newsprint against his fingertips, the smudge of ink. But nothing he does lifts the paper now, not his touch, not the breath he blows on its feathered edges.

Weekdays, Maureen is up and out early. Simple clothes, slacks often, no jewelry except three bangles that slide down and collect at her left wrist. No rings. He's yet to see her dress up for an evening out—a few longer items hang from the closet bar, still in plastic from the cleaner's, but it's hard to tell how they'd look laid across the bed, or on her.

Once in a while, during these hot afternoons, Evan hears the telephone, six rings before the answering service intercedes. Even the rings are different, thinner, chirpier than he remembers. If it rings when she's home in the evening, she barely acknowledges it—if she does pick up, it's only someone trying to sell her something. When she needs to return a call, she often starts by apologizing for having failed to answer. Her voice is low-pitched, almost hoarse. It can be teasing, can feign disbelief—*Oh, uh-huh, I'm sure*—but more often seems guarded, wearily alert. Sometimes, Evan's noticed, she talks aloud to herself, punctuates thoughts—*Oh, right, right, right, right*—as she sifts through papers, sometimes addressing herself with a sharp derisive tone, as if she's more than one person: *Why can't you keep your mouth shut?*

Extraneous noise seems to trouble her—whenever the house rattles or settles or a sound from outdoors seems too close, her shoulders give a jerk, she listens hard, head tilted, as if one ear's better at picking up threats than the other. But every so often, Evan sees her push back from the computer table, rise abruptly to her feet, and put on music. Never a voice he recognizes—another reminder (as if he needed one) that time has kept pressing forward. But the singer she plays most reminds him of Janis Joplin. That outsized fury. Not as boozy a voice as Janis's, the vocal cords not as shredded yet, but, holy mother, what a sound.

Later, in the kitchen, Maureen will suddenly belt out a line herself:

It's four in the morning, babe, and I'm deep down alooone—

Explodes into it, no self-consciousness. And she isn't bad, either. Halfway up the stairs, she'll freeze and hit it again, insistently. Then, the rest of the night as she sleeps, the lyric will beat in Evan's head: *deep down alooone—*

Evenings, if she's not on the bed reading, she's downstairs glued to the computer. Sometimes Evan stations himself at her shoulder and scans what she's scanning. Endless squibs of news. Bombings, celebrity split-ups, murder trials, pedophile priests, breakthroughs in digital camera technology, Botox. The regular onslaught. And so ephemeral, most of it. He keeps thinking that this window of time—late twentieth century, early twenty-first—will seem like the Golden Age a hundred years from now. *Why didn't you work on the air and water?* he hears future citizens demanding. *Or, for Christ's sake, population? Why didn't you save something for us?* And yet, admittedly, he's curious, he can't stop looking. *So this is how the world plays out, this is what happened after I died!* Even the date is startling: 2002, the palindromic year he sees stamped on postmarks and sales receipts, stuck to the rear tab of Maureen's car. He'll never get used to it.

When she's writing, Evan only skims the words as they scroll by, enough to see what's what, but not so much that he feels like a vampire. She types in bursts, her shoulders rolled over as if she's practicing an etude. Sometimes, thoughts wandering, she stops and looks up at the room, twists and looks behind her, her gaze sweeping over Evan. Then another blizzard of keystrokes.

Several times, she's written to the brother mentioned in her father's letter, her tone casual, big-sisterly, but saying little about herself, just that she's settling in, she was lucky the clinic was short-handed and she could get regular hours, only the occasional weekend, which is OK because she can use the money. She says she's very sorry to hear about the situation with Gillian, but he's probably just going to have to accept it. She says:

> Once somebody changes their mind about you, it's not that likely to change back again, that's been my experience, Toby. I wish I could say otherwise. And you know, the grand gesture . . . I mean in real life it doesn't work so well. She'll only think you're desperate and want to back off all the more.

There's nothing about their father's plan to subdivide the orchard, nothing about going home for a visit.

At the bottom she puts:

> xxx
> M.

Sister kisses. But below that:

> —Look, Toby, I don't have so hot a track record myself, I'm sorry. I'm just saying it's not about fairness. She feels what she feels. If you don't honor that, you're nowhere. OK?

There are a few others she writes to, including a girlfriend back East. Maureen's more candid here, more conspiratorial. She talks about her *decision*, about trying *to take charge of her life*. Still, it's clear she's not a woman who puts it all out for people to see. Even those she confides in only get a piece.

What Evan *can't* do is find out more about her. An irony: When he was a man who could research whatever his heart desired, his heart quit desiring. He remembers telling the doctor during another of those dreary office visits, *It's like I've lost the point.* He'd meant: Of seeing what the next day had in store. He didn't *need* to see it. He was indifferent to anything outside the gates of his misery. Anything within he'd seen too much of already.

But now the point seems shiningly obvious, not the least bit hidden: To watch, to gather more information, to act on it.

As if he could.

He'd love to know if his father's still among the living. It's not hard to picture Donovan as a flinty old crank in his eighties, unless the decades at the forge finally caught up with him, the iron shop's bad ventilation. Or his bulging prostate. Or, more likely, something not on the radar.

And Evan's one sibling, his grumpy sister, Gayle, what became of her?

When he'd first awakened here—he calls it *waking*, having no other word for it—he was profoundly groggy, the barest fleck of consciousness. He could see and hear but not *think*. Only later, looking back, did he process what he'd taken in: Gayle making her way up the staircase, followed by their father with his hawkish gaze, his white-bristled scalp. They'd halted in the doorway of the master bedroom, but neither could refrain from entering, Donovan producing a single syllable of gross disgust back in his throat, Gayle staring stolidly, finally tugging at Donovan's sleeve as if to say, *OK, enough. You saw it, let's go.* And a few days later, it was Gayle, not Claudia, who returned alone and sorted through Evan's things, his effects. Culling, making piles, boxing, bagging.

Two of Claudia's friends eventually appeared and carted away her few remaining possessions and that was that. Even so, he waited to see if she might come. At least drive into the turnaround and stare at the house a few moments before driving off. But she never did.

So here's a thought Evan knocks against ceaselessly: If the gods had meant to punish him, unambiguously, they'd have kept Claudia right here, right under his nose, or else materialized him wherever she now lives. They'd demand that he see her anguish in its raw state, then make him watch as her memory of him began to silt over and be buried by time. They'd make certain he was on hand to see her undress and slide into bed with a new partner, whenever that occurred. And all the rest of it: intimacies, indignities, life proceeding, her body aging, wearing out, dying.

Thus, he can assume only that this purgatory is something other than unalloyed punishment. He can only think that he's meant to observe this queue of characters who pass through 12 Madrona Street: Kuhls, DiNobilos, Fessendens. And now Maureen Keniston. That's if there's any design at all—and on that score, oddly, he's as unenlightened as ever. But he's grown more and more convinced that his fate, for want of a better word, is to keep his eye fixed on the current resident.

And so he does.

Stowed

HIS BODY WAS STOWED in a black bag, carried on a gurney down the narrow staircase, wheeled outside, and transported off-site. By then, his organs were worthless for transplantation, he assumes. What a waste. It's possible his body was autopsied, though likely not. Later, it was buried or cremated, which would've been carried out according to his wishes—had he *had* specific wishes; had he made them known. But as far as he remembers, he'd left no instructions.

There'd never been a regular burying ground for the Molloys. Donovan's father had been swept off a merchant vessel into the icy North Atlantic during the 1930s. Catholic in name only, Pad Molloy, Boston-born. *His* father, the Irishman, Evan doesn't know enough about to fill a shot glass. And Evan's own mother, dead of sepsis in the Third World? A tin of ash. And not even *this* returned to them, having been misplaced in the warrens of international bureaucracy, beyond the reach of attorneys, congressmen, deputy ambassadors, and the like. So, there were no plots to visit. No withered mums, no lichen-infested lettering to scrape clean with a penknife—and no logical resting place for Evan's remains.

He can't think of this without remembering the song about the drowned sailor from whaling days who reappears among the living. Wheezy concertina, raw-scraping fiddle. From an obscure album of Cape Breton music Evan once unearthed among the family LPs, it made a distinct impression on him at age thirteen or fourteen. Maybe it was the link to his grandfather's fate, or simply the image of a man confronting the dates on his own stone slab—not that Evan will get the chance, since he's confined to this quarter-acre of ground. And then he's obliged to recall a certain set of art history slides: a medieval sarcophagus in Padua with two tiers of carved stone, the upper showing the dead man in repose, splendidly attired, the lower presenting him naked and worm-ridden—either a radical statement of hope or gruesome realism, depending on how you read it. But for all that, Evan thinks: Let his own remains remain wherever they've wound up, in whatever shape they're in.

He estimates that two full days elapsed after the gunshot before he had the first twinge of awareness. Except for its severity, his stupor wasn't drastically different from mornings he'd surfaced after a medicated sleep, apprehension filling his nostrils like a draft of car exhaust. So, strangely, there was no one instant when it hit him straight on, when he thought: Jesus Christ, what's going on here? Incrementally, sensation returned to his limbs, his skin. It was the same for his powers of thought. As the spring of 1992 gave way to summer, he grew into this new state, his mind sharpening as if, at last, pure oxygen were reaching starved precincts of his brain.

Only then did the questions begin bombarding him. Why had he been singled out—was it for taking matters into his own hands, offending the natural order? Was it indefinite, a sentence without appeal? And what did "indefinite" mean in a situation like his? Would he be here to see the house rot and tumble down, and another rise on the same patch of dirt, and ditto for that one, ad infinitum—until what: the comet hit, the sun blackened?

And if *not* indefinite, would he have to die again?

Or maybe he's only marking time here and is actually headed elsewhere? But what a welter of problems when he tries getting his tongs on that one. *What* elsewhere? Based on whose say-so, what reckoning? *Not a fart's chance in a windstorm,* the old Evan might've observed. This Evan's not so sure.

After the gunshot, the house sat unoccupied for a time. A commercial cleaning service mopped up, two young Vietnamese-American men in gray-striped coveralls. Evan's blood was fan-shaped on the wall, some of the splatters a fine mist, now oxidized, granulated enough in spots to require scraping with a wide-bladed putty knife. The drapes were unhooked from their hardware and rolled in plastic, a steam cleaner was passed back and forth across the carpeting, though eventually—change of plan—the carpet was ripped up, the plaster with its gouges and muted stains was crowbarred off, falling in brittle hunks. Sheetrock was nailed over the skeleton of old lath, the molding and baseboard re-mitered, the floors sanded and sealed, and the room painted an off-white called Chelsea Fog, though the wall surface was too new-looking then, too glossy-slick. The next owner, Roberta Kuhl, instinctively found it wrong and had it wallpapered with a print of bamboo leaves, pale-green spear points. *That's much better, don't you think?* she asked her husband. Distracted, sad-sack Stephen Kuhl, who'd be muscled from his job with the city a year later. Anyway, the bedroom wall? He had no opinion.

If they were to ask Evan—but nobody's going to ask Evan anything.

He watched realtors show the house, watched couples trail through the rooms, nodding. They were tightlipped on the subject of the house's recent history, these realtors, but one of the neighbors, a retired longshoreman named Quimby, repeatedly made his way across the cracked cement of the turnaround, hipsprung and red-nosed, in order to let prospective buyers know the score. *Those buzzards won't tell you nothing, they're only in it for the you-know-what.* Evan stood not three feet away as this public service was performed. He'd scarcely known Quimby. Why such zeal? Evan listened to an agent's promise to check into this rumor and saw she was about to say, *All houses have their sorrows,* but caught herself.

Had the Fessendens known? Did they warn Maureen? *There's just this one thing, probably I shouldn't even mention it—* But he's never heard the topic raised when Maureen's on the phone, never caught her directing any cold stares at the upstairs wall.

Does she sense she's not alone?

No, she *is* alone. If Evan's learned anything, it's that there's no point of contact between these two—even now, he's unsure what to call them. Zones? Conditions?

One February afternoon during the Kuhls' tenancy, a day both were home, Roberta sequestered in the bedroom with a headache, blinds drawn, Stephen downstairs with the kindergarten-aged son, Greggie, watching basketball and sorting through bank statements at the card table. The boy was sweet-tempered, methodical, with his mother's poise, not a child you couldn't let out of your sight for a moment or two, but when the phone rang it was Stephen's supervisor, calling him at home on the weekend (not a good sign), and the boy took this opportunity to retrieve the other half of a tangerine he'd abandoned at lunch. Chewing, he found the cellar door unlatched—neither parent would claim to remember not fastening the hook and eye; neither could say exactly when they were last down there. In any case, a steep bank of stairs with a black plastic runner. The boy's stocking foot slid from under him, and trying to right himself, he overcorrected and pitched headlong toward the cement wall where the stairs angled near the bottom. This would have been the moment for Evan to intervene. If his hand were capable of holding a door shut, this would have been the time.

The TV was going, Stephen Kuhl was still on the phone, trying to concentrate, his cheek against the receiver. It was Roberta upstairs who heard the one rasping wail through the ductwork, and came, even then graceful, without wasted motion. And when they got the boy into the car, a dead weight inside the crocheted comforter, Roberta clutching him, her ear next to his dry lips where his breath came in ragged drafts, tangerine-scented, Evan scrambled into the back seat and bent forward between the two parents. Stephen slammed the car into gear, and it lurched backward into the turnaround, then plunged ahead. Abruptly, Evan found himself outside again, arms in the air where they'd rested on the vinyl car seat. The rain was coming down a little harder—it chilled him without actually getting him wet.

No one returned that night. It wasn't until the next afternoon that Roberta stopped home, showered, changed clothes, and drove off again, all within twenty minutes. Later, Stephen did the same. They were absent another night. Whatever blaming they'd done was temporarily out of their systems by the time they brought their son home on Monday, around lunchtime. It had been replaced by a tenderness, a benevolence that kept its sheen on them, intermittently, for days afterward.

The boy's face was scabby and inflamed, his elbow and forearm were the color of charcoal, one eye was swollen to a slit, the brow shaved and crosshatched with crusted stitches. His neck was circled by a foam collar. Stephen Kuhl said he had to put in an appearance at work. Roberta told him yes, he should go, they'd be fine. *But come home early if you can.* She played with the boy in his room, then read *Amos & Boris* to him, her voice a steady incantation (Evan listening from the privacy of the dormer, eyes closed). She never interrupted herself to say that her son had to be more *careful,* had to not *scare* his parents so much. The boy dropped off to sleep. She covered him and went downstairs. Evan paused over the child a minute, then followed after the mother. She'd begun making coffee. As it gurgled and dripped she glanced at the hook and eye, fastened now, then looked away, maybe thinking the same thing Evan was: Next time it will be something else. He saw her long pretty arms, the fatigue bluing the skin below her eyes. She was resting on a balance point, he thought. The convulsive desire to do something swept through him again, but his hands were as ineffective on her shoulders as they'd been on the cellar door. After this incident, chastened, he refrained from trying to touch anyone who lived in his house.

Mr. and Mrs. Donovan Molloy

Evan's father had come out of the navy at the end of 1945, and while some of his buddies went to school on the GI bill, Donovan Molloy apprenticed with a blacksmith, a Milanese named Crespi—forge artist, designer and fabricator of massive iron gates, fences, and sculptural and architectural pieces. The Northwest was suddenly in the grip of a building boom, and funding for style and ornament began to flow. Crespi won the bid for the façade of the Olympia Bank building—he and his crew worked for months at the forge, then on intricate scaffolds, installing the soon-to-be-famous design of staggered peaks and sunrays, a Northwest icon.

Since Crespi had a son (to say nothing of a nephew and numerous second cousins), Donovan broke away after a few years and established his own shop along the ship canal in Ballard, a rambling structure of corrugated tin down among the sheds of the boat builders. It was rough going at first—Evan was barely in school at the time, Gayle a toddler. But Crespi began to throw commissions his way, and there was word of mouth. If Donovan was a stubborn and tireless craftsman, he was the same sort of self-promoter. He began to prosper. He annexed two more buildings, hired other smiths, spent more of his time sketching, researching, making alliances with the people connected to money. But he never quit hammering metal, never completely delegated, always took part in the crating up and installation.

In other ways, he was a self-taught, self-created man. He read fanatically, eclectically. *The Autobiography of Benvenuto Cellini*, Frank Lloyd Wright's lectures on architecture, monographs on metallurgy, meteorology, and macroeconomics. He subscribed to obscure journals and newsletters; the drafting room wall was a mélange of clippings and postcards and notes scribbled on torn graph paper. Over time, he became a local institution. There was even the pricey coffee-table book, *Donovan Molloy: Works in Iron*. Gigantic leaping salmon, totems and spires, postmodern gargoyles, female bodies draped and undraped. Donovan Molloy, face fiery from the forge, dripping sweat, or decked out in a snappy suit, eyeballing blueprints with the mayor, accepting an award, being inducted into this and that.

Even now, cruising the property, Evan sometimes feels the muscles of his lips tighten a certain way and knows they're forming a particular expression of his father's. Donovan withdrawing a bar of white-hot metal from the coals and going at it with the hammer, the blows dull and leathery like fists on a punching bag, *tuth, tuth, tuth,* then stopping to check the progress, letting the tool hang for a second—*that* moment, the look of unhurried assessment, though the iron was rapidly cooling. *Keep going or quit now?* And, whichever, proceeding without a second thought, without remorse. He was never one to belabor the past, Donovan. A shrug, a bit of the brogue: *What's done 'tis done.*

And Evan's mother? Taller than Donovan by a good two inches, reedier, the source of Evan's long limbs, his eyes, called *droopy* or *soulful* on Evan, depending on who was talking, but on his mother they seemed worldly and knowing, as defining an aspect of her as the lazy ironic laugh or the Tareyton lodged between two extended fingers of her left hand. But she was long gone. Mrs. Donovan Molloy, who never liked the sound of *Mom* or *Mommy*, who begged Evan and Gayle, once they'd reached school age, to for heaven's sake call her by her name, which was Patricia, a perfectly good name, after all.

She was barely nineteen when she'd first met Donovan—he'd shown up at a dance in Bremerton, along with her brother and a few older boys from the shipyard. The war in the Pacific had been underway a few months, but they were deferred for working in a defense plant. Except that Donovan had given up his exemption and enlisted. He was waiting to leave for naval gunnery school. Patricia had ten weeks with him. *It was all so accelerated,* she told Evan when he was old enough for such a conversation. *Things were hot and heavy, but then came the Battle of Midway, and suddenly he was five thousand miles away, being shot at, bombs dropping near him. And what* was *it between us? We'd had such a short time, Evan. I was terribly confused. Everyone was encouraging me to see other people, so I did for a while, but then I started to realize that seeing other people was pointless. It was your* father *I wanted. I couldn't believe I'd been so unclear about it at first. He was gone almost three years, but I waited. I felt like one of the wives already, dreading the news reports—*

And then he was back. He was so big and immediate, his presence in the room, his body still in one piece. Here Patricia wavered a moment—what else would she say about Donovan's body? Even if you were in the habit of speaking openly to your children, there were limits. She went on, *For a long time he just seemed miraculous to me, that's what I'm trying to say.* But as far back as Evan remembers, his parents had been physical with each other. It didn't matter who was watching: horseplay in the kitchen, sighing neck rubs, impromptu dance steps, kisses on the fly. Not to mention the innuendo, the scraps of private jokes surfacing, the rolled eyes. All along, there'd been the heavy vibe of sex in the Molloy household—but it was only later that Evan understood it for what it was. Patricia and Donovan had been ferocious lovers.

Why had it stopped? That was one of the great mysteries Evan was left with. He was never sure whether the marriage had frayed in such slow increments that he'd been mostly blind to it—they *did* argue; they *did* sometimes act hopelessly exasperated with each other—or if Patricia's attachment to his father had suffered one massive fracture later on. There was the story put out for public consumption: The partnership had run its course; Patricia had a desperate need to feel useful on her own terms. It wasn't exactly untrue, Evan could see that. But it left you unsatisfied. It omitted things.

However long the plan had incubated, Patricia waited until Gayle had begun her last year of high school to set it into motion. She took an apartment, enrolled in the university, and began retooling. Less than four years later, she was at work on an anticholera/malaria project for an international aid outfit in East Africa. Even now, when there's all the time in the world to contemplate it, Evan finds her transformation stunning. Where had this resolve come from? It was as if she were carrying through on a pledge she'd made while nobody was watching, as if she couldn't live with herself unless she made restitution for the soft life she'd been granted.

I seem to have scoured down a bit, she said on one of her trips back to the States. It was true. The new Patricia bore only an oblique resemblance to the mother Evan had known. She dressed more simply, opting for neutral fabrics that packed well. She'd given up her contact lenses, and her only makeup seemed to be a vermilion-tinted lip balm. There was a forthrightness, an abruptness—she might touch your wrist and you'd stop what you were saying because it wasn't sufficiently to the point. But she was funnier, too. She told stories, did people's voices. Here was the local magistrate with his puffed-out cheeks and unruly brows; here was the earnest young Baptist boy from Indianapolis.

How badly had Donovan been injured by his wife's defection? He wasn't of a generation that paraded their hurt about in the open air, nor was he bitter or vindictive by nature. He didn't bad-mouth Patricia, didn't go out of his way to belittle this reincarnation of hers. *It's her life,* he said, *she can do what she pleases with the rest of it. I wish her Godspeed.* But how could you take that at face value, after twenty-four years of marriage? You couldn't. Surely Donovan suffered, but all that showed was the murderous schedule he was maintaining at the forge, his fury if anyone mistreated tools or forgot a message, and the fact that he sometimes spent the night on the office cot instead of driving home.

Eventually, his funk lifted and there came a time, during the early seventies, before Patricia began to be out of the country for extended periods, that the Molloys reconvened now and then for a crab feed at the house in Ballard—all four of them (five counting Claudia). Why not? It wasn't as if they didn't care about each other. But also, Evan thought, his parents seemed intent on proving that you didn't need to live so conventionally, that this could be pulled off without the traditional animosity. He even harbored the hope that Patricia might sleep over one of those nights. It was unrealistic, only a daydream, he knew that. But it pained him to see the end of their bodily connection. Didn't he have a stake in it, after all? *That* flesh and *that* flesh?

Inevitably, replacements were brought in. First came Corinna, the daughter of one of Donovan's patrons—gorgeous, high-strung, scarcely older than Evan. Nearing sixty, his father had the upper body of a light heavyweight, hard-packed shoulders and forearms, a midsection that could still take a blow. His hair, formerly white-blond, was now white, cut tight to the skull. His eyes were disarmingly blue and direct. Obviously, a man who still did things in the world, a man whom women were drawn to. But this was a doomed, slightly ludicrous affair, ending in a public blowout at Ray's Boathouse. *You should've just gotten the Jaguar,* Gayle told him. Evan found it harder to be glib. He'd grown up in Donovan's shadow, gotten hooked at a tender age on the belief that he was a second-stringer compared to his illustrious dad. He understood that Corinna was thoroughly out of his own league. All the same, he hated seeing Donovan humbled or embarrassed.

After Corinna, Donovan played it closer to his vest. When he took in a jazz show, when he appeared downtown at some fundraiser, he often had company: one or another woman friend with her black sheath dress and cashmere shawl. If any stayed over, if there was more going on than rudimentary companionship, Evan didn't hear much about it, nor did he ask.

Until, finally, there was Liz. She was just past forty when Donovan first encountered her. She'd recently moved to Bellingham to look after her emphysemic father; Donovan was up there inspecting the site for a commission. She'd traveled before that. She'd been a stringer for newspapers; she'd written grants and worked on campaigns. Her face was full and olive-toned, and she had wild wiry hair, still mostly black except for a white swath down the left side, where, she said, her one original idea had escaped. Not nearly as combustible as Corinna but good-spirited and sexy. Donovan was smitten. He began referring to her as his "bosom pal" in a way that managed not to be hopelessly cloying. In 1980, she became his second wife.

And on Patricia's side there was Pieter. A lean South African, four or five years her junior, good-looking in an entirely different way from Donovan, rather cerebral, cool-eyed, with a fringe of soft beard, low on the jaw like an Amish husband's. He accompanied Patricia on her last trip home. Evan's impulse was to dislike him, to be put off by the slightly fussy accent, the reserved demeanor. In fairness, Evan thought, he might not like *anyone* his mother slept with. But the truth was, his resistance to the man had started to burn off during their first meeting, and he guessed they'd wind up friends. Yet before this had the chance to develop, it fell to Pieter to call the Molloys with the news of Patricia's hospitalization—and then, only hours later, her death.

Robie's Sister

THERE WAS A BOY who'd worked for Evan's father—Robie, short for Robichaud, or Robillard, some French-Canadian name. His sister used to come around the iron shop, a tall girl with black twitchy hair. She was usually accompanied by a girlfriend. They were nineteen or twenty, driving a dented car the color of a swimming pool. This friend was always trying to cajole Robie into taking her out, trying to drag Evan into the fray: *You think he should go out with me, don't you?*

But it was Robie's sister who snagged Evan's attention. Not what you'd call a hippie, but certainly *different*. In retrospect, maybe she had smoked dope already, though this was a year or two before everyone did, Evan included. Or tried something harder. In any case, his thoughts gravitated toward her, and for reasons other than ordinary lust. She was neither pretty nor homely, simply a stringy girl with an offbeat look, who acted as if her looks were fundamentally beside the point. She was at least two years older than Evan, yet seemed to value what he said, sometimes touching him in encouragement as they talked in the car.

A hand on the leg of his work pants, a tug on the sleeve of his T-shirt.

At seventeen, Evan was just starting to see how bland his education had been. There were other entire categories of things to know about, whole other ways of seeing. She knew writers he'd never heard of. His first taste of the Beats came from her. It was from her he first heard names like Carl Jung, Henry Miller, St. John of the Cross, Tagore, and others he's since forgotten. She was no college girl, either—all this feverish reading was strictly on her own. He couldn't imagine her discussing any of it with her girlfriend, who'd taken to disappearing with Robie among the boatsheds. The same was true with music—she knew of singers and bands you wouldn't hear on the radio in a million years. Donovan prided himself on his assemblage of oddball jazz recordings, hard bop and post-bop and whatnot, but Evan got the sense that Robie's sister was unearthing even stranger stuff. There was a certain gesture she made, opening her eyes comically wide when she got to a good part of what she was explaining, mimicking an astonished person. He knew in his gut that what she was after, the obscure signals she was trying to pull in, was *crucial*, to use one of her words.

Evan and this girl—why can't he remember her name, *Denise? Danielle?*—got as far as holing up on the front seat of her car a few afternoons so the friend and Robie could be together. What if he simply drove off with her? Just *went*. Would sex enter in at some point (Evan was still uninitiated), or were they comrades in a greater cause and therefore sex was inappropriate? It was hard not to think about sleeping with her—and yet this other possibility tantalized him, too.

But then he was out of the car and back in school. It was winter, rain and fog. One night at suppertime, he overheard Donovan talking on the phone: *Slit her wrists, slit her fucking wrists in the bathtub. No, no, Christ, that sister of Robie's—* Evan stood listening in the vestibule, frozen. Donovan hung up, caught sight of him and said, *You heard that?* All Evan could do was nod. Donovan gave a grunt. *Twenty goddamn years old,* he said. *Makes you sick.* He stared at Evan for a long moment, pointed with his chin, and said, *Go wash up.*

So she was the first, first he knew.

Robie didn't work for Donovan much longer—Evan never spoke to him again, never had the chance to say anything. Robie wasn't much for talk, anyway, so who knows how he'd have reacted? Evan wondered if they said a Mass for her, or did she have to be shunned now? Did they have to start writing her out of the family story? Evan wasn't even sure what *he* thought. The whole thing just knocked him sideways. He hadn't seen it coming. And why *hadn't* he? Because he was seventeen, so self-concerned he noticed no undertones in what she'd been saying? Or had it blindsided her, too?

Maybe, he thought, this was one of the dangers of being someone like Robie's sister, dissatisfied with regular life. Maybe it could just dawn on you one day that you'd seen enough, you didn't need to stay for the rest. Evan couldn't avoid the image of her naked body in the tub. Or knowing that she'd had to transfer the blade to her other hand in order to do both wrists, and that the open cuts must've burned like crazy when she plunged them into the bath water. Unless the tub had been empty. But the idea of the porcelain being cold, her legs with goose bumps, and the blood flying all over, that was too much, that was where he made himself think of something else.

Patricia Discusses the Afterlife

Evan figured that one reason people belonged to churches was to have a coherent-sounding story when their offspring asked about dying. But Patricia was antichurch; Patricia was a dedicated advocate of the here and now. One evening when he was ten or eleven, Evan had crashed on the couch after supper, worn out from swimming. He woke later, hot-faced and confused, unable to tell from the wan light at the window whether it was morning or still the same night. Someone had turned off the TV. The house seemed lifeless, airless. He felt horribly empty, unable to remember who he was. This had happened to him before, he knew everything would come rushing back in just a moment—it was as if his body had raced ahead and his mind needed to catch up. And it *did*. He was Evan Molloy, lying on the sofa in the den. But instead of relief washing over him, the horrible feeling only intensified. He found himself imagining time gaping away, billions of years, and his place in it no bigger than a spark. And then he thought about the darkness after the spark. He jumped up, banging his knee on the coffee table, and dashed into the hall. No one was around. It didn't matter; he couldn't outrun this.

Then he saw Patricia on the deck outside, her face hovering behind a veil of smoke. Moments later, she was stroking his head, asking what the trouble was. Evan managed to blurt it out. She smiled sadly, nodding, as if to say, *Oh, so it's that. What happens after.* When he'd settled down a little, she said, *People go into the Beyond, Evan.* Looking back, he realizes that she'd probably had this speech saved up for when she needed it, but now that she was saying the words aloud it sounded like flimsy stuff to hand a kid. But she went on, trying harder, *It's a mystery, honey. If anyone tells you otherwise, they're only guessing. I can see how much this is bothering you. But don't you think I'm the one who should worry? I'm so much older than you. It's a long ways off for you.* Evan was on the wicker ottoman, touching the shiny cool skin of her knee. *If you're not worrying about it, why aren't you?* he might've asked had he been older. Patricia told him that odd as it might seem, people mainly went about living their lives, raising their kids, trying to keep their chins up, and not thinking too much about the end of things. A bat was crisscrossing the air above the Norfolk pines. Somewhere a mower quit, flooding the neighborhood with the absence of sound. *Once in a while they get overcome with, I don't know, a moment of, well—* She waved at the smoke as if noticing it for the first time. *Nothingness,* she was going to say, he knows that now, and he can see her calculating what more to add. *I suppose it's only natural to wonder these things, Evan. There's no avoiding it, I'm afraid. People who go to church believe certain things, they think they have the inside scoop, but that's always seemed to me—* She broke off, stopped short of calling it virulent wishful thinking. *Come here, sweetie,* she said finally. It embarrassed Evan to feel the plush of her breast, but for a short time he managed to relax and breathe easily and let himself be held.

Evan had assumed Patricia's death would come when he was middle-aged, at the soonest. But he'd been only thirty. The truth is, he'd never really adjusted to having her gone or to the way everything went haywire so fast. The fever, the hasty cremation, the urn vanishing down a rat hole, the absurd volley of calls to and from Africa—it would be black comedy if it weren't happening to him. He'd lived another dozen years himself, and from time to time, he was ambushed by the thought that he and Patricia hadn't said a proper farewell. A sudden queasiness, an acrid taste dripping down his throat. And yet what he had or hadn't said to Patricia no longer disturbs him. From where he stands now, those last-minute declarations seem immaterial, a stilted formality. When, after all, was his heart ever a mystery to his mother?

What concerns *this* Evan is the hour of Patricia's death. Tanzania's rainy season had begun, Pieter had reluctantly explained. She'd been transported in the back of van to the referral hospital in Mbeya, an extra two hours with the mud and washouts. Pieter had stayed with her, of course, so she hadn't been alone. But still, Evan thinks, the strangeness of her predicament must've been intolerable. And the pain—she was undermedicated, her lips had cracked, her head and joints ached, her limbs shook. Whatever she'd been given was impotent against this fever (hundreds would die of it over the following half year). Within minutes, Patricia progressed from fighting it to babbling delirium to shallow coma. Pieter was patient and civilized, addressing their questions as best he could. But for Evan the story never illuminated what needed illuminating. Had Patricia understood what was happening to her? Did it *matter?* Or was it all just *I heard a fly buzz when I died?* No transcendence, no respite, no moment of final understanding? And whenever he tries to picture the wardroom, he sees a host of savage green-winged African flies, driven inside by the rains. But the worst of it is imagining Patricia's last lucidity eaten by terror: *What have I done? What on earth am I doing in this place?* Patricia, who'd addressed his boyhood fear of death by telling him with such loving futility, *People go into the Beyond.*

As a grown man, Evan had replaced Patricia's version of the afterlife with—actually, he'd never replaced it with anything. Nothing religious, anyway. He took the visible world for what it was, particles or waves (depending on how you looked at it) coalescing into things you could touch or smell or listen to. Was there *more?* He'd need evidence. And why *shouldn't* he? If people were modeled on God, why should they have to dumb down their powers of judgment? It was demeaning and senseless. But what he really believed was that it simply worked the other way around. The fact of being alive was so unfathomable that people had invented a super-parent to shepherd them through the experience—one both wrathful and loving, aware of individual sparrows and sand fleas but at the same time extraordinarily reluctant to get involved. And then, having created this confection, they defended it, using the most tortured illogic. It was all perfectly human, Evan thought, perfectly understandable. Even beautiful in its way. But, still, a story.

And *this* Evan? What does he think now that his old conclusions appear, if not truly wrong, then woefully incomplete? The fact is, Evan doesn't know *what* to think. He's as baffled as ever— *more* baffled, actually. What's new is the bafflement itself. No longer does it bang around inside him causing trouble, icing his gut whenever his guard lets down. It's just there, every minute of every day, like breath: in and out, in and out.

Ned

O<small>NE</small> <small>NIGHT IN JULY,</small> Maureen answers the phone, and when she hears who it is, the first thing she says is, *How'd you get this number, Ned?* Listens, then interrupts, *I don't care about that, I need you to tell me who it was.*

Evan has been sitting on the stairs watching night come on. The house is stuffy, breezeless. But he notices a current of something stirring in himself.

No, I can't talk to you, she says. Her head shakes nope, nope, nope in the half-dark. But she listens another few moments, her chest rising and falling, then lets the hand with the phone drop away and hang at her side, and finally deadens the line with her thumb.

After a short time, she comes alive again, punches in a number, and when she starts talking, it takes Evan a second to realize she's leaving a message on someone's answering machine.

It's me, I wish you were around. Someone coughed up my number. Anyway, he just called here. I don't want to deal with this, I really don't. I know it wasn't you, but it was someone. *I can't have him hounding me, that's not going to work. I've got to have some goddamn— Well, OK, call me, unless it's like three in the morning, will you?*

She returns to the kitchen where the lights are on. Evan hears her tidying up, the familiar *scritch* of the dishwasher mechanism. The rest of the evening, no one calls—not the one she wants to hear from, nor the one she doesn't. Eventually, she climbs the stairs. Her face is moist at the temples, flushed. Evan stands aside but notices the subtle rise of temperature as she passes— what a bare wall might feel when sunlight crosses it.

In the bedroom, she strips off her shirt, lets her shorts drop, yanks back the bedding, and lies atop the bare sheet in her underwear, but hardly five minutes later she's up again, poking at the lighted numerals of the phone.

Just please ignore that last message. Call me when you get a chance. I'm fine.

Outside, a moonless night, clear, the air cooling at last to the dew point. Two planets hang in the eastern sky. The deep black overhead is crossed by a plane's blinking wing lights. Rustling in the cedars, in the thick braids of clematis vine. The odor of cut grass decomposing.

Evan stands at the foot of the bed, arms crossed. She never sleeps on her back, never uncovered. Sleeping this way she snores, light ragged drafts. He lets his weight ease down into the room's one straight-backed chair so its unglued dowels won't squeak. But of course they don't. How is it he still forgets?

Later, she wakes anyway, groping for the sheet. She rolls onto her side, then her other side. Evan stares through the gelatinous gray light, hears her limbs rearrange themselves again, hears, *Fuck, fuck.*

Molloy & Son

DONOVAN MOLLOY: *I hope this doesn't come as a major shock, but I don't want you to think about working here for the long haul, Evan. I'm not unsympathetic, but I found a calling, and you have to, too. That's how it is. You hear what I'm saying?*

Crespi & Son, but not Molloy & Son.

The smithy had been big medicine for Evan from as far back as he could remember. He'd worked there since he was fourteen—summers, some Saturdays, and Donovan had been known to pull him out of school to ride along on installations. What a rush *that* had been. But it was always assumed he'd go to college. Donovan was only stating the obvious, that Evan was Patricia's boy. Maybe if he'd been more like Robie—thick-muscled, a purple panther tattooed on the upper arm—or the other forge rats Donovan had hired over the years, with good backs, an affinity for heat and noise, able to stay zeroed in (Donovan had a huge contempt for inattention and negligence). Evan was no ninety-seven-pound weakling. He could handle the tools. He didn't wilt; he didn't keep making the same dumb mistakes. Still, he was cut out for other things. Gayle proved to be the one who inherited the Molloy genes responsible for undauntedness. She and Donovan even looked alike: blunt-faced, with the same ruddy skin that colored easily, the same penetrating, almost beady gaze. Donovan had taught her to work at the anvil, too, and she showed signs of being good at it, but midway through high school, she lost interest.

Donovan Molloy: *And listen, stay out of the goddamn war. I don't want you messed up in that horseshit. Get your degree, but don't be in a big hurry. Maybe it'll be over by the time you get out.*

OK, there was something they agreed on.

But the war *wasn't* over when Evan graduated from college—the fall of Saigon was still five years off. The president ordered the bombing of Cambodia that spring, and the National Guard used live ammunition on student protesters in Ohio. Days later, a song about it was pounding from the speakers of the car radio. Evan had used up his four years of draft deferment, and as soon as he left the university he was reclassified 1-A—he'd been subject to the first lottery and had drawn a number of tantalizing ambiguity. He waited to be called for his physical, put in a few hours a day at the iron shop, and (still in partial denial about the army), mailed out job applications to any company or agency in greater King County that could conceivably put his talents to use.

Though it was hard to say what his talents were or exactly what a major in humanities had prepared him for. He'd read *The Lonely Crowd* and *The Wretched of the Earth*. Freud's *Civilization and Its Discontents*. Lucretius and Marcus Aurelius. He read *What the Buddha Taught, Common Sense, The Rights of Man, The Second Sex, The Well of Loneliness, Walden*. Camus, Neruda, Dante, some Levi-Strauss, some Gaston Bachelard and Raymond Chandler. He'd prowled the Suzzallo Library, written papers, taken blue books. He'd stood, in fright and exhilaration, to deliver oral reports. By his own estimation, his undergraduate performance had been respectable but not incendiary. He was young and bright without being one of the bright young prospects.

He may have cast off the fantasy of working alongside Donovan, but nothing had replaced it. The truth was, he didn't think about his future much. How could you plan with the war lying across your path like a mud slide? The only plan Evan had was to keep himself out of the military. And even that was hazy—starve himself to be underweight for the physical, head up into British Columbia, refuse induction outright and be jailed?

There was also the problem of what he actually believed. Was it ethical to not go if it just meant somebody else had to? In the Civil War, he'd learned, rich boys had bought their way out of conscription—either paid a modest fee or rounded up a stand-in. He took it as an article of faith that this war was evil. But, really, what did he know? He was twenty-two, no whiz-bang on *realpolitik*. What did he know beyond what he absorbed from Walter Cronkite or the underground press, beyond Patricia's occasional screed against Nixon and Laird and Kissinger (*those cocksuckers*, he'd overheard her say one night. His *mother*). But maybe he was deluded, maybe the Domino Theory was the unvarnished goods after all. Maybe, down inside, he was scared shitless of fighting in a war, and this morality business was nothing but a smoke screen—and what made *his* fear any more worthy than the next person's?

In the meantime, just after Labor Day, he received a call from a company he'd written to, a consulting company named Blauser-Ammons. Could he come for an interview? Evan was fuzzy about what consulting companies actually *did*. He'd included several in the Big Mailing based on recruitment materials in the Placement Office. But two items had stuck with him: 1) they didn't look down their noses at liberal arts degrees (they did their own training), and 2) they wanted people who could think straight and write lucidly (that he could do). He had his hair trimmed and borrowed a striped tie from Donovan. Then, twelve floors up in the Wofford Building, he sat in a straight-backed chair, answering question after question, sweat rolling down the inside of his shirt, cool, like slug trails. When he was asked about his draft status, he told the truth. This seemed to shine a new light on everything.

Donovan had said to swing by the shop on the way home, so he did, but squirmed at the thought of laying his failure out before the old man. Donovan surprised him, though. *That one was for practice,* he said. *Go change and come hammer some iron.* Later, as they washed up—Evan had always loved the sight of his father drying his big grimy forearms with a shop towel—Donovan asked him what the day had taught him. *I hated how I sounded,* Evan said. *Superficial. And I didn't know shit about the company. The other thing is, nobody's going to hire me if I'm 1-A.*

What about next time? Donovan asked.

Do my homework, Evan said. *And keep my mouth shut about the army.*

His father hacked and spat. *That's good,* he said. *But go ahead and put it all out there. You don't know how the army thing's going to play out yet.*

Yeah? Evan said.

He wasn't convinced there'd be a next time. But soon he heard from a second consulting firm, a smaller, younger competitor of Blauser-Ammons. He had a week to pull together some research. Then, the day before the interview, still debating what to say about his draft status, the morning's mail brought him a letter from the Selective Service. Isn't this exquisite fucking timing, he thought. He could hardly bear to rip it open. But it wasn't what he'd feared. Miraculously, he'd been reclassified 1-Y: eligible in the gravest national circumstance, but no longer under active consideration.

You live a charmed life, Patricia told him.

Which all depends on the part you're looking at, Evan thinks. No, not really. His life *had* been charmed. How could he deny it, even considering its outcome?

So he breathed a sigh. He sailed off to the next day's interview, did well enough to be offered a follow-up, and was eventually hired. But, looking back, it's so clear: As necessary as preparing had been, what truly fueled his performance, what made him seem expansive and worth taking a chance on, was having learned that he had a future. He'd scarcely been able to contain himself.

Claudia

ONE NIGHT the following spring, Evan worked late, then (overstimulated, too fidgety to go home) stopped by a party he knew was in progress on Minor Avenue—friends from a house he'd lived in his last year at the university.

The dope-smokers were laid out across the rug, bestowing their attention on a strew of LPs. Evan glanced around for a familiar face, but all he could see in the candle flicker was hair and legs, so he moseyed through a scrim of wooden beads into the high-ceilinged kitchen where the light was better. There was a girl leaning back against the radiator, a freshly lit Benson & Hedges in one hand, the lid to a peanut jar in the other. Long-waisted, a little tomboyish. She was wearing cutoffs and a man's white dress shirt, tails out. Evan watched her tap the ash. His very first view of Claudia. What if he'd simply polished off his work, headed back to his apartment, and tried to sleep?

Instead, he pulled a beer from the fridge and walked up to this girl and said brightly, *Sorry I'm late.*

With only a microsecond's hesitation, just enough time for her eyes to widen and take him in, Claudia said, *But you're not late.*

They were blue eyes, though her hair was glossy black, cut in bangs. She wore unstylish black plastic glasses in the manner of Clark Kent's. She was smiling, provisionally. Evan had been dating someone else, but he knew, the first hour of the first night with Claudia, that this other relationship was nothing—paltry, already over but for the shouting.

After a while, Evan and Claudia moved to the fire escape. They sat dangling their feet, trading life stories. Between buildings, a sliver of the black bay was visible, intersected now and then by the lights of a ferry. The night got chillier, but it only made Evan more alert, and Claudia seemed not to notice the cold at all. She was younger than he'd thought at first, not yet twenty, and still lived at home with her mother in West Seattle. But she'd skipped the last two years of high school and was taking night classes in math and business now, working half-time at Weinstock's Photo Supply. What really fascinated her was computer science—she read whatever she could get her hands on, she told him. God, did she ever have a look, Evan thought. Smart, eyes on the prize. And there was how she *didn't* look: flirty, cooler-than-thou, needy.

At some point, the girlfriend she'd come with stuck her head through the window and asked if Claudia was staying or going. *Staying,* Claudia said.

When the party thinned, they walked up the street to an all-night diner and kept talking. Evan didn't push; he didn't try to win her over. There was no seduction, unless the two of them were equally seduced away from their own vagrant lives, seduced into the gamble of partnership. They came out of the café into the early light, jazzed but finally drained of words, fingers interlaced, and walked through a light mist, then, for the first time, separated.

One evening years later, Claudia said, *I admit it was fast. But I never put a mystical spin on it—like fate engineered our meeting out of all the people in the world. To me it seemed like we were heading down some road together. We just fell in with each other and kept walking. You always claimed I was so independent, but I had no desire to take after my mother, to go it alone. I really didn't think I would hook up with anyone so soon, but then I looked at you and I recognized who you were, the person I was going to love. And I did love you, Evan. I loved you to pieces.* Evan said, *That's how I saw it, too.* Claudia couldn't help responding, *I just wish you hadn't stopped seeing it that way so quickly, Ev. To this day I can't believe you did that.* What could he say? There was no more apology left in him by then.

Compared with his own mother, Claudia's mother, Sadie, seemed ordinary—generally cheerful, plain-faced, and plainly dressed, an account manager with the electric company. However, there was this: She'd never married Claudia's father—in fact, Claudia had no idea who he was. Whoever he was, whatever the relationship, Sadie was mum on the subject. Evan found this amazing. *I mean, Donovan's such a force of nature,* he said. *I can't imagine having a void instead.*

Claudia said you didn't miss what you never had.

Evan didn't exactly buy it. *But there's a whole story there,* he insisted. *How can you stand not knowing?*

Claudia said, *I guess I just can.*

It doesn't bug you?

She shrugged. That was all she was prepared to say.

But as he got to know her better, Evan realized that her hunger for the information had simply never exceeded her desire to let Sadie keep it a secret. Furthermore, like his own father, Claudia was essentially self-created. Her idea of who she was didn't require this mysterious figure. She wasn't incurious—not in the least—but her curiosity was pragmatic, aimed at what she could use. The rest she allowed to fall away.

A free-floating memory: rendezvousing at Dick's for burgers in the few minutes Claudia had between work and class; Evan saying, *Glad you could squeeze me into your busy schedule;* Claudia kissing him, rocking from foot to foot, both of her salty hands on his face, saying she *loved him, loved him, loved him.*

Why hadn't they slept together yet? Weekdays, from a window at work, Evan eyed the cobbled alley below, giving this question serious attention. He thought about it as he bounced along on the Number 4 bus, and in the shower, letting the jets prickle his backside. Why didn't they fly straight into bed? It wasn't as if the times were advising forbearance. But somehow holding off seemed a necessary element of their new alliance—not for the sake of caution, but to let things unspool at their natural speed. OK, maybe there *was* some caution. What if they weren't compatible? What if sleeping together was the beginning of the end?

Evan figured Claudia didn't have an extensive sexual history—she was young and didn't seem like the type (not that he was a terrific judge of that). His own sexual history wasn't extensive either: four girls in four years, and one of these hardly counted—a very stoned, very fumbling encounter in someone's loft. But he didn't pry. Some nights she was at his apartment late and they ended up crawling into his studio bed, snuggling to a point close to sex, and *still* held off.

It was as if, having waited, they needed a sign now, some augury. It got to be a joke. Walking along the water one evening, Evan told her about the Roman practice of ornithomancy. He pointed out a line of cormorants dotting a heavy ship's cable. *For instance,* he said, *seven birds in a row like that, that would be extremely significant.*

Claudia glanced over at the birds, seven black silhouettes. Just then one of them shook out its wings and flapped off. Against the sky it looked more like a pterodactyl.

Not that I put any stock in that stuff myself, Evan said.

Right, Claudia answered.

They bumped hips and walked on. But here was the thing: They couldn't just *screw* at this point. There had to be more to it than that.

A week later, Evan went to see a crony of his father's, a gimpy semiretired charter boat operator named Toshi. Countless times since boyhood, Evan had slipped over to Toshi's mooring, helped with the scutwork, or just hung out, soaking up Toshiro-san's outpouring of fact and embellishment.

Evan explained what he had in mind.

Next full moon? Toshi said.

Uh-huh, Evan answered. *Night of the twenty-fourth.*

Toshi said, *And you don't want to go out.*

No, tied up here is fine.

Toshi took this in, nodding soberly, but seemed to be having trouble keeping a straight face. He said, *There's special rates for things like this.*

Evan nodded back, looked at his shoes a second, then said, *And what would be really good is if you could not say anything to the old man.*

That's extra, Toshi said.

You know I'm good for it, Evan said, trying to keep up his end of the banter. But, in truth, he was a bit unnerved. He was always a little sheepish to find himself in the presence of Big Life Events, to find that he too would partake of them.

Two weeks later, Evan swung by Claudia's and told her to grab a toothbrush and come with him. Earlier that day, he'd put a set of high-thread-count straw-colored sheets on the bed in the main cabin and smoothed out a cotton quilt he'd found in the cedar closet at home. He'd filled a bagful of narrow-mouthed jars with daisies and put them around. He'd rolled a few nicely shaped joints in licorice paper.

So where we off to? Claudia asked in the car.

Sorry, Evan said, *not at liberty to divulge that.*

They stopped for takeout on the way to the marina. Evan checked the sky. Streaky clouds. *I think there's a full moon tonight,* he said casually.

He ushered Claudia down the floating dock, past the *Doretta*, past *Mack's Beauty* and the others. It was mid-August, hot stale days around the boatyard, but as they came aboard Toshi's boat, there was a breeze out of the northwest — you could almost smell the Olympics on it, fir and rock. Evan gave her a quick tour, all but the bedroom, then led her up a ladder to the top deck, where he'd put out a couple of canvas-backed chairs. They ate, passing the white boxes of lo mein and cashew chicken back and forth, Claudia picking out the ears of baby corn with her chopsticks, now and then stopping to look at Evan with the poorly suppressed grin he remembers so readily from that time in their life together. The sun finished its fiery dive into the skyline and the moon broke out of low clouds over Lake Washington exactly as he'd wished it to.

Deep in the night, Evan woke with Claudia's long body stretched out alongside his, her cheek against his arm. The floor of the cabin rocked slightly, a stray jiggle of chrome glint played on the wall.

Not incompatible after all.

He woke again. He'd been dreaming of rolling swells on the open ocean. The light seeping into the cabin was pale, shadowless. He realized he was alone. He scanned quickly and saw nothing of Claudia's, then had to fight off the idea she'd fled while he slept. He yanked on his pants and stuck his head into the passageway. Simultaneously, he smelled coffee and saw Claudia outside on the bow deck. She was balancing one of Toshi's white porcelain mugs on her knees, looking off at the thicket of swaying sailboat masts, at the gulls blowing by, white on gray. It was a sight he could watch forever.

In a little while, she came inside, smiled a wordless good morning, refilled her cup, and padded back into the cabin. She was wearing his light chambray shirt from the night before. He followed and sat on the bed. She handed him her coffee and undid the buttons of the shirt and removed it and then she was standing in front of him, totally at ease, it seemed. How is it our modesty just vanishes? he wondered.

She stepped forward, slipped her hand onto the nape of his neck, and drew his face to her chest. After a moment she said, *I know what you're thinking.*

Evan stopped kissing her skin long enough to murmur, *What?*

She said, *You're thinking you've died and gone to heaven.*

Evan said, *Oh god, I have.*

She pulled back from him sharply so they could look each other in the eye. *Me too,* she said.

Really? Evan asked.

She said, *Yes.* Then she flopped onto the sheets and said, *Now please, please, please.* Seconds later her legs were locked around the small of his back.

At some point, they made fresh coffee and had an English muffin. They didn't make love for the third time until nearly eleven o'clock that morning.

Ten months later, June 1972, they were married.

In the spirit of involving his father, Evan had gone to Donovan and said he had kind of an odd request. He and Claudia were thinking of having the wedding out on the water, so how would Donovan feel about approaching his friend Toshi? *You want to get married on the boat?* Donovan asked. *What's your mother have to say?* Evan said he'd come to him first. *Jesus Christ,* his father said, *I don't believe that for a second* (and naturally Evan *had* discussed it with Patricia already). But Donovan actually looked taken with the idea. He said he'd see what he could do.

So, early the following summer, the wedding party motored down the ship canal, through the locks, and out into Puget Sound, Toshi at the helm. People on shore waved, and the wedding guests waved back, holding up glasses of champagne the same color as the evening light. Nobody but the skipper knew what significance the boat had for Evan and Claudia, and he kept his mouth shut.

Sadie and Sadie's frowzy mother, Frieda, were there, Claudia's boss, Harry Weinstock, a couple from the neighborhood, her girlfriend Holly, and a small contingent of others she'd known since grade school. The women wore billowy cotton or silk, some with shawls in case it grew chilly on the water. Claudia's dress was off-white with eyelets in the bodice, the hem ten inches above the knee. Her legs were muscular, bare, and lightly oiled.

Every now and then, Evan looked up and caught Sadie and Frieda eyeing him and conferring. *They're still not sure I should be handed over to you,* Claudia teased him. Maybe it was a joke, and maybe it wasn't. Evan suspected that Sadie had never taken to him as wholeheartedly as Patricia had to Claudia. And who could say what was on Frieda's mind? Evan had been around her only a few times, but she seemed to have a daffy bohemian air about her—how could she not like him? He smiled in their direction, raised two fingers in a small salute.

But, of all on board, only Evan's sister, Gayle, was truly out of joint. She was in a Marxist phase—she'd been pestering Evan for weeks, saying marriage was *bogus, obsolete, reactionary*. How much of this talk she believed was anybody's guess. Patricia and Donovan's breakup had been amicable, supposedly, but Evan suspected it had gotten to Gayle more than she let on, that it was really the divorce, not philosophy, behind her rhetoric. She'd be into her thirties, as it turned out, before she trusted anyone enough to cohabitate with him. By then, the revolutionary jive had burned off and she was selling commercial real estate. At the time of Evan's wedding, Gayle was still living at home, nominally to keep Donovan company, but she'd taken over the loft of the garage and came and went as she pleased. One evening, Evan had stopped by and found her on the outside stairs, a joint the size of a Popsicle stick tucked in the corner of her mouth. She passed it off and immediately started lecturing him again. Evan listened a short while, then told her to stuff it. *Look, we're getting married because we feel like it,* he said. *It's what we want. No one's coercing us.*

That's what you think, Gayle said.

Evan told her he wasn't having this argument.

She offered her trademark curl of the lip, and said, *Fine. Just don't expect me to show up. Don't expect me to be a party to it.*

Evan looked off into the twilight. *You know,* he said after a minute, *there are girls who look up to their big brothers.*

In the end, she did come. And behaved herself, though she kept a pace or two away from the center of the action all evening, and every time Evan spotted her she had a fresh drink.

Both Evan's parents were there on the boat, of course, each alone. Gregarious, glad-handing Donovan, Donovan in charmer mode, doling out the Moët & Chandon, working an arm around Claudia's mother and grandmother, leaning in, confiding. And Patricia, almost three years into her makeover. Tonight she was a balm for Evan. She spirited him away long enough to say how good he looked in his new linen suit, touching the coils of burnished hair spilling over his collar, telling him how much she liked Claudia, kissing him on the forehead, saying, *I see great things for you two.*

Evan couldn't speak for a moment. When he recovered, he told her thanks.

Patricia smiled back at him. *Now go find your wife,* she said.

He and Claudia had promised each other lifelong loyalty, succor, forbearance, etc. A considerable laundry list. They'd stood shoulder to shoulder while his best man read a poem from the thirteenth century and two musicians spooled out a midtempo waltz. The squeeze box player was Evan's old friend Sonny Nicolette. Open-necked embroidered linen shirt, wispy rust-colored Vandyke. Seventeen years later, clean-shaven and mostly bald, in his first term on the bench in Snohomish County and going by the name Bruce Nicolette, Jr., he would marry Evan and Claudia again.

The boat scudded along in the lowering sunlight. They stood watching the froth of its wake.

I'm so happy, Evan said, dumbstruck to be granted this euphoria.

Me too, Claudia said. *It's amazing, isn't it?* She was gripping him around the waist for balance.

Earlier, just before the pictures, she'd handed him her glasses. It occurred to him that her memory of the night would be a blur, literally. Now he fished them out of his jacket pocket and slipped them on her. Claudia did a little double take, as if to say, *Oh my god, it's* you.

Animals Who Lay Down Together

Then a week's honeymoon in Friday Harbor.

They slept late, read books, rode bicycles, relived the high and low points of the party, ate waffles with strawberries, wrote post-cards, chatted with strangers, played backgammon on the breezy porch, fished (Evan), took picture after picture (Claudia), show-ered (Evan and Claudia simultaneously), napped, woke up, made love whenever they pleased.

After Friday Harbor, Claudia returned to Weinstock's and continued her night classes. Evan went back to work downtown. He'd recently been upgraded from a researcher passed among the project managers to a member of a senior consultant's team. This man's niche was process analysis, so Evan began to spend days in the field, poring over manuals and business plans, interviewing production managers, heads of inventory, HR people, QA people, shop stewards, drivers of forklifts, fabricators of fiberglass boat hulls, distributors of canned salmon, burly flour-covered women with hair nets, climate control engineers, and the like. He grew fascinated with the division of labor; he couldn't look down on the roof of any windowless industrial space from the interstate without having his thoughts zip ahead to what was going on inside.

Evenings when they were both around, they traded off cooking —Patricia had insisted that Evan not be a lout with no domestic skills—or one of them brought home takeout. They shared beers at the laundromat. Free hours they often walked around the city, Claudia toting her camera. Weinstock's gave her cut-rate supplies and developing—color was sent out; black-and-white she printed herself on nights she didn't have school. The tall plaster walls of the kitchen and hallway filled with sheets of photo paper, new ones supplanting older ones: architectural detail, lettering, stacks of rebar, scaffolding, ventilators, jackhammered concrete, bales of rags. People only if they were part of a street or construction site shot (and now and then she photographed the two of them, using her cable release). The subjects changed, but you could tell the same person had taken them all—what they had in common was harder to identify. Maybe it was just that she liked *stuff*, Evan thought. Things without a lot of interpretation. Things by themselves.

So now he was married, a married man.

He went around constantly aware of it at first, of being not-single, joined-to-Claudia. It must pulse off his skin like heat shimmer, he thought. He even found he'd grown more sanguine about the state of the world. The distinctly queasy, apocalyptic feeling that began afflicting him in college whenever he thought about Vietnam or the world running out of oil or smothering in population or the fact that the Cuyahoga River in Ohio was so clogged with waste that it *caught fire* during his senior year had begun to wane after he entered the work force—but only now, flanked by Claudia, was he really aware of the difference.

Some evenings, they lounged around the pebbly rooftops of their friends' buildings in ratty deck chairs, smoking weed, speculating, storytelling. Sometimes they slipped away to the shadows to grab at each other (considered in bad taste since they were married now).

One night, as Claudia was stripping down for the shower, Evan saw a patch of angry brick burn on her backside. *Jesus, where'd that come from?* he said.

She put her hand on his cheek and let it slide slowly down, as if to say, *Price of doing business.* She stepped up into the tub and slid the curtain, leaving Evan thinking, How can I not have known that was happening?

Another memory: Evan and Claudia and a handful of others taken to a spaghetti joint by a friend's mother in the mood to treat. A noisy, good-spirited meal. Over coffee and melting spumoni, the woman singled out Claudia and Evan, and told them, *It barely gets interesting until after the first fifteen years.* Claudia stared back, nonplussed with wonderment, a look Evan's never forgotten. *I'm perfectly serious,* the woman said, gums bared by a fierce smile. *May you two find it out.* That sound was the whoosh of time pinning Evan's ears back.

You know what the best part of my day is? Claudia asked in bed one night.

Lemme guess, Evan said.

She said, *Well, I like that, too. As you're completely aware. No, I like that we're just two animals who lay down together. You know?*

Evan smiled. *Lie,* he said. *Lie down.*

Claudia gave him a little punch in the chest. *I can't help it,* he said, grabbing for her, pulling her to him. *Patricia drummed it into me. Lie, lay, lain.* Claudia got a hand over his mouth. Evan worked it free. *Lay, laid, laid,* he said.

Oh yeah, you're good at that part, she said.

Evan went at her where she was ticklish. *OK, OK, OK,* she said, howling, wriggling.

Later, as they lay quietly, Evan said, *But I do know.*

What? she said, drowsy now.

Evan said, *Two creatures.*

She said, *Animals.*

Evan said, *Animals, creatures—*

And so their first year of marriage became history.

They decided that Claudia should quit work and throw herself into school. Just get it over with. Money-wise, it was a stretch, but there was Evan's modest salary, student loans—and Donovan could be approached, if it came to that. Even with overloads, it took her another eighteen months to graduate. They celebrated briefly, then came a spell of *So now what?* as Claudia sorted through her prospects. Before June was out, this was shattered by one simple phone call: her former advisor, explaining that the director of the university's computer center was looking for a new graduate to train. Claudia's plan had been to find an entry-level position in a local company and build up experience while she researched ideas for starting some venture of her own. The university job would be a detour, and lower-paying; on the other hand, it was *computers.* She recognized it for what it was, a private tutorial she couldn't have bought. A day later, she spent an hour hashing things out with the advisor, then they strolled over to the computer center and she was introduced to the director. All very casual; it came out that the two men were longtime rowing partners. That night, Evan saw how energized she'd become, how confidently she'd already switched gears. Suddenly, he was frightened for her (a new sensation), and he was torn between telling her not to get her hopes up—undoubtedly, others would interview—and not wanting to rain on her parade. The present-day Evan can only shake his head at this old life-strategy of his: Avoid hope so you won't look naive when things don't pan out. What a ninny. Every night that week, he helped Claudia map out what to say at the formal interview—they even talked about the outfit she'd wear. But Friday, while Evan was at work, there was a second call: the director asking when she could start. That was it. The whole thing had been an inside job. Truly amazing, Evan thought. But Claudia had that effect on people—everyone wanted her on their side.

Not long after that, one of the founding partners broke away from the firm where Evan worked, siphoning off a couple of the senior staff, even a few younger analysts, a development that caught Evan totally off guard. He was going to have to be a whole lot more astute if he wanted to survive. The partner who remained had always struck Evan as less than classy—brilliant, maybe, but a little slippery.

In short order, the office was reorganized. The mood grew testy. There was a new aggressiveness, a new emphasis on speed; at the same time, the size of the project teams was cut. More work, fewer workers. Evan tried to adjust. He needed the experience, and he and Claudia needed the money. After the shakeup, he was reassigned and mostly did market research now, which bored him. It seemed to lack the clarity of the step-by-step analysis he'd done before. With the accelerated turnaround times, he often found himself signing off on work before he was satisfied with it, and couldn't shake the feeling that he'd missed something potentially major. His main motive now seemed to be dodging trouble, avoiding the public upbraidings that had become a feature of his work landscape.

Considering how fired-up Claudia was by her job, Evan tried not to dwell on his—and if he'd learned anything from Donovan, it was how unimpressed the world was with whiners. But eventually he had to level with her, had to admit that he'd started dreading his workdays. She listened, she encouraged him, she told him he'd get with it again. *And if I don't?* he said. She didn't look troubled. She said, *Then we'll cope with that.* She was straightforwardly upbeat without seeming oversweet (he never could've married a Pollyanna). He renewed his vow to suck it up and go on. Then, suddenly, one Tuesday morning after the start of the new year, he simply gave notice and walked out. No irons in the fire, nothing.

Hey, good for you, Claudia said that night. Evan's spirits brightened. Then he realized that she thought he was kidding. He had to spell it out. He hadn't expected her to be overjoyed, but the look she gave him now—he hadn't really expected *that* either, the open-mouthed stare through the black glasses, the step backward to lean against the doorjamb.

Did you want me to stick it out there forever? he said.

It's not that, Claudia answered. *It's just, wow.*

Evan stripped off his jacket and slung it on the chair back. *People quit jobs all the time,* he said.

She said, *But, I mean, Ev, it's not like you're washing dishes. This just seems kind of—* She stopped before she accused him of going off half-cocked, or however she was going to put it.

Evan felt the blood rise to his face. He turned away and hunted in the fridge for something to drink, in no rush to turn around again. He'd seen what he'd done more in terms of standing up for himself, following his instincts; now he was filled with doubt.

What do you plan on doing? she asked his back.

Evan grabbed a bottle of orange soda and straightened. *Finding something better,* he answered (how phony he sounded suddenly). He popped off the cap and let a long swig wash down his throat, then pressed the bottle against the hot skin of his cheek.

She said, *Ev?*

Only now, meeting her gaze again, did he start to get it—quitting wasn't the issue, not the main issue; it was having left her out of the decision, neglecting their partnership.

Then it was January, February, March. Raw gray skies, soaking rain. Every morning, Evan got up with Claudia, made coffee, and hung out with her as she dressed for work. Sleeping in seemed like a very bad idea. He tried to stay busy—sending out feelers, following up on leads. But the economy was dead. He got some poorly paid technical writing through a college friend, even put in a few days at the iron shop. His mood ebbed toward a persistent low-grade glumness.

Another month passed.

It made him uneasy to be home while Claudia was working. He didn't believe he needed to be the big breadwinner, but not keeping his end up felt strange. His life seemed off kilter. He couldn't help but wonder: How long before this left a mark on their marriage?

He'd just about talked himself into going back to school, taking something *practical* this time, when Dimond & Associates called him for an interview. Contrary to his worst fears, this came off well. His jitters gave way to a calm voice telling him if he wanted the job, he could have it, but first he'd need to sound like a guy who knew what he was capable of, a guy who'd reward the company splendidly—in short, not the droopy fellow of the recent weeks, but his best self, the one who prevailed, the one joined to Claudia.

But it was at Dimond he met Frannie Marx.

Years later, during one of his periodic heart-to-hearts with Donovan's second wife, Liz, Evan heard himself say that his breakup with Claudia sometimes seemed like a byproduct of the marriage itself. If it hadn't been for the charge being married put in him, how it made him feel capable and potent, he'd never have gone after Frannie. Wouldn't have had the raw nerve, the heedlessness. *Let's see if I have this right*, Liz said. *Claudia made you feel so good you started screwing Frannie?*

Evan said, *I wasn't offering it as a defense.*

And the capacity to betray, had he carried that with him all along, like a faulty gene—not that this was an excuse, either? Still, if he bore Claudia no ill will, if he had every intention of staying married forever, how to explain it? That the zeitgeist frowned on men who didn't pursue their curiosities—you had to *get it on;* you didn't want to be *repressed, hung-up?* That monogamy was a daydream, no match for human biology? That sneaking around was one slick drug? That there were *two* Evans, each with a lover?

Smudge

ONE AFTERNOON before Maureen has returned from work, a man crunches up the drive on foot. He eyes the house, circles around back and stares in the window, then sits on the steps. He has strong, precise features, cropped graying hair like iron filings. Smartly dressed, silk shirt, tie. Evan looks down on the thinning whorl at the back of his head and waits to see what he'll do, which is to check his wristwatch intermittently over the next thirty minutes before slapping his palms onto the knees of his slacks and rising to leave. But he needs to peer inside once more, hands cupped to the glass, his nose leaving a smudge.

Ned of the late-night phone call, Evan guesses. He follows the man across the dusty grass and down the drive, going as far as he's able, then watches as Ned strides up the empty sidewalk, stopping once to see if he's been observed, then disappears down a cross street. Must've parked where the car wouldn't give him away, Evan thinks.

Is it only dumb luck that Maureen, who shows up at more or less the same time each afternoon, is late today? When she climbs out of the old Mercedes, two plastic Safeway bags droop from her wrists. She unlocks the house, backs in, goes about unpacking her rations on the tile counter, unaware that the house has been trespassed upon.

Others

IN 1968, when Evan was twenty, Patricia's friend Alice Wolfe swallowed a lethal dose of Nebutal once it became apparent her breast cancer had metastasized to her brain. She'd driven alone to the cottage on Grays Harbor that she rented for two weeks each summer. Evan had been there with Patricia once; he could picture the sun-faded drawings on the walls, the simple rooms with their water view. Alice had been a recovery-room nurse, Patricia's older friend. Bowl-cut hair the color of concrete, wire-rimmed glasses. She was steely in her judgments, yet thoroughly decent—she'd doted on Evan, told him he had a sweetness the ladies would love; he'd know what she meant later on. A day or two after his mother had received this news, Evan stumbled onto her in the pantry. How rare to see Patricia weep. Her forehead was creased from where she'd pressed it against the edge of a shelf. Evan didn't know whether to stay or go. He put his hand on her back where it shook. *Oh, Evan,* she said, her indignation shocking him, *life is so* mean *sometimes.*

Still, in the Molloy household Alice's act was held to be reasonable, possibly even heroic. Not sinful, certainly. Sin at the Molloys' was a matter of acting selfishly, small-mindedly. Alice had only herself to answer to, and she hadn't left behind too grisly a mess for others to clean up. Evan had no hard evidence but always felt that somehow her death had hastened the demise of his parents' marriage, that it pumped fuel straight to Patricia's ruminations about last things.

Then, the year Evan met and fell in love with Claudia, he learned that a friend named Ira Pfeiffer had leapt from the nineteenth-floor window of his parents' apartment in New York City. As undergrads, Evan and Ira had taken literature seminars together and often hung out over coffee. Evan found himself awed by the force of Ira's opinions, his drive to get to the bottom of things — in fact, witnessing Ira in action was one of Evan's earliest clues that he wasn't cut out for a life of scholarship.

Everything about this death was confusing. Ira had taken a leave from his Ph.D. program and spent ten months in Trieste, translating and writing commentary for a diary kept by a Yugoslav woman in the extermination camp at Jasenovac (it had turned up among papers belonging to Ira's uncle). But according to Ira's New York friends, he was changed when he returned. No more bold assertions, no more wit — he'd grown touchy and apathetic. Yet, the night before he jumped, he and his father had arranged to play tennis the next afternoon: Ira, competitive in all things, had been a high school champion. *It could've had to do with what he was working on,* Evan was told long-distance. *It was grim enough stuff. But people here are wondering if he had a brain tumor or something, considering the personality shift. You should've seen how he looked at us after he came back — as if it were taking gobs of energy just keeping us in focus. But then, who knows?*

Alice Wolfe's death hadn't really gotten to Evan, hadn't *penetrated*. She'd been in her late fifties — it seemed old to him then — and he'd been aware that her cancer was considered terminal. Also, coming when it did, the late summer of 1968, it had been crowded out of his thoughts by public tragedy—the assassinations, first of Martin Luther King Jr., then of Bobby Kennedy. Evan had been up late watching the California primary returns, he'd listened to Kennedy's victory speech, and gone to bed thinking, OK, maybe there's hope after all. It wasn't until morning that he learned what had happened only seconds after he'd punched off the TV. Then, in August, came the head cracking outside the Democratic Convention in Chicago, the gassing and mass arrests. The country seemed to be disintegrating, edging toward a kind of Third World chaos. All of which felt more real to Evan, more consequential, than the loss of his mother's friend.

But Ira had been *his* age, *his* friend.

Evan had a tough time figuring out what he actually felt about this. *Grief* seemed too bold a word. It was more like a pervasive sorriness, a disappointment with how the world was. Now and then, for the rest of his life, he'd hear a voice with an accent like Ira's and the same staccato delivery (in an airport, a guest on the radio), and before memory had a chance to kick in, he'd think it *was* Ira, then think, No, Ira's dead, followed a split second later by a shot of bodily revulsion—it was like turning over a piece of fruit and finding it sodden with mold.

Maybe there *had* been an organic reason for Ira's desperation, but the more Evan contemplated this, the less difference it seemed to make. Something had set Ira apart—not from the general run of people, but from those who'd gone to the window, had a look, and eventually turned away. That's what Evan kept returning to, that *something*. And the tennis date—it meant that as different as Ira had seemed to people, no one had truly seen this coming. Or hadn't known what they were looking at.

Ira's death had one other outcome for Evan. It brought back Alice Wolfe's death and made him see it with greater clarity. Also Robie's sister's. He discovered that certain events didn't grow fuzzier over time—if anything, they got sharper as the clutter around them fell away. And he realized that, for him, these three suicides were not isolated occurrences. They were the first three names on a list that would continue to grow, which made him wonder who the next would be.

During his early thirties, Evan reconnected with a friend from high school named Terry Harker. Terry and his older brother had been original members of the Buzz Bombs, the third of the local bands to make it semi-big, a few years after the Sonics and the Fabulous Wailers. Summer evenings, once the Spanish Castle had shut down, Evan had often cruised out to the Regal or the Pacific Ballroom for shows. Then the band had a single that garnered national airplay. They went on TV and began touring—the Midwest, up and down the East Coast, trips to Hamburg, London, Liverpool. Later, they underwent some personnel changes, broke up for a time, re-formed, became embroiled in a pair of lawsuits. At that point, Terry threw in the towel. He came home, bringing his new wife, Ruby, an ex-pat Brit he'd met in Boston. Evan didn't much care for her at first—she seemed like a poseur, a throwback to the likes of Twiggy or Penelope Tree—the ironed hair and raccoon eyes. But soon she grew on Evan. He saw that she loved Terry, and what he'd taken as affectation was, in fact, the lid over a well of insecurity.

While Ruby figured out what to do with herself, she found work hostessing at a supper club. Terry bought into a guitar and drum shop in the Denny Regrade but devoted most of his time to setting up a nonprofit to help young bands with legal advice, contracts, bookings, and press releases. Before long he was performing again, in a pickup group with one of the numerous ex-Sonics. As Ruby kept saying, half-seriously, *Bad scene when the man doesn't get to bang his kit. Know what I mean, rat in a cage?*

One Friday night they were setting up at Moxie's. Evan had come along for the hell of it. Terry realized the wrong cymbal case had gotten into his van—apparently the good ones were in with gear Ruby had lugged back from the loft where Terry kept his practice set. Evan offered to telephone and have her run them over. Terry said she was at the movies. Thus, Evan found himself driving to their place. It was maybe half-past eight, mid-October. The apartment was fully dark. Later, when this morphed into a story, Evan said he'd suspected something was wrong, but the truth was harder to explain. The cymbals were right where Terry said they'd be. Evan grabbed the case and was headed out when he stopped and, for no obvious reason, detoured toward the kitchen. The swinging door was blocked. He nudged it open, saw that pillows had been placed along the floor on the other side. Then the gas smell hit him.

He went first to the one tall window, heaved it up, and only then, in the weak light, made out Ruby's body—she was kneeling, arms crossed on a folded bath towel. How long did it take to die this way? He dragged her toward the window and thrust her head out, but in the process of flipping her over he struck the window frame and its weight crashed onto her shoulders. *Ah, fuck me*, he said aloud, wrestling it back up, his other arm about her rib cage. She started to retch. A spume of stomach acid and red wine splashed onto the sill and down Evan's jeans as he tried to clear her airway, and then she was violently coughing, slapping at him like a drowning woman. Finally, he let her droop to the floor and rushed to shut off the gas valve, then hit the exhaust fan, which slowly clattered into service.

It was a fluke—ten more minutes and she'd have gotten her wish. Maybe five. While he waited for the EMTs, Evan wiped her face with a wet cloth. Her color was awful, livid, black stains around the eyes, streaking back across her temples as if she'd been crying into a big wind. *Can't tell Terry* was the first coherent thing she said.

Evan told her not to talk.

She said, *You can't, oh promise.*

Evan said, *I need to go open the door, please don't move.* While he was dashing to the other room, it occurred to him he'd left her alone with a kitchenful of knives, but when he found her again she'd risen only as far as all fours, her face angled toward the fresh air. The medics arrived at last.

Ruby went off, saying, *I didn't mean it, you can't say anything.*

And for a second, Evan *did* ask himself if there was any way to keep Terry from knowing. But that was foolish, not to mention impossible. He looked up the number for Moxie's and called.

I honestly thought she was over it, Terry said, later that night, Evan's first clue that a pattern was at work. They were in plastic chairs outside the Harborview ER. *But what can you do if someone really wants to kill themself, not a fucking thing, when you get down to it.*

Evan nodded soberly. But was it true? Could you stop a person for good? *Should* you? He closed his eyes, pressed his thumb to a spot between his brows that had begun to ache from the gas.

After a while, he said, *All she could say was not to tell you. It seemed so—*

Terry said, *Pathetic?*

Evan said, *No, no, I meant sad, I guess.*

It's OK, Terry answered. *It's sad, it's messed up.* He was a big man, blond and balding. *This is the fourth time I know of,* he said. Seeing Evan's look, he added, *The first two were before I knew her.* He blotted the moisture on his high forehead. He said, *When she comes around she'll be like,* Oh, Terry, I don't know why I did it, I don't want to leave you, it's crazy. *I kind of believe her. It builds up in her system like a craving, except with her it's a craving for oblivion. But I mean it's not like she acts more and more de-*

pressed all the time, not that I see. Maybe I'm blind to it. Or maybe she's playing me. She could be. He gave a tired shrug, red-eyed, squinting off as if something might have changed down the corridor. *I don't know, four times, four failures. If she really wanted to—*

Yeah, but if I hadn't gotten there, Evan said.

Terry shook his head. *I know,* he said. *I know.*

When Ruby was back on her feet, she called Evan and asked him to meet her for coffee. A month had passed. Evan said sure, he'd be glad to. He didn't know what to expect, whether the gas had left permanent damage. He assumed that Terry would be with her, but when he saw she was alone, he began to understand how intimate today's encounter was, nothing to be witnessed by a third party, even a husband.

Her hair was in a simple shag now and she'd ditched the dramatic eye makeup—she had the pallid stare of a woman without her glasses. Sitting across the table, Evan found himself monitoring her flow of words, listening for anything off-kilter, but except for the lingering whiplash (where the window had struck her), she seemed all right. Maybe a little subdued.

So they drank their coffee. Ruby acted as if Evan knew all there was to know about her now—and, worse, as if she'd peered inside him and spotted a kindred spirit. Evan thought, Don't lay that on me, I'm not that way. All month he'd been turning the episode over and over almost against his will, but now, across the booth from her, it hit him with a fresh bluntness: Here she was, living, breathing, giving off heat and scent, and it was because of what he'd done, and had he *not* done it, this exact same flesh would be (after thirty days of decomposition) unbearable to look at, or smell.

Ruby took his hand where it lay on the tabletop and held the ends of his fingers, rubbed them lightly. After a few moments,

Evan said, *I keep thinking I should apologize to you. Isn't that funny?*

Ruby said, *For calling Terry? I know you had no choice.*

Evan said, *No, for the rest of it. Did I do the wrong thing? Are you angry?*

Ruby kept looking at their hands. *You didn't have a choice about that either,* she said. *It's too much to expect a person to turn and walk away. It's wired into us, isn't it?*

Evan said it must be, then he found himself about to add that it was her business what she did, nobody had the right to judge her. But he held back. He wasn't sure whether he believed it or not. And he didn't want her taking it as encouragement.

After that it was hard to find anything to talk about. Outside on the street, minutes later, she rose onto tiptoes and kissed Evan near the mouth, said, *Don't—* Then, *No, I'm not going to say that. I'm not. OK, bye-bye, luv, be a good boy.*

He watched her go, head erect, as if balancing spinning china on the end of a stick. He was left to wonder how she was really doing, and what she hadn't let herself spit out. *Don't think badly of me? Don't feel sorry? Don't think your own day won't come?*

From then on, he saw less and less of the Harkers. They were grateful—at least Terry was—but Evan's part in the event had tainted him. Just the sight of him was a reminder, he guessed.

One night in 1984, Evan was out with friends in Ballard and there was Terry drumming for a cover band. Evan sought him out at the break and they passed an uneasy ten minutes. Ruby was great, he said. Getting exercise, doing yoga, maybe going to open a shop.

Terrific, Evan answered. *What kind?*

Terry said they were still working out the fine points.

Evan said, *Well, give her my best.*

Terry nodded.

That winter, by pure chance, Evan saw in the paper that Ruby Lynne Harker, thirty-seven, had been struck and killed by a Metro bus.

Even now, these others still barge into his thoughts, thrusting their riddles at him. Robie's sister selecting the tub she'd been bathed in as a girl, where her mother likely stole twenty minutes of peace for herself every few nights. Ira Pfeiffer, jumping out a window at his parents' apartment, when as far as anyone knew he'd been nothing less than a devoted son. Or Ruby, resting her cheek on the enameled door of the same oven she'd used to bake Terry brownies.

But she wouldn't have been thinking of brownies, or the oven left uncleaned. She'd be homed in on the jet hiss and the thickening smell—not the gas itself but a sulfury additive called mercaptan. Almost too wound up by the discovery that this, after all, was the day, almost too excited to keep still and let the gas do its job.

Frannie

Evan had no complaint about his wife. They'd been married three years now and he hadn't grown tired of Claudia's girlish body, her white white skin, flat belly, slender legs nearly as long as his. He loved sleeping beside her and waking to find her asleep beside him. He wasn't sick of her nasty habits: the inability to find things in plain sight, or the resonant mucousy smoker's hack she greeted him with, mornings after they'd stayed up late—her smoking gained momentum as the day wore on—or even her bodily impatience when he'd take too long getting to some point he was making. Familiarity hadn't shaded into contempt; anticlimax hadn't dulled married life. He liked Claudia's company. There was no one he'd rather argue with, no one whose opinion he valued more, no one he couldn't do without.

And yet, Evan was profoundly attracted to Frannie Marx.

She had big liquid eyes, a compact but womanly figure—she was a year or two older and had been at Dimond long enough to be an old hand. She wasn't flirtatious around the office (the only place he saw her at first), nor did she have an especially sexual demeanor in public. But he knew, he *knew*. Whatever age he lived to, Frannie would be the most beautiful woman he'd ever hold naked in his arms.

One morning when he'd been at the new job less than a year, he was at Frannie's worktable when a project manager named Zukofsky came looking for him. A fussy, oversized man with suspenders and a showy belt buckle and tawny curls wetted with hair oil. Evan listened to his spiel and was about to explain why he wasn't actually in the wrong, when Frannie flared her eyes, warning him. When they were alone, she said, *Never go straight at Zukofsky. He's* way *too attached to his victories. You have to go the other way.*

Side door, Evan said.

Frannie bestowed her smile on him. *Exactly right,* she said.

Evan found it hard to believe every male in the place wasn't breathing down her neck. Possibly they were put off by her nervy intelligence, or something else he didn't see. And why wasn't she already with anyone? A mystery. But he did learn that she'd been married once. The week she turned eighteen, she ran off with her biology teacher. Her *biology* teacher? No, it was a true story. He surrendered his job two months before the school year ended, and they fled to another state. He found work in a lab that tested meat for contaminants. Frannie started community college, later switched to the university.

Many afternoons, Evan and Frannie had coffee together. Clearly, they were hitting it off. She knew he was married, but her attitude seemed to be that was his business, that was between Evan and his wife, why should it get in the way of *their* friendship? Dimond & Associates wasn't an uptight workplace—Bill Dimond was a decent, genial guy and it filtered down. It's possible that amid the general camaraderie, Evan was slow to realize how linked to Frannie his mood had gotten, and not just those conversations at break, but glimpsing her throughout the day, hearing her voice in the hall. Days she was out in the field, he felt oddly inert, deprived. Gradually, it seemed to Evan, they both came to take it for granted that had circumstances been otherwise, they'd see where the relationship went. Until, one afternoon when they were by themselves, she looked at him with her chin on her fist and said, *You know, I think we could get together. I'd like it, I would. Just so you know. But you have to decide. I don't want you to think I'm putting you under any pressure, Evan.*

Right, right, he thought, no pressure.

There came an evening when Claudia met two old girlfriends to go swimming at Haller Lake. Evan had intended to work late or catch the early movie, whichever; he didn't mind a night left to his own devices. It was July, an easy wind slipping between the buildings. Then he was walking Frannie to the lot where she kept the ragtop Karmann Ghia and they were driving along the viaduct, windows down, Frannie poking through the ashtray for a decent-sized roach, asking Evan if he couldn't duck down and get it lit, which he did, and they stopped later and bought Cokes and watched the peaks of the Olympics turn slowly to silhouettes from the turnaround at Alki Point. Evan kissed her. It was a kiss without edges, a slippery engulfing kiss. He pulled back and they studied each other. Evan wouldn't have thought there was any room for amazement here, because it was pretty obvious what was up, even if neither had said much over the rushing air and the Ghia's noisy gearbox, and he figured her for an advanced amount of sophistication with regard to moments like this, but there it was: They were both virtually hammerstruck.

Frannie's apartment was reached by means of a double flight of outside stairs, wooden planks, once creosoted. She had a clay pot of primroses on the landing. Evan pressed against her softly as she worked the key.

Inside, the apartment was spare, picked up, indisputably the apartment of a single woman with her own sense of design, of habitation. She went around raising the windows, then disappeared into the bathroom. Evan wandered, discreetly, breathing in the smell of the place, sandalwood maybe, oranges. Here were the spines of her books, here were things she'd collected and laid out, a set of carved ivory figures, yellowed, no bigger than horse chestnuts — a laughing Buddha, a sleeping cat, a mermaid with braided hair, a geisha. He couldn't keep from picking one up, rubbing it with his thumb.

Then Frannie was back, smiling, changed into civvies. Shorts, a sleeveless T-shirt. Even her upper arms were beautiful, the olivey muscles.

What would you like to do now? she asked.

Come here, Evan said.

Frannie laid her open palm against his chest. He felt his pulse bumping in pressure points throughout his body. In just a moment, it would all start.

After his first visit to her apartment, they still had coffee together at work, but often in the company of others. Evan learned to affect a certain nonchalance. *Frannie?* Oh sure, absolutely, they were buds, she was helping him get his footing at the firm. Sometimes he asked if she'd be able to give him a lift, or maybe it was Frannie who'd say, *Going to need a ride tonight?* But otherwise they stuck to the unspoken ground rules: Nothing intimate would be said at work, no matter how secretively. Evan wouldn't ask if she saw other men, nor would he chat innocuously about his life with Claudia. Frannie would never call him at home. She'd refrain from giving him little presents. If she couldn't meet him, for whatever reason, he wouldn't cajole, wouldn't let himself go jagged with frustration.

Could he say he loved her? he wondered. Would she allow it, welcome it, insist on hearing it whether it was true or not, or tell him no, don't say that, please don't even think it? *Did* he love her, or love *it,* the whole situation, the sudden complexity, the danger—Evan, for whom risk taking wasn't a first language?

The sex took place in her west-facing bedroom, the remains of the sunlight strained through a thin cloth curtain with a pattern of cornflowers. Their skin ran with sweat. Rivulets, soaked hair. Sometimes Evan broke down laughing. At work, Frannie was pleasant but focused, definitely not a giggler, not a woman who'd be interested in hearing your hilarious new joke. Only in bed did her comic side emerge. Evan would be grabbing a split-second breather, hoping to postpone the inevitable, poised *right there.* Frannie would make a face and that would be it. She'd say, *So soon? I'm not impressed, Molloy. You should learn some self-control, women dig that.*

Despite the old wisdom, Evan wasn't sad after sex with Frannie. Often he was so used up he didn't know he'd gone to sleep until he woke fifteen minutes later, Frannie's leg twined with his, her fingers, cool now, drawing lines on his forehead. With Claudia he was frequently restless, even claustrophobic, after making love, especially if it was afternoon or early evening, still light out. He'd have to get up and move around, drink a long swill of cold water at the sink. He'd gotten used to hearing her voice from the bedroom, *What're you doing out there, honey?* It wasn't about *her,* though. Sometimes, after coming, a burst of shame tore through him—that he could want sex so much, that anyone could know this fact about him. It was gone an instant later, just a small fit of chemicals in his brain. But how depressing to be reminded that it was *all* chemicals finally—the anticipation, the raging eagerness, even this self of his wondering about it. He had to hang on until that thought, too, was purged.

Strangely, at Frannie's he felt none of this. Though he could never stay long, he woke happy, as if exempt from time. Frannie never seemed sad then, either. She appeared to love the way they pummeled each other, the clowning, teeth-clamping urgency, but he began to think that her true domain was the brief hiatus that followed; her stillness reminded him of a hollow in the grass where a deer has slept.

One of those first visits, he found himself propped up against the headboard, blissfully gazing at their limbs. *You don't have any clothes on,* he said.

Perfectly true, she answered.

When I see you at work, Evan said, *I'll think of you like this.*

Cool, she said. *But that goes two ways.*

Evan said, *I think I get the better deal.*

She said, *Think what you want, mister.*

Evan had vowed not to talk to Frannie about Claudia or his home life, so he ended up talking about his boyhood fascination with the iron shop. He described the slack tub—half an oak whiskey keg, charred inside, still smelling of sour mash—where the hot metal was plunged. He described the dirt-packed floor, the bellows noise, the sunlight spiking down through gaps in the tin sheeting. Donovan had gone to propane in later years, but Evan always remembered the forge as coal-fueled, making the air thick with smoke, and giving the place the aura of standing outside time. The smithy was the province of grown men, that's what he was getting at. *It spoiled me for office work,* he said, then laughed at how he sounded, so damn earnest. It was mainly bullshit. For one thing, the office suited him fine—he liked his yellow tablets, he liked *thinking,* analyzing how things worked. And, for another, he had to remind himself, Donovan spent a good piece of his work life cantilevered over the drafting table, half-lenses slipping down his nose, his hand dirtied by nothing more manly than pencil lead.

For her part, Frannie talked about Mr. Basko, the biology teacher. The white shirts fresh from the laundry, the pleated trousers with suspenders, an uncommon man, almost forty but never married. She saw him in the lab room or the teacher's lounge—as office aide she came and went freely, putting out the mail, observing, overhearing whatever there was to overhear. She said, *He had one of those old-style leather briefcases. I watched him working the brass latches on it one morning, how precise and dignified he seemed, but also powerful and full-grown. I had a kind of intuition. The boys in my own class hit on me, but they were so raw or something, so juiced up on themselves. I hadn't gone all the way with anyone yet. Suddenly, I had the feeling that sex was going to play out differently for me than for my girlfriends. It was going to involve this teacher and have another whole set of consequences.*

I know how this sounds, Evan. Either I was a predator or he was, I needed a father figure, he was into schoolgirls—believe me, we talked about it from a hundred angles. But I had to know if there was anything to my premonition. I started dropping by the biology room after last period and we talked while he checked out equipment for the next morning. Later in the year we'd meet for coffee at night or go for drives. At some point we fell in love, the way normal people do. Everyone says it was his job to not let that happen—and you can argue that, but in our case, I mean, why couldn't we have this? I was almost eighteen, nobody was twisting my arm. Finally, we just went, Screw it, we're going for it.

And, you know, it was terrific for a while. We were like expatriates—in a strange land but together, that kind of feeling. There were all these stereotypes about our situation, but we really wanted to disprove them. We thought we were up to the challenge.

She rolled onto an elbow and looked at Evan. *My fascinating life,* she said.

I'm *fascinated,* Evan said. He lifted her fingers to his mouth, brushed his lips against them.

After a minute, Frannie said, *He was a sweet man. Well, still is, I'm sure.*

You don't have any contact with him? Evan asked.

Not anymore, she answered. *What would the point be?*

Evan nodded, as if to say, *I see.* But this chilled him a little—actually, more than a little. People broke up and moved on all the time, that's how it worked. What about the girl he'd dated before Claudia? He didn't have the first idea about her life after him. Still, to be as intimate as Frannie had been with the biology teacher, and then *nothing.* Evan was having a hard time figuring out what was so troubling about this, but guessed, finally, it was that pledges you made straight-faced, with total conviction, could turn out to have been provisional after all.

Before leaving Frannie's, he always took a quick shower, toweled off in the steamy air, marveling at her cosmetics arrayed on a narrow glass shelf. Brushes, tubes, screw-top jars that Claudia didn't have.

Robe about her loosely, Frannie kissed him at the apartment door and stepped back, giving him up for the night. The tenderness of this gesture nearly broke him. Then he was down the outside stairs and up to the bus stop in long strides, cutting through bands of thickening shadow. A ten-minute wait, lights coming on now, the smell of a brazier in the slow-moving air. Then riding the Number 7, eyeing his fellow passengers, caught up in the illusion that they made a small community. Often, the same two Chinese women with their mesh bags, the student with the glossy blue-black skin, spindle-limbed, regal-looking.

The waitress with her prayer book and scuff-shot white waitress shoes. He remembered thinking, not so long before, that
the condition of marriage had radiated off him for all to see. He
wondered now if the state of visiting Frannie did as well. But
he knew better. No one gave him a second thought. He closed
his eyes and jounced along, feeling the still-wet hair against his
neck. Guilt sometimes whispered at him, *What do you think
you're doing?* A background noise, like the sizzle of the trolley
wires overhead. He smiled to himself, opened one eye, saw
where he was. Another two stops, then he yanked the cord. The
double doors hissed, he stepped onto pavement, picked out the
cowled light above their building's entryway, and made for it.

Liz

FRIDAY EVENINGS during the mid-eighties, Evan often stopped by the old house in Ballard and had a beer with Liz and his father while the freeway cleared. No disrespect to Patricia, but Evan couldn't imagine his father without Liz now. She managed his calendar, took care of correspondence, the requests for donations, and so on. She dealt with the accountant, the assessor's office, the insurance people, Social Security. She was loyal yet independent; she didn't lose her cool. She kept Donovan from eating crap food and got him to cut back on the long hours. In short, Liz handled him in a way Patricia never had, called him on some of the BS, letting the remainder roll off like spring rain.

She always gave Evan the two-cheek kiss, *smack, smack.* Evan had never been the hugging type, but he liked this ritual, being drawn into her warmth and scent for a second. They'd gotten close almost at once. He could confide in her—she'd turned out to be the sister his own sister had never been. Evan was now in his mid-thirties. He and Donovan got on decently these days— bouncing along in his father's wake had already taken whatever toll it was bound to take, he figured. But he was intensely grateful to have Liz present, grateful it wasn't just himself and the old man, nursing drinks and trying to manufacture a conversation.

Evan asked her one night if she was sorry not to have had kids. They were talking on the deck while his father was inside taking a call.

I did want to, Liz said. *I'm actually kind of surprised it never happened. Maybe if I'd been five years younger when I got together with Donovan.*

She gave a little shrug, finished her drink, and slung the ice over the railing.

They sat without talking. It was early fall, still warm enough to sit outside, but some of the plants in the glazed pots had already been cut back, and a dogwood was shedding red leaves onto the deck. It was Liz who spoke finally. *You've got to watch out for your second thoughts,* she said. *Regret's an acid, Evan. My dad kept going on and on about that. Nothing's more potent than regret. It's the strongest thing we feel.*

No argument from me, Evan said.

A moment later she asked gently, *What about you? Children?* They'd discussed his marriage; she knew the lay of the land but never interrogated him, another thing he was grateful for.

Claudia was counting on kids, Evan answered. *She had her work in front of her first, but there seemed to be plenty of time. We'd get to it down the road.*

Then there wasn't *any road,* Liz said.

Evan nodded.

In a moment, he said, *It's just that lately I've been feeling kind of spooked that none of me will go on. Not even my DNA. It's sort of hard to describe.*

Liz gazed at him. She said, *Here's another thing my dad used to say:* You haven't lived your whole life yet. *He was a great font of wisdom, my dad. Not unlike yours.* Evan smiled a little. Liz said, *What I mean is, don't count it out, all right?*

Evan said, *I just feel like I missed my chance.*

But the conversation ended there because Donovan came bustling onto the deck, rubbing his hands. *Hey, we're losing the light,* he said. *Let's get the grill going. You're staying, right, Ev?*

Evan said no, he really should be going.

Donovan gave him that look. *Jesus Christ,* he said, *I came into a big windfall of prawns. You don't need to run off.*

So that was a night Evan ended up staying. And he had to admit there was something vaguely hilarious about the spectacle of his father manning the gas grill after standing at the forge all day.

But, another of those Friday evenings, Liz took him aside before Donovan got home, sat him on a kitchen stool, and told him he wasn't looking so peppy, he'd seemed careworn lately. *How long since you've been to the doctor?* she asked. Evan shrugged. *Do you* have *a doctor?* she asked.

Not exactly, he answered. *Not at the moment.*

Liz said, *Well, you need to get checked out. Have a physical. Will you do that?*

If it were anybody else, Evan would've dug in his heels and insisted nothing was the matter. Patricia, for instance—he'd *hated* worrying her. But it was almost a relief hearing it from Liz. It was true he'd been feeling off lately—headachy, unfocused. Careworn? Not a word he'd have chosen. Drab maybe, but at the same time sort of fretful.

Liz touched him on the shoulder. She said, *Don't blow me off, OK? Because I'll keep asking.*

Evan nodded. He said he knew she was right; he'd make an appointment.

Two weeks later, she called him at home and asked how he was coming with the checkup. Evan said he didn't have a lot of progress to report. Liz said, *Did I not say I'd keep bugging you?*

No, you made that pretty clear, Evan answered.

A few days after that, he was grocery shopping when he simply went to pieces. All at once he felt *terrible.* The only thing he had to compare it to was the stomach flu, or possibly food poisoning—those last seconds before throwing up, when his heart rate spiked and his skin went rubbery. But vomiting wasn't going to relieve this. It was a dire, hurtling sensation. He bowed his head under the store's florescent lights and gripped the cart with both hands, begging whatever it was to stop. Then he abandoned the basket and began walking toward the exit. It was all he could do not to break into a dead run. *Don't want to die,* his inner man was crying, but at least it wasn't aloud, at least people weren't cranking their heads to watch.

Out in the parking lot, he couldn't remember where he'd left the car. Drizzle collected in his hair and trickled down the neck of his jacket. Where was the fucking car? He couldn't stand still; he felt like pumping his arms and legs up and down like a four-year-old. He loped between the aisles of vehicles. Oh Christ, he thought, is it getting worse? Please don't let me pass out. Then he spotted the car, the silver-blue Honda with the rusted quarter panel. He got in and started the motor and sat squeezing the wheel, telling himself it was insane to drive in this shape, but he had to, he had to keep moving, he had to get home. Moments later, merging into traffic, he remembered an incident Patricia had described once, about an older gentleman steering his big boat of a Chrysler to the curb of a downtown street in the midst of having a coronary, her point being his heroic effort not to plow into a crowd of bystanders. But, *Jesus*, Evan was thirty-three, he wasn't having a heart attack.

He made it to the house, bounded upstairs, and lay on his bed taking slow breaths, but had to get up again. He dashed around turning on lights, wondering if this was the moment that would be judged later as his last chance to call for help. He checked his pulse again: still very fast, but not irregular. He walked through the house, then outdoors, up Madrona a ways and back in a heavy mist, then he tried the indoors again. He took his pulse. Slower, closer to normal now, but the beats were huge and hard —he unbuttoned his shirt and he could actually see them inflating the wall of his chest. He lay back in the stuffed chair downstairs and did the slow breathing again, and now he felt the last of whatever it was washing out of him. He pulled a blanket over himself and did nothing for a while. He told himself to get up and eat, but he didn't feel like eating and was afraid any activity would set it off again. He felt so *susceptible* all of a sudden.

Strangely, he woke the next morning in good spirits. Lucid, hungry. He showered and dressed. He remembered the previous day's episode, but it didn't seem to have happened to *him*—it was more like a scene from a movie. He was happy to disown it. At the same time, he knew he couldn't let himself be fooled. It *had* happened to him and could recur. Today, tomorrow.

So that was when he went out and found a doctor, an internist, Dr. Bonney. Roughly Evan's age, curly-headed, prematurely jowly. He talked in a scratchy whisper, with an East Coast accent Evan couldn't quite place. Evan sat on the exam table and explained the situation. The doctor asked how long he'd been that way. Evan said a couple of months, at least, probably longer.

The doctor asked how he'd been sleeping. Evan said not that well.

Can't fall asleep or you wake up early?

Evan said, *I wake up.*

Like four or five o'clock?

More like two or three, Evan said. *Usually I get back to sleep around four.*

The doctor made a note on his clipboard.

Evan described the panic attack (in the three weeks that had passed he'd learned what it was). The doctor asked if there'd been anything traumatic in his life recently. Evan said not really. The doctor waited as if expecting more. *It's been ten years since I got divorced,* Evan said. *Five since my mother died.*

The doctor nodded.

Kind of old news, Evan said.

Dr. Bonney said, *You and your mother were close?*

We were, actually, Evan said. *Pretty close.*

The doctor wrote again.

Later he did a physical exam. Tapped on Evan's chest, listened to his lung sounds, looked around in his mouth, snapped on a glove and checked his prostate. He told Evan he wanted him to have a fasting blood test.

Except for his cholesterol, the numbers turned out to be more or less normal—thyroid, hematocrit, glucose levels, white count, and so on. Evan was prescribed the first of the sleeping remedies, told to exercise and give the caffeine a rest.

Things kept deteriorating anyway.

His ears rang, his eyelid twitched, his hands often had a fine tremor. He felt *unwell*. He made no mention of this at work—flying under the radar seemed like the best plan. He juggled his schedule. The days he was shakiest, he came in midmorning, then stayed into the evening to catch up. With everyone gone, the offices had a stillness that helped his concentration. The downside was that working late often left him too wound up to sleep when he got home. And sometimes, unaccountably, the failing light outside made him feel intensely vulnerable—and sad. He took to dropping the office blinds well before sunset. Hours later, when he left the building, it would be night and the city lights would be blazing. Night itself wasn't a problem.

Several times, stirring around the house after midnight, he tried smoking a joint. He hadn't really smoked dope since his mid-twenties, but he kept a small amount in the freezer. He'd already given up on wine at bedtime—the drowsiness was nice, but as soon as the alcohol metabolized he woke with a vengeance, revved but brittle. Dope didn't do that. A few tokes in front of the TV—he loved the smell, *grass,* that first wave of buoyancy and benevolence. What he used to like was how silly everything seemed when he smoked. And *sex*—boy, he'd loved it when he was stoned. Talk about disappearing into the cosmos. But one afternoon when he and Claudia were climbing into the sack, he stopped to light a joint, and a look came across her face, a quick flare of disappointment (she smoked, too, it wasn't that). He knew enough to set the joint back in the ashtray and let it go out. She'd seen that even if he did want her, simply making love with her wasn't good enough; it needed *enhancing.* That was the last thing he wanted her to think, so from then on, no dope before bed, unless it was her idea.

But there was no silliness now and no sex. Pretty soon he remembered why he'd *stopped* smoking dope. After the first half-hour, the benign feeling segued into apprehension. Not paranoia, exactly—he wasn't afraid storm troopers were about to bust in. It was that he seemed to lose his *self*. He'd gotten close enough to see that it was made of pixels, then seen them wink out randomly until there was no picture left. So now, alone in the house and unable to sleep, he found himself wondering how long before the goddamn dope wore off and was grateful when it did and his wits came creeping back.

Pretty soon he was at Dr. Bonney's again. *We may have to start you on one of the tricyclics,* the doctor told him. *You should also have a tranquilizer.*

Isn't that sort of extreme? Evan asked.

The doctor had a way of lowering the clipboard before he said important things, a paternal gesture that got Evan's back up. He said, *There's various things we can try, Evan, but unless you cycle out of it on your own, we'll have to get this under control with medication.*

What are the odds of it just going back where it came from? Evan asked. The doctor said he really couldn't answer that. Evan frowned. *I hate to think of being all whacked out,* he said. *I've got to go to work and everything.*

Then again, the doctor said, *you have to ask yourself how well the work's going as it is.*

Reluctantly, Evan nodded. After a moment, he said, *It's not just taking it, it's being someone who* needs *to take it.*

The doctor wrote on his prescription pad. He said, *It'll take some getting used to, but I think you* are *someone who needs it, Evan.*

Evan was resistant. There was something he didn't trust about this doctor and his pharmacopoeia. He came away feeling stained, guilty of an obscure sin. He remembered how Patricia had hauled him off to the pediatrician as a boy, his stomach crampy and painful to the touch for no good reason. The thought of his body crapping out on him—really, it was appalling. The whole idea of being inside a body with its own sinister agenda, sometimes it seemed beyond belief. Who'd dream up such a scheme? Why *shouldn't* you be prickly with dread? These weren't new thoughts, nor was the chemical turmoil being churned out by rogue elements of his brain totally unfamiliar. It was just so *relentless* now; it was asking so much of him.

And yet when spring finally arrived that year, he *did* begin to cycle out of it. Slowly at first, then more rapidly as the days lengthened. He began to feel like himself again. He slept; he ate regular meals. He could sit still and pay attention to something outside himself.

Reunion

PEOPLE SOMETIMES REFERRED to his *ex-wife*. It jarred him, even into his thirties. Claudia, they meant. Part of him had never adjusted. For a few years, he heard about her through mutual friends—learned, for instance, that she'd left Seattle and relocated to the Bay Area. But then, for a long time, nothing.

Once, in the early eighties, he saw Sadie on the sidewalk in Queen Anne. He'd been to an early movie and was still mildly hypnotized as he emerged into the winter light. It took him a second to recognize her, and his impulse was to turn away and investigate the COMING SOON posters under the marquee. Instead, he straightened and watched her approach and finally called out. Only then did it occur to him that they hadn't been face to face since before his separation (then divorce) from Claudia.

Oh, it's you, she said. There was a moment of eye contact as Sadie seemed to sort out her own impulses. She'd never rebuked him properly. She owed him, but not out on the street like this; she didn't have it in her to make a public scene after six years. Or even just cut him with an icy stare: *Would you get out of my way, please.* She readjusted her grip on the string bag in her hand. She said, not quite a question, *You didn't stay with that girl.* Evan shook his head. Sadie gave a single nod in reply, as if to say, *Yes, that's how it usually works.*

Headlights were coming on and the air had an edge. Sadie said, *She remarried, Claudia. Did you know that?*

I hadn't heard, Evan answered.

He hoped to god he didn't look as slammed as he felt. *Well, would you tell her*— he started to say, stalling. What *did* he mean to say? He tried to get a handle on it, but Sadie preempted him, waggled her free hand in the air separating them. *No, Evan,* she said, *I'm sorry, I'm not going to tell her anything.*

And so Evan said his goodbye and let her go. He set off in the opposite direction, clammy under his clothes, overheated even in the cold.

As to his own love life, he'd eventually started getting out again and later drifted into an affair that consumed a couple of years. Semiregular sex, weekend trips—but there was no *combustion* really. Even the breakup was strangely tepid—a miscommunication, time passing, a final meeting clotted with lapses of attention on both sides. In its wake, Evan found himself thinking of Robie's sister again, not her death (though it wasn't far from his mind) but how it had felt to be in the car with her outside the iron shop, their sweaty backs against the doors, their legs crossing in the middle of the bench seat. Not exactly a private place, yet he was far removed from life as he'd known it. He couldn't remember exactly what he and this girl had talked about so feverishly. Stuff she'd turned up in her reading, undoubtedly, clues about living authentically, taking the blinders from your eyes, and the like. He was afraid it would all sound sophomoric now—he'd lost his tolerance for the pseudo-mystical, for credulous hippie wisdom. But she'd *shaken* him; that was the point.

She'd gotten him to see that there was more to the world than you got from tuning in the regular stations. This was precisely how he'd expected college to make him feel: on the threshold of great secrets. But when he reached the university, he found that it rarely did. Just often enough to tease him—the occasional jolting exchange with a prof, the occasional mind-blowing passage in some reading. The majority of the time, he lingered in a state of low-grade disappointment.

Now, in his mid-thirties, unattached, he worried that this same discontent would dampen *any* relation he had with a woman, no matter who it was, no matter how thrilling their first attraction to each other, how thrilling the first sex, how much intellectual edge or style she had. The letdown would set in. Was it a condition of the world, or specific to him? Why was boredom so close at hand? He began to believe his capacity to love was somehow stunted and had no idea what to do about it.

After Claudia had abandoned their apartment on Healey Avenue, Evan stayed on, hoping the marriage might yet heal, then lingering a few months longer, hating the symbolism of quitting the place they'd moved into with such confidence. He rented an apartment, within walking distance of work. But that one he never settled into properly—it had a mossy smell and the light was gloomy. He moved again, this time taking the top floor of a house in an out-of-the-way neighborhood above Lake Union. Much better. He might've remained there indefinitely if it hadn't been for his sister. Gayle had begun to rag on him about buying before prices went higher, reminding him over and over how stupid it was to keep paying rent, telling him he was just pounding money down a rat hole.

Several Saturdays, Evan let her drive him around, and later, alone, more and more taken with the prospect of living outside the city, he began looking farther to the south, and finally discovered the house at 12 Madrona Street: FOR SALE BY OWNER. A late-1920s bungalow, brown-shaked, with a generous upper story and graced by morning sun. He listened to the owner's spiel, nodding attentively as the timbered ceilings were pointed out, the original tile work in the kitchen, the art-deco sconces, as he was told that the water heater was virtually new, also the roof shingles, guaranteed for twenty years. Evan asked a few questions, thanked the man, shook hands, and drove off. But that night and over the next few days, he found himself picturing the layout in his mind's eye—slipping from room to room, roving the yard, seeing the sway of the cedar branches and the blackberry-thick terrain where it dropped away toward the water. He thought, Yes, this one. Already it seemed his. He hurried back and plunked down earnest money.

A few months after the end of their relationship, Frannie had quietly given notice and left Dimond & Associates. Evan assumed she had let others in on her plans, but, in fact, no one seemed to know where she'd landed. Or maybe she'd sworn them to secrecy. Sooner or later, he thought, a rumor of her would waft back. He tried to picture how it would be if they bumped into each other, a year or two down the road. Then he tried not to. As things turned out, though, there *were* no rumors. Evan never saw her again, never heard a thing.

Evan had left Dimond before long himself. Only then did he really appreciate how the affair had cost Frannie her job—as cool a customer as she was, continuing to work near him had proven untenable. Maybe everyone had known about them, after all, he thought. People weren't stupid. In any case, Evan had made a valiant effort to keep the wreckage of his private life private and was pretty sure that if he just kept facing forward, his composure would return, and whatever taint was on him professionally would gradually wear off. Though he'd been promoted once at his first job, he'd always felt he was playing catch-up there, that he'd be the perpetual apprentice. But at Dimond he'd gotten his feet under him. He liked the teamwork. He liked the client base, emerging companies usually. He liked how the assignments changed every three or four months—crossing the floor of a plant, or threading his way back through a maze of desks and workstations, he'd get a blast of relief that he wasn't chained to one spot, one numbing task. He liked doing interviews, picking through data, getting it in order, pinpointing where the flow of actions bogged down, and so on. Problem solving. And when he made his follow-up visits, and saw that the clients had actually put his recommendations into action, and that his predictions had been correct—it was satisfying, even more than that sometimes: These businesses were typically in the throes of their first radical expansion and Dimond's analysis was literally what kept them alive. But, for all that, Evan knew he had to start fresh.

He borrowed one of Donovan's shop vans, took off into the Cascades, and spent three weeks alone. He read beside small campfires, ate charred hot dogs off a stick, listened to the coyotes yipping and barking, wrote entries in a journal—notes to himself, observations. Not exactly forty days and forty nights, but enough distance from ordinary life to see its shape. He was twenty-nine. He'd come by his occupation more or less by chance. If he wanted to change horses, now was the time to figure it out. But what he brought back to town was the understanding that he really *didn't* want anything else.

He dropped the truck off at the iron shop, thanked Donovan for the loan, then shut himself in the shop office and put in a call to Harry Glover, the partner who'd split from the firm where Evan first worked (Evan had kept loose track of him ever since). They met for lunch the following week and talked the better part of two hours. When he'd interviewed in the past, he'd been obliged to conjure up a hypothetical Evan Molloy—quick learner, ripe with potential. Now he had a track record. He answered questions without feeling that a trapdoor was about to open under his chair. Harry said he'd be on the road for a week, but Evan should swing by the office when he got back. Evan thanked him, said he would. At the end of that second meeting, Evan was hired.

And then, one evening in 1987, twelve years after their divorce, Claudia called. Could he spare a few minutes to catch up?

Actually, I can, Evan said. He'd been undressing and was now sitting on the edge of the bed in his boxers.

She told him she'd been in California most of the time they'd been out of contact but had recently moved back. She was working for a software company called Acropolis; Evan recognized the name, that was about all—computer audio, he thought.

And I have a daughter, she said. *Janey. She's almost ten.*

Amazing, Evan heard himself say.

Before he could inquire, Claudia told him that her marriage to Janey's father was over. Evan asked if he should be sorry.

No, don't be, she told him. *Anyway, it's getting to be old news.*

Evan waited to see if she'd elaborate. Instead, she asked how *he* was doing. The first thing that came to mind was the previous winter's malaise or illness. He almost started describing it, then didn't. He was fine now, why muddy the waters? He said simply, *Holding my own.*

Too bad you can't find someone else to hold it, Claudia shot back, an echo of the silly repartee they'd used on each other years before.

He had to smile. *Don't I know it,* he said.

A little dead air.

It's very strange to be talking to you, he said.

I know.

Why had she called? Just reopening the lines of communication? He reached back over his head and snapped off the lamp. The streetlight came through the blinds, throwing slats of shadow across his legs. He said, *You moved back for the job?*

It was too major an opportunity not to take, she said. *I was a little homesick, too, I guess. Work had been good, kind of frantic sometimes, but I always liked it that way—no, I just never felt like I belonged down there. It seemed a little like being in exile.*

She left it at that. A moment later she asked how his father was.

Same as ever, Evan answered. *Bigger than life.* He told her about the marriage to Liz.

And Mama-san? she asked then.

So no one had told her. Instantly, his mother's death seemed very fresh again. He felt himself start to sag but shored himself up and gave Claudia the story.

She said, *God, Ev, I wish you'd tried to reach me. Really. Sadie would've passed along a message.*

I don't think I'm her favorite person, Evan answered. *Anyway, I thought you'd rather I left you alone. It was a judgment call.*

Poor judgment, Claudia could've fired back. But all she said was, *I'm so sorry to hear this, Evan. It just seems really—I don't know, I can't believe it.*

In the end, Claudia never did say why she'd phoned. Whatever the motive, Evan thought, it would come out sooner or later.

The following week, he found himself going back over what they'd said and reflecting on their three-year stint of marriage. He discovered that, surprisingly, he could hold his mind to it without flinching, without the spikes of queasiness. One of them would call a second time, or else not. Evan's inclination was to let it be her, unless some urgent reason presented itself.

None did. Another four months passed. Then, as it turned out, *he* was the one. Just dialed her up without a dime's worth of forethought. She answered immediately and they talked again. He realized that she'd been holding back before. She sounded freer now, able to let down her guard. They both could. But she also seemed—well, not sad, maybe a little fatigued, as if her bodily energy and self-assurance weren't boundless, after all.

A few days later, she called back to see if he wanted to meet her daughter. *I'm not asking anything in particular, Evan. I mean it. It's just I feel like you and I have some connection, and Janey really ought to—*

Get an object lesson in the perfidy of men, Evan thought. But he said, *That would be good.*

They decided to meet on neutral ground. A walk around Green Lake, then a simple lunch at a nearby café. It turned out to be a decent day for the off-season, high forties, the sky broken, the clouds like molten pewter.

Janey was a beanstalk with a blue tam and thick-lensed glasses. Behind them her eyes were like Claudia's, intelligent, alive—yet different, shadowed by reluctance or skittishness, he couldn't tell quite what it was. Her head came up to his shoulder, and already she held herself like a tall girl, apologizing for the sin of size.

Evan gave his hand. She shook it formally. *I'm happy to know you,* he said. Janey nodded, taut-lipped.

He turned to Claudia, noticed that she'd done away with her glasses. He smiled, said, *Contacts?* She gave a quick nod. She wore a leather jacket snapped at the waist, a red scarf. Her face was fuller, less blanched-looking, the plain bangs replaced by a perm of loose black ringlets. She leaned in, they touched cheeks, then began to walk.

Second Sight

IT WASN'T LOVE at second sight.

Still, Evan was amazed at how little rancor Claudia displayed, how uninterested she seemed in airing old grievances. It felt good to be in her company again. More than good. Yet, he wasn't entirely at peace. He couldn't help wondering why he should receive this gift. He waited for her to yank him up short: *Look, Evan, please don't get the wrong idea here, OK?* He even asked himself whether Claudia's amity belonged to an elaborate, as yet to unfold act of revenge, but this he wrote off as unadulterated paranoia. Alternatively, he wondered if she was courting him. That didn't seem to be the case, either. The dynamic between them was trickier to put your finger on. But he couldn't deny what she'd admitted on the phone: Despite the time apart (and what had necessitated it), he and Claudia were still, in a way, connected.

Sunday afternoons, now, the three of them often saw a matinee, then Evan cooked at his place. He began stocking the beer Claudia liked and cream soda and cocoa for Janey. Occasionally, during the week, they had supper at a street-front spot in

Claudia's neighborhood, then Evan accompanied them back to the apartment but never stayed long. He tried to be friendly to Janey, without being patronizing or assuming he automatically had authority over her. For her part, Janey didn't act as if he were an interloper—so far Evan had managed to escape hearing a sneered, *You're not my father*.

He often saw her on the floor of her room, bent over a spiral notebook. Her writing was spidery and back-slanted; she had the left-hander's indelible ink smudge down the heel of her hand. Now and then, possibly at Claudia's insistence, she'd ask him for help with schoolwork. It was here, one on one, that Evan began to appreciate how frequently Janey seemed to have multiple, often competing scripts running at the same time. For instance, as to the homework, she wanted his help—she had a finely developed fear of being wrong—but received it grudgingly, as if angry at Evan for knowing things she didn't. Fortunately, Evan sniffed that one out early. Slyly (he hoped), he started talking up the value of ignorance—as opposed to stupidity. This had been one of Donovan's big themes. Ignorance was a natural state that led to invention and revelation, but stupidity gave him conniptions. It could get you killed, you and those around you. Evan seemed to make some headway on that score—increasingly, she was willing to ask him questions—but she still seemed a chronically mixed bag of emotions.

One morning, not long before the school year's end, an earthquake rattled through Puget Sound: Richter 6.4, epicenter off Vashon Island. Evan had been standing in his shower, water drumming on his skull, so he'd been oblivious to the subterranean rumble others reported. Without warning, the tiles underfoot began to shudder—it was like a freight elevator jerking to life. He thought at first it was happening *inside* him. Another attack, coming from nowhere. Buckling knees, faint-headedness. He grabbed wildly for the shower curtain and only then realized that everything in the bathroom was jiggling along with him. A pill bottle danced off the shelf; water sloshed and plumed up out of the toilet.

Thirty miles north, Evan found out later, Janey had just strapped on her book bag, left the top-floor apartment, and started downstairs to the bus. Suddenly, she heard what sounded like a big jet flying dangerously low, but the noise was caroming all around the stairwell, coming from everywhere at once. She dropped to her knees and clutched the uprights of the iron railing. In California, she'd felt dozens, maybe hundreds, of minor quakes; she'd been drilled in how to save her life, but now she froze. Claudia's building stood in a part of the city with loose subsoil, actually fill, and was very sensitive to movement—they routinely felt heavy trucks banging over rough seams in the street. As Janey held on, head down, eyes pinched shut, praying for it to end, a chunk of stone cornice broke off the neighboring building and fell two stories onto the skylight above her. Chips of sooty glass rained onto her hair and shoulders, the bigger fragments as well as the cornice piece thundering down beside her, clear through to the ground floor. Even in the din, Claudia heard the razory wail that came from her daughter, but by the time she reached her, the quake was over. A few last slivers of broken skylight ticked onto the terrazzo. Inside the walls, a joint settled with a small wince, then, except for Janey's panting, the stairwell was as still as a mine shaft after a cave-in.

Janey and Claudia described all this for Evan when he arrived; he'd set off as soon as possible, but the trip took forever with the backups and closed bridges. The three of them stood in the high-ceilinged kitchen—it hadn't suffered gross damage, but things had a jostled, displaced look. Claudia asked Janey to sit again, then to Evan she said, *I think it's all out of her hair. We washed it in the sink and I combed it* (an aluminum comb was still dangling from her hand), *and then I tried going over it with the flashlight. I thought if there was any fine dust—*

Evan nodded. *Jesus, what a thing,* he said. He turned to Janey. *But you're OK, right?*

She shook her head noncommittally. Then, as if showing him stigmata, opened her fists to display the red creases in her palms from the square edges of the railing bars.

Evan wasn't sure how to play this—emphasizing the freakishness of nature seemed like a poor idea. He said, *Wow, you got a front-row seat, I'm jealous.* Before she could object, he explained about being in the shower when it hit. *I thought I was going to have to run out into the yard stark naked,* he said. *But please don't picture that, OK?* He looked at Claudia. *You either,* he said. That seemed to cut the tension.

You know about aftershocks? he asked then. Janey nodded. But it was hard to tell what she knew, so he said, *There may be more shaking in the next few hours, but it's a natural part of this quake, not a new one. Understand?* She nodded again. After that, Claudia made coffee and they watched the coverage on TV—the local network affiliates, but even CNN had it. Evan got out the road atlas and marked the epicenter for Janey, and drew squiggles where he thought the major fault lines ran. Putting it back into the realm of the knowable, that was Evan's way. He'd handle it the same if he could do it again, but he'd give her more of a chance to recount her onrush of fear. How selfish grownups were sometimes, urging the child to confirm that yes, she's fine, couldn't be better.

Maybe a month after the quake, Evan and Janey sat on the sofa and watched a 60 *Minutes* segment about newly excavated tombs in the Valley of the Kings. Later, at dinner, he described seeing the King Tut exhibit in 1978. He'd entered the maze of gold-filled rooms at midnight, among the day's last group of visitors—the lights were extinguished behind them as they went, giving the place a distinctly hushed and tomblike feel, but that part he kept to himself. Janey asked him how mummification was done, then what a Canopic jar was. *It's where they stash the internal organs of the person who's the mummy,* Evan answered, amazed that he'd been called on to produce this nugget of arcane information. She said, *They don't still do that?* For a second, he wasn't sure what she was driving at. *You mean to people like us? No, not as a rule.* She nodded solemnly. A few days later, she asked about autopsies, if everybody got one. Evan said only if the circumstances were fishy, or they needed to be totally certain how a person died. At this point, Claudia threw them both a dire look: *Enough with the morbid stuff. What's with you two?* But Janey didn't strike Evan as morbid exactly. Oversensitive, maybe, trying overly hard to get her ducks in a row (Evan had had his own duck problems over the years). Anyway, he thought they got along fairly well, all in all. Even had a certain rapport, he sometimes believed.

Yet, other nights she'd turn owly and implacable for no obvious reason. Just put a wall up. *What is it?* he wanted to ask her. *Can't I do something for you?*

The answer was no. There were times she wouldn't make eye contact, or instead of answering his question, screwed her mouth into a rodentlike expression; he couldn't believe it wasn't meant to be comic, but it wasn't. Or she'd slip into the third person, saying things like, *Janey's not tuning in your station*—remarks that might sound hip coming from a twenty-five-year-old, but from Janey seemed disturbingly off-the-wall.

You can't take it personally, Claudia told him when they were alone. *I'm sure it's all about Luc and me. I'm sorry you have to be on the receiving end.*

Lucas was the second husband. Evan had seen Janey's thicket of photos in their sleek Plexiglas frames: Lucas beside a blue marlin hung from a chain. Lucas piloting a bumper car as Janey squeezed his upper arm and shrieked. Lucas eating a hot dog, taking care not to dribble mustard on his shirt. And the black-

and-white studio shot: Lucas in a business suit, hair glistening, freshly razor cut. His skin had a smoky cast, his eyes were almond-shaped, disappearing into hooded lids. An entirely different gene pool from Evan's. Hungarian, Magyar. He had the gaze of a second-generation immigrant on the make, Evan thought.

I know I shouldn't, he said. *I mean, I don't take it personally. It's just kind of capricious.*

Claudia shook her head softly.

One Saturday, Janey went off to her grandmother Sadie's for the weekend. Claudia and Evan spent a peaceable afternoon inspecting the antique warehouses under the viaduct, then dawdled at Ivar's over steamers and beer. Later, at the apartment, she asked if he'd like to stay over.

Up to this point, they'd been chaste, two survivors of an old calamity. For weeks, he'd wondered if sleeping with her again was inevitable—or was it the one thing that was *never* going to happen? But now that the moment was upon him, he knew he'd been shielding himself from the truth of how much he wanted her and was suddenly scared he was going to blow it. Relax, he told himself. But he didn't want to relax; he wanted to feel the excitement sparking all through him.

Claudia was sideways on the sofa, sleepy-eyed, one long leg folded beneath her. Evan was beside her. Sounds drifted in from the street.

The thing is, Evan said after a while, *I didn't bring a toothbrush.*

Oh, darn, she answered. *I guess you'll have to go, then.*

Evan reached a hand out and rubbed the glossy skin over her anklebone.

She said, *Is this nuts?* It sounded rhetorical. She lowered her head and laid it in his lap. Evan cleared the hair from her face.

After a few moments, she said, *You know what I'd really like? Just to have you in bed with me.*

Evan said, *So this is what you might call a limited offer?*

Let's just see, she told him.

But what was he supposed to wear to bed? How tacky would it be to keep on the undershorts he'd worn all day—clean that morning, but still? He took a quick shower, gargled with toothpaste water, then came from the bathroom, towel about his middle. Claudia was in thin cotton bottoms and a T-shirt washed halfway to oblivion. She folded back the comforter and got into bed, then looked in his direction, eyebrows raised. Evan switched off the light, ditched the towel, and slid in beside her.

She ran a hand down his bare flank. She whispered, *Your jammies—* Evan smiled up at the darkness.

You'd like to sleep? he asked.

Claudia went, *Mmmmm.*

He felt her lips vibrating on his skin. *Sleep then,* he said.

You're OK with that?

Evan said, *I'm good.*

Claudia said, *This is such a—*

What?

—a luxury.

In no time, her breathing slowed. Evan hadn't slept a whole night with anyone in—well, too long. Unsettling to acknowledge, but there it was. He lay hearing the muted noises of the street. He floated, vigilant, trying not to think. Maybe he dozed a little, but then Claudia's whole body gave a hard jerk, her fingers seized the straggle of hair on his chest as if grabbing at dried weeds while falling off a cliff. It was all he could do not to yelp out loud.

She woke anyway, panting, confused. She tried to sit up. *God, she said, I was, I don't know—*

Evan said, *Shhh, you're fine.* He jockeyed himself around so he could hold her from behind. He touched his lips to the hollow below her ear. *All right?* he asked softly.

She murmured something and took his hand between hers. Soon she fell asleep again.

He woke after dawn, alone among the sheets. The apartment was soundless except for the tick of rain on the fire escape. He pulled on pants and went barefoot down the hall and stood in the kitchen doorway. Claudia was sitting with her coffee, looking out a window, smoking. Eventually, she turned, swept the hair from her face and saw him. *Spying?* she said.

Evan said, *Not really.*

She asked if he had to leave.

Not for a while, he answered.

He *had* been spying, of course, having a look at how she was these days, Claudia at thirty-seven. It might have been better if he'd pulled away right then, saving them both from the future, but he felt no foreknowledge of disaster, no special wisdom emanating from his body, just the prickle of excitement.

He watched her hand seek out the lighter and fire up another smoke. *You know it's a shame smoking's so bad for you,* he said. *You're really good at it.*

Claudia looked at him, trying not to grin. *How'm I supposed to take that?* she asked.

Evan said, *Another in a long history of mixed signals.*

He peered into the icebox and drew out a bottle with two inches of apple juice. *May I?* he asked.

It's yours, she said.

Evan drank.

Thanks for last night, she said.

My pleasure, he answered. He went off to find his shirt. Behind him, he heard the bathroom door, the hiss of the shower. He stood buttoning up, eyeing himself in the full-length mirror, trying to comb his hair with his fingers. The shower stopped with a pipe clank. There was Claudia, dripping wet. *You still here?* she said.

Evan turned. *Here's something I haven't seen in a while,* he said.

It looks OK? Not too saggy?

Not saggy at all, he said, which was both true and the right answer.

Claudia toppled him onto the unmade bed, gathered her wet hair back and kissed him. *You taste like apples,* she said, rising up to see his face. Evan smiled. She said, *What're the chances of talking you into something?*

He let his fingers trail down her breastbone. *You have the whitest skin,* he said.

But even after that morning in early April, they didn't go full-speed ahead. They took their time. As much as Claudia wanted Evan to know her daughter, she was clear about not injecting more confusion into Janey's world. And, really, what exactly was going on between them? Maybe only nostalgia, maybe just the undoing of old tensions. It seemed more substantial than that — but how *much* more, how much weight could it bear?

So they went slowly, avoiding grand declarations, keeping watch. If I give my word, will it be worth anything? Evan wondered over and over. Can I be a safe harbor this time? He tried to imagine dishonoring Claudia again. The thought of it gave his gut a shot of the same woozy repulsion as the sight of an operation on TV, a body sliced open in full color. He wasn't the same man he'd once been. Though he was still superstitious about predicting the future—wasn't it just begging to be tripped up? And those months, the previous year, when his nervous system betrayed him, what about that? But you can't live always assuming catastrophe. And so, despite the rustle of misgivings, Evan began to view the situation as that rarest of things, the second chance.

Pamela

For a few days after Ned's call, Maureen plays telephone tag with the woman friend she left messages for that night. Then, one weekend morning, a woman Evan assumes is this friend appears at the house. She's bearing a white bakery bag. Taller, darker than Maureen, fuller through the hips and a couple of years older, wearing a tie-dyed sundress, her coarse black hair in a ponytail coming undone. Maureen makes coffee. She and Pamela go outside and settle in canvas chairs, shadowed by the cedars, the lemon bars on a blue glass plate beside them. Two women talking, a Saturday morning in summer, a day that will later blaze but has enough of a breeze now to clack the bamboo wind chimes the Fessendens left behind and toy with the hem of Pamela's dress.

Close by, Evan sits cross-legged on the brickwork patio he laid here ages ago. It's gotten wavy from tree roots over time, and the gaps between the bricks are tufted with moss. He listens intently. It's now that he begins to piece things together: that Ned's a doctor—a radiologist, he guesses from other things that are said—that Pamela works at the same hospital or clinic where

Maureen used to work, and that the affair with Ned reaches back a couple of years at least.

Don't let me eat all these, Pamela says, licking powdered sugar from her fingers. She has a big smile, big teeth. Her sandal dangles off her foot, jiggling rhythmically as she talks.

You know what, Maureen says, breaking a lull, *I haven't been entirely straight with you.*

Pamela waits for her to go on, but Maureen only gives a twist of her mouth. *Don't tell me anything you don't want to,* Pamela says.

They look at each other another few seconds, then Maureen says flatly, *I got pregnant.*

Yuh? Pamela asks, big lines appearing in her forehead.

Maureen nods.

Pamela says, *But you're not now.*

No, Maureen tells her, she isn't now.

These things happen, Pamela says then, but Maureen isn't buying her nonchalance. *Not to me they don't,* she answers. *It was stupid, stupid.* There's that fierceness Evan witnesses at odd moments.

You didn't put it there yourself, Pamela says.

I don't care, Maureen snaps. *I have no excuse. Zip, zero.*

They leave it that way for a moment. Now it's Evan who waits.

And this was when exactly? Pamela asks.

February, Maureen tells her.

Pamela nods. *But weren't you tempted to—?*

Maureen says, *Go through with it? About two-thirds of one very crappy night.*

The two women stare back and forth until Maureen finally says, *It wasn't going to happen, Pam. It wasn't. It was a fantasy. I wasn't going to raise it alone. And Ned—It wasn't going to happen.*

Pamela says, *He doesn't know about this?*

Maureen shakes her head and the accompanying look says she's taking this information to her grave.

As it all sinks in, Pamela's gaze drifts away. Suddenly she's looking straight at Evan, almost seems to be *focusing* on him. Her expression falters, goes dead blank for a long instant. Before he can stop himself, Evan says, *Pamela?* Then again, more sharply, *Do you see something?* But, that quickly, the look vanishes. She bends, replaces the sandal strap on her heel, turns back to her friend, and says, *So he thinks what, that you just broke it off on general principles?*

Maureen takes one of the lemon bars and holds it in her open palm but doesn't lift it to her mouth. *I don't know, I told him I couldn't do it anymore,* she says. *I said I was tapped out. I knew that wasn't going to be enough, I knew I had to get out of there. But then, finding out I was knocked up, it was like, OK, rub my face in it, you know what I'm saying? I mean, even now, I'm just kind of—not right.*

Oh, babe, Pamela says. *Why didn't you say something? I wish you'd told me.*

I feel like I shouldn't be telling you now, Maureen says.

Pamela studies her, sympathy laced with impatience—it's an old dispute between them, Evan guesses, Maureen's desire to go it alone, to keep her own counsel.

After a moment, Pamela says, *You know they never filled your spot. They've just been using temps. I wish you'd see about coming back. I know if you talked to them —*

Maureen says no, she's here now; she's not coming back. People are going to have to get used to it.

Well, I miss you, Pamela says.

Evan sees that Maureen is about to say something almost cutting, something she doesn't mean and will have to apologize for, but she stops, diverts herself by tipping her head and fixing her eyes on a swath of empty, washed-blue sky. At last, strangely distant, she says, *I'm not one thing and I'm not another, that's how it feels.*

We all feel like that. At least, part of the time, Pamela tells her.

But Maureen's obviously in no mood for platitudes. Pamela lets it drop. Switching gears, she says, *I don't know how he got your number. But you can always get a new one.*

I just got this goddamn number, Maureen answers.

Pamela jumps in, *But if he's harassing you.*

It's not — Maureen starts to object, but then says, *I don't know what it is he's doing.*

Pamela says, *I can't stand the thought of anything bad happening to you.*

I don't know if it is or not, Maureen answers. *I overreact.*

Pamela says, *You're entitled to overreact, don't you think? You've gotta take care of yourself.*

I am, Maureen says.

Pamela says, *Why am I not convinced?*

A look passes between them. After a minute, Maureen says, *I'm just in limbo land, that's all.*

Then it's just the bamboo chimes, barely touching, and a single crow rasping as it waddles along the gravel lane.

Pamela breaks off half a lemon bar, eats unhurriedly. *You know what,* she says finally, *I passed a farmer's market on my way here, why don't we have a look.* And before her friend can raise an objection, she says, *Come on,* standing, gathering up plates and cups.

Evan watches Maureen. Hesitation, then acquiescence. The fleeting crinkle at the corner of her eyes, not a smile, not a grimace.

The two women slip around the corner of the house and Evan feels a little suck of abandonment. A few minutes later, he hears Pamela's van door slam, then a second door, heavier, the old Mercedes, followed by the rattle of the diesel. Then the two cars back into the turnaround and are gone.

For a while, Evan doesn't budge from the cool bricks. Delicious human talk—he could've listened the rest of the morning and all afternoon. But eventually, he gets up and begins his slow navigation of the property.

A day like this, Riley would ordinarily be stretched full-length on the stone step of the shed, taking the sun. Or dozing in the speckled shade beneath the rhodies. Except that since Evan no longer sleeps, the cat probably doesn't either, so—as Donovan used to say if anyone caught him nodding off during a Husky game—Riley's no doubt just *resting his eyes.*

That first summer, profoundly ignorant about his new station in the scheme of things, Evan had wondered if perhaps the cat had been assigned to him as a guide; Riley's collar tag read *1986,* which gave him seniority. The folly of that idea was soon obvious. In other words, Evan thought, the afterlife was as short on explanation as life had been. Later on, since they'd evidently been alive at the same time, he asked the cat, *How come I don't remember seeing you around?* Riley gave a few perfunctory licks where Evan had been petting him, as if to say, *Not my fault if you weren't observant.* But the cat bore no grudges. He often walked along at Evan's heels, high-stepping if the grass was dewy, going so far as to occasionally join Evan on the shed roof (the view was great). *How'd you get up here?* Evan asked the first time, then thought, Right, same way I did.

But the cat's AWOL today. Again it occurs to Evan that he hasn't seen him for what's getting to be quite a while. So no Riley, and now no Maureen. The lift he'd gotten earlier, overhearing the two women, has already begun to fade, giving way to a more sober mood.

Intangible

W HEN TWILIGHT ARRIVES that evening, Maureen's still not home.

Evan revisits the idea that the friend, Pamela, seemed to catch a flicker of him. Are there, after all, a few people who see what others don't? He never had any use for psychics or channelers or would-be spoon-benders—he was like Donovan in that regard. So has he changed his mind? But that's the thing: His mind *itself* is different, not so wedded to the definite as it once was, more vulnerable to the fragile air of the intangible.

He finds himself recalling an incident that took place when the DiNobilos lived here.

He hadn't much liked this couple. They were bland, seldom a raised voice or squeal, seldom an obscure remark for Evan to turn over in his mind. In any case, Mrs. DiNobilo's sister had been visiting from Pennsylvania. It was late afternoon, going dark. The two women were in the kitchen. *I need to tell you something,* the sister said. Her name was something like Cilla or Cia—Evan can't get it back. *Yes?* Mrs. DiNobilo said.

Eric brought a girl home a few weeks ago, Cilla or Cia said. *Her name is Zoë. They haven't been together long but seem taken with each other. I couldn't tell what she was like really. Focused and well-mannered, I suppose, plainish hair, no makeup to speak of. She plays the pipe organ, that's one unusual thing. Anyway, Eric had taken his truck out to the quick-lube place and Zoë thanked me for having her and said she'd like to give me a reading with her cards in return, if I didn't mind. Well, you know how I feel about business like that, but I was caught off-guard, I couldn't duck it gracefully.*

Tarot cards? Mrs. DiNobilo asked.

No, the sister said. *Just simple white cards with drawings of things: a shovel, a needle and thread—like what you'd find in one of those brain-teaser games. She asked me questions, then laid out whichever card went with what I answered. Pretty soon there were sixteen cards in rows of four. It was all very low-key, but even so I was uncomfortable, I have to say. I told her,* You know, Zoë, I really don't care for this, it's not my cup of tea. *Then I kind of laughed, thinking of reading tea leaves, and all like that. She smiled in a perfectly pleasant way and said lots of people have that reaction, why didn't I just look over the cards and tell her if any in particular were making me apprehensive. So I looked, and actually there* were two or three. *One was an ink bottle and another had scallopy lines that I guess were waves. When I paused at those cards—it's hard to describe. I just didn't want to linger on them, they were sort of stirring me up. Zoë said sometimes she puts out the cards and nothing much happens, they're inert—that was her word. She also said you couldn't take the pictures literally. For instance, the card with the waves didn't necessarily mean you'd be going on a boat trip, it could just be you were remembering a day at a lake, or something like that.*

Evan saw that Mrs. DiNobilo was about to interject the same sort of mild reproof she often directed at her husband but held back. Her sister said, *I know, Sheila, but can you listen to this please?*

Mrs. DiNobilo said, *You can't—*

Listen first, the sister said, then after a second went on. *So, OK, she moved from card to card, talking normally, then she said,* Oh, hmmm, *and proceeded to ask if there wasn't something I'd never told anybody, about Daddy? I said,* Well, I don't know, Eric's grandfather and I were quite close. *She said,* Yes, I can tell. But is there something from around the time he died? *And I felt the hairs all up and down my arms shoot up. I knew what she was going to tell me, and she was right, it was something I'd never told anyone, not even you, I'm afraid.*

About Daddy? Mrs. DiNobilo said. Her sister nodded. Mrs. DiNobilo said, *I hope it's not one of those repressed memory things, I hope you're not going to try to get me to believe that—*

It's nothing bad, her sister said.

Evan stood observing, his shoulders back against the pantry door. It was the most intriguing conversation he'd heard the entire time the DiNobilos had been in his house.

The kitchen had grown dim and finally Mrs. DiNobilo had to rise and put a light on. Evan had the sense that no matter what her sister said next, it would be discounted, coming as it did in a long line of transactions between them. Then again, maybe not.

The sister said, *The day after Daddy died, you and Mom were at the airport picking up Sari and Stew. I was all crampy and I'd been in the car for hours myself, of course, and I just wanted to crash. I took a codeine and got in the tub and was up to my chin in hot water when I got the distinct impression Daddy was there. Like in the bathroom. I almost felt I should cover up.*

I heard him say, It's OK, doll. *It was like in the Bible where the angel goes,* Be not afraid. *Well, I wasn't afraid. I know you're prob-*

ably thinking it was simply a delusion, wishful thinking, or what-ever, but his voice was very real, very calming. Clear-sounding. His voice from before he was sick. I remember thinking that if you'd been sitting there on the toilet seat keeping me company, you'd have heard it, too. It wasn't exclusively in my mind is what I'm try-ing to say. It even rang a little on the tiles.

So I said—

Out loud? Mrs. DiNobilo asked.

Out loud, yes. I said, Are you here? *Daddy said,* I know you've been thinking about me. *I said,* Well, of course.

He said he was sorry to bug out on us so soon, but at least the three of us were more or less grown. Then he said he'd love to get to see his grandkids, but he knew they'd be fine, and he knew I'd tell them about him and so on. I said, Do you mean *my* children? Children I'm going to have? *He said,* Right, your two kids. *Then he asked if I wanted to know their names. I didn't hesitate, I said,* Oh, please, yes.

Eric and Kristin, *he said. I said,* Tell me—

He said he'd get in trouble if he told me any more, he shouldn't have said that much, but he wanted to give me a going-away pres-ent. I said, How much more trouble can you get in?

He laughed a great big laugh, he said, You'd be surprised, doll. *And then suddenly the bath water—*

She twisted up her mouth. *I'm* never *going to be able to explain this. It was like being up to my shoulders in liquid silver, slightly cool but not cold, and above the tub the air was lit up for three or four seconds. I felt myself shudder, it was almost like, well, it's sort of embarrassing. And then I was alone.*

Anyway, that's what she told me after seeing how I reacted to the cards—not the whole thing but some of it, and the details were, I mean, Sheila—she described the flowers in the tiles.

Mrs. DiNobilo said, *Mother's fleurs-de-lis.*

She told me it's like she concentrates on where the cards line up with each other, and when she focuses her attention there, sometimes she sees what amounts to little film clips, or hears music or talking as if from the radio. Sometimes it's nonsense, but sometimes not.

Sometimes what she saw or heard was about the future, but frequently, as in my case, it had to do with the past, and even though, granted, you can't prevent something that's already happened, how you think about it is constantly evolving, and sometimes the readings help to—

But here Mrs. DiNobilo's sister seemed to run out of steam. Her shoulders flagged inside their cotton sweater. She folded her hands on the table and squinted off. *No, that's enough,* she said finally. *That's what I had to tell you.*

Evan saw that Mrs. DiNobilo had her own reasons to be disturbed. Why had this taken years to come out, why hadn't she been told before this? More to the point, why hadn't the father seen fit to visit *her?*

But it seems to me, she said, still sounding reasonable, as always, *you must have named the kids after what you imagined in this, well, whatever we're calling it, and not the other way around. It's perfectly explainable—and after all, Eric's a family name.*

That was the trouble with stories like Mrs. DiNobilo's sister's, Evan thought. They were like trying to round up globules of mercury. The events were always a step or two removed, always happening to other people, always requiring that you take somebody at her word. It was never yourself, never now. Or so Evan had believed when he was alive and fortified with skepticism.

The Evan who overheard this tale had his own questions. Why was the father in and out so fast, when his own confinement appeared endless? Why the voice and not the rest of him? If it's true she could hear it, why couldn't she hear *Evan?*

He broke down and tried addressing her directly. *Listen, forget old Sourpuss,* he said. *Over here, by the pantry —*

Nothing.

After a moment, he came and settled onto the vacant stool beside her. *Just lift your eyes,* he said. At the very least those sensitive hairs on her arm should spring to attention.

Evan said, *You're not ignoring me, are you?*

She sat rubbing one hand with the other, no doubt still lost in the memory of her father who, departing, had made the air shine and her skin quiver.

Evan smiled. *It's OK,* he said finally. *I don't take it personally.*

Reluctantly, he slid from the stool, drifted off into the front part of the house where it was dark, leaving the sisters to their own devices.

But, now and then, he returns to that non-encounter — whenever something like Pamela's curious gaze this afternoon tempts him to wonder if there might be anomalies in the physics of his state that he's not aware of, special conditions under which he, too, could be heard. That it hasn't happened yet no longer strikes him as an ironclad reason that it never will.

Later that evening, the twilight almost gone, Maureen's car pulls up. Evan listens for the screen door; he watches her silhouette crossing the kitchen. Her purse hits the chair; the light comes on. She checks for messages, then roams the house aimlessly, eventually runs a tepid shower, lies atop the bed with wet hair, tries reading, but after a few minutes lets the book slide to the floor and does nothing for a while. Evan remembers what that was like—as soon as you told yourself to sleep you were doomed. But then, at last, she does fall asleep, the tin-shaded lamp still burning.

Watching her, Evan thinks: How amazing it would be, to take shape in the soft air and say, *Be not afraid.*

Tell Me Something's Different

Early evening, the conclusion of another hot day.

This time, bolder, Ned drives straight up the drive, comes to a slow crunching stop on the gravel. The car is European, the color of pencil lead. In the corner of the windshield, a blue sticker that grants him access to the physicians' lot. Evan watches him get out, cross to the house, take a skip-step onto the low porch, and try the screen door. It's unlatched, but the heavy inside door is firmly locked. Ned rings the bell, flicks his knuckle a few times on the narrow window to the right, looking back once as he waits. Nothing for a while. His hand comes up to hit the glass again, but now the door opens. A crack, then wider.

Evan is still out of earshot as the first words are exchanged, Maureen with her arms folded across her chest, Ned more animated, gesturing. Evan wonders, approaching, what would happen if Maureen tried to close the door on Ned, if he'd jam one of his expensive shoes in the opening and force his way in. But to Evan's surprise, Maureen steps aside and, head down, lets Ned enter.

The screen door slaps shut. Evan stares at them through the mesh. Did Maureen know the man was coming, did Evan miss a phone call between them, or is it just that she's accepted Ned's showing up as inevitable, only a matter of time?

Evan slips inside. They're in the front hall, an awkward distance apart. They haven't touched. Chin squared, Maureen says, *Can you do me one favor? Don't say how much you've missed me.*

What would you like me to say? Ned asks.

She answers, *Tell me something's different.*

The one thing he can't do, Evan sees.

She says, *If nothing's different, why are you here, Ned?*

You know why I'm here, he answers.

Maureen looks at him. Finally she says, *Because I'm so freaking fascinating.*

Ned says, *You know I hate it when you sound that way.*

The screen doors are open at both ends of the house, but it's useless. There's no breeze yet. Ned swipes at his forehead with the back of a hand. *What if we went for a drive,* he says.

Don't do it, Evan thinks. Stay on your own turf.

I'm sorry it's hot, Maureen replies, *but I'd rather not go anywhere.*

It'll cool, she adds without conviction.

Ned looks around, confirming what his glance through the window told him: that the place is underfurnished, a bivouac. *You know, honestly, Maureen*— he says.

She's wearing her standard around-the-house outfit, the camisole and jeans, her wooden sandals. Willfully not putting on a display. But she's showered—Evan can smell the gingery residue of shampoo coming off her still-damp hair, and there are the two hard points that are her nipples through the off-white rayon.

I've got iced tea, she says. *Would you like some iced tea?* She turns and heads into the kitchen without waiting for an answer. Evan follows, then Ned. She roots in the freezer for ice cubes and clinks them into two tumblers and lifts out the pitcher. *There's no lemon,* she says. Light comes slantwise through the back window. The tea is the color of her freckles. Ned has no choice but to sit where she's put the glasses, and she sits opposite, straddling a turned-around chair.

Judy is well? she asks, the question coming with all the dispassion she must have intended.

Ned furrows up. Nothing about this is going to be easy for him. *Judy's fine,* he says. *Jarrod is fine, Shan is fine also. As is the wolfhound. All are fine but the master of the house.*

The other day, Evan took him for an impatient man, a man used to giving orders and having his needs routinely met. Now he seems more complex, his good looks not so run-of-the-mill. He's more interesting somehow, the wakeful eyes, the delicate hands on the beaded glass. For a few seconds, Evan remembers how it feels to sit in your lover's kitchen, a fugitive from time, from real-world rules of conduct, only the chemical rush to answer to. But there's something else about Ned—a chilliness, a mercenary quality Evan distrusts.

But I do miss you, Ned says. *I understand how you thought you needed this time by yourself.*

Maureen says, *I don't think you do.*

OK, whether I do or not.

She says, *You don't, Ned. No offense.*

The thing is, Ned begins again.

This was one of Claudia's expressions, Evan recalls sharply: *The thing is, Evan, I'm not sure you're really trying to help yourself.* Looking for a beachhead of precise assessment. Here in this same kitchen, a different table but identical postures, the middle of some night that's gone as gone can be.

You needed to draw a line, I get that, Ned says, and holds his hand up this time so she won't interrupt. *I was willing to see if being apart would work out. But it hasn't, OK?* Maureen is looking elsewhere. He stalls until her gaze returns, then says, *You've got to understand there's a limit to what I can —*

Maybe he was going to say, *put up with,* but he holds off. Now both men are watching her, both absorbed by her austere, offbeat beauty, the bony hook of a nose, the lower lip with its slight outward curl, the fine freckles anywhere the sun has touched. Evan doesn't have to see Judy to know she's conventional, nice to look at, well-preserved, capable, and fully deserving of loyalty. None of that matters in the end. He knows what Maureen is to Ned. And understands more vividly now that there's another whole aspect to Maureen—it's been banked, tamped down, as long as Evan's been observing her. She's got her spirit in protective custody.

Ned says, *I'm unable to give you up.*

But she's heard all this before, Evan can see. Cheapo words. Not worth the air they're stitched on. Not unless things have changed. Have things changed? No, nothing changes. Except Ned sounds so earnest suddenly, so civilized. Against her will, she sputters out a laugh, then turns away again.

What? he says. *What?* Ned takes her wrist; she slips it away. He lifts both palms to the naked air in a gesture of exasperation, but controlled, muted. He says, *You hear what I'm saying?*

She says, *Do I hear it? Will I ever stop hearing it?*

Maureen, he says.

She says, *I shouldn't have let you through the door.*

Ned answers, *You don't believe that,* and she says, *You don't know what I believe, Ned.* He has no handy comeback. After an exhausting few seconds, she goes on, *You know what kills me, even if you left her, at this point, it wouldn't make any goddamn difference. Things are just completely —*

Ned stands abruptly, an agile, tactical move, taking her shoulder, giving her no room to back away. *Look,* he says. *No, look at me. Have I really done this to you? Has this only been misery? Nothing more?*

She eyes his hand on her, then stares off again. He touches the top of her backbone where it's exposed, rubs with his thumb.

What it used to be is what it used to be, she says finally. *You don't get that yet, but I do. I have to, Ned.*

I still want you, he says.

The force of these words simply stops her cold. She doesn't even bother to say what a blight it is, all this wanting. She just says, *Yeah?*

Yeah, he says.

Lucas

CLAUDIA OWED EVAN certain facts about her ex-husband, and gave them, but didn't linger. Lucas had been one of the vendors with accounts at the company where Claudia worked in San Mateo. *He was always coming around, taking three or four of us out to eat,* she said one afternoon. *But then it was just me. He was very charming at first. The snakiness didn't come out until later.*

What was so snaky about him? Evan asked.

They were inching along in traffic, on their way to pick up her daughter at martial arts. Janey was the last girl you'd think would take martial arts, which was why Claudia had signed her up—to help with her coordination, to make her less panicky about her body. Tuesdays and Saturdays, hangdog, Janey went off in the flapping white outfit, her glasses secured with a Croakie. Evan watched, suffering a pang at the rigors of childhood.

Claudia shook her head. She didn't want to get into it. Evan persisted, gently. She said, *Well, for one thing, he had a bookie. Still does, for all I know.*

Evan said lots of people have bookies.

She gave him a look. *Do you?*

Evan said, *No, I don't—gambling does nothing for me. But people bet on stuff all the time, ballgames, whatever. Remember in* Guys and Dolls *where they're betting on the cheesecake?*

Claudia turned to him and said, *Evan, this is real life. Name one person you know personally who has a bookie.*

OK, he couldn't.

She said, *Lucas was very snaky about money. Secretive. I realized I couldn't trust him when he talked about our finances. We were both making decent money—but, you know, where was it? He said it wasn't liquid. It was more like it had vaporized. I started trying to picture our future and I didn't like how it looked. Even so, I hung in there way too long.*

Evan said, *But it was good at first.*

A small flat smile from Claudia. *Oh, well, at first,* she said.

Evan said, *He pursued you.*

She answered, *Let's just say pursuing is one of Luc's strong points.*

It dawned on Evan that barely three years had elapsed between the end of their marriage, his and Claudia's, and Janey's birth—an awfully short time, now that he stopped to think about it.

What other strong points did he have? Evan asked.

Claudia left this alone. But a little later, she said, *I never felt for him what I felt for you, is that what you'd like to hear?*

Evan glanced over. *I'm not fishing,* he said.

She said, *Uh-huh.*

He said, *It's just I like to know what's what.*

They were on the Aurora Bridge now, amid a grand procession of brake lights in the late sun. There appeared to be an accident up ahead. Far below, boats glided along the waterway, glints and shadow. Just to the west, though you couldn't see it from here, were the galvanized roofs of Donovan's smithy.

Claudia said, *It's not my way to rehash every single thing, you must know that about me.*

Evan said, *I guess I do.*

She went on, *With you I had what I thought was a soul mate—I'm sorry, Evan, I don't know how else to put it. Lucas and I were never going to be soul mates. I was under no illusion of that, but I didn't care. In fact, I thought it might be good to be with someone where I could keep more of myself back. It wouldn't be the same kind of marriage, but I was up for it, I was optimistic. This isn't a slam against you, it's just how it was. He wanted me, I liked the attention, he appealed to a side of me that was—well, he could be very attentive in his way, let's leave it there.*

She broke off for a second, then said, *But I'm trying to remember how it seemed at the start. He was old school in a way, he wanted to scoop me up and take care of me. You wouldn't think I'd be susceptible to that kind of treatment, but apparently I was. Just goes to show.*

Evan nodded. *Goes to show what?* he asked.

Claudia said, *What's it show?*

Right.

Claudia gave a rueful little headshake. *Shit if I know, Evan. That I can get fooled as easy as the next person. That no one's immune to flattery.*

A little later, she added, *That part of me was hungry for it.*

A couple of weeks after this conversation, they were walking in the Market. Across the cobblestones came a black-haired girl with big black glasses. She looked ten months' pregnant. *That how you looked?* Evan said.

I was way *bigger,* Claudia responded immediately.

But in bed that night, she said, *Actually, Janey was a fairly small baby, just over six pounds.*

Evan found himself asking about the labor. *You don't* really *want to hear this?* Claudia answered. He said sure he did. *Well, it was lots of work, actually,* Claudia said. Evan was up on one elbow, his other hand at rest on her belly. *Luc in the delivery room?* he asked. She didn't answer right away, and Evan thought, OK, don't press. But then she said, *It wasn't Luc's idea of the high life, my being pregnant so soon, I'll tell you that. For a while I honestly thought he'd bolt. It took real effort to bring him around.*

She added, *And then, I mean, later on it was like the whole thing had been* his *idea. Mr. Family Man.*

Evan shifted his weight until he could look her in the face. He brushed the hair out of her eyes. She said, *It wasn't a good pregnancy, Evan. It was crappy. I was so toxemic. I wasn't positive I'd survive it.*

Evan said, *You?*

What do you mean, me? Claudia answered. *It was ugly. Really, Ev, there were times —*

Evan said he hadn't meant anything; it was just hard to picture her laid low.

You make me out to be some kind of superhero, she said. *It's not fair.*

Evan said he just admired her strength, he always had. What was so wrong with that?

After a moment, Claudia covered his hand with hers. They lay like that, not talking. Finally, Claudia said, *I wanted a baby, I didn't want to wait until I was into my thirties. I wanted to do a good job of it, to really concentrate and have it go well. But then, being sick—it seemed like such bad luck. And I started to notice resentment seeping in. I thought, Oh god, don't let me take it out on the baby, please don't stick something between us.*

I'm sorry it was like that, Evan said. Claudia studied him for a moment, then nodded.

She said, *Lucas was traveling a lot, so he hired an LPN to take my vitals and so on, a Ukrainian woman, but she was kind of dour, not much comfort. And very* Slavic, *full of these scary Ukrainian proverbs.*

Luc also had his mother come by. I never knew if she meant well or not. She was really nosy, for one thing. She'd ask about these intimate things between Luc and me, and expected me to open right up to her. But I'm not that way—and who was she, after all? Not my own mother, not my girlfriend. When I tried to explain this, she acted as if I was just being difficult. A prima donna.

And there were other things. Luc has a bunch of siblings and cousins, a big extended family on his mother's side. Her brother, Luc's uncle, is like the godfather of the whole shebang. Somehow I got the feeling that I was having the baby for them, that I was meeting an obligation to the clan.

I probably could've handled all this better if I'd felt decent, but I didn't, I felt rotten. And there was no talking it out with Luc. I couldn't ask him to choose between me and his family, or his mother—I had that much figured out.

And, really, there wasn't anybody else. I didn't know many people down there—a few women at work, but not well enough for this. I mean, they were work friends.

So I just tried to hold myself together.

What about Sadie? Evan asked.

Well, yes, Sadie, Claudia said. She disengaged from Evan and reached over for a cigarette. She'd been trying not to smoke in the house as much—this was the first she'd had in hours. She sat back against the headboard, her legs out on top of the sheets.

In a minute, she said, *I pictured myself trying to explain all this to Sadie, but the thing was, she didn't like Lucas to begin with. I think she was tuned into the snakiness long before I was. Anyway, I couldn't bring myself to admit that anything was wrong, I couldn't stand the idea of somehow lowering myself in her eyes. I still wanted to be the golden girl. So I downplayed it as much as I could, I just said I was a little tired, she didn't need to come.*

Evan stroked her leg as she smoked. *Sorry,* she said when she was done, meaning the cigarette. *I had to.*

Evan said he'd live.

After a minute, he caught her eye again and said, *I think Sadie had a pretty good bead on the first husband, too.*

Smiling a little, Claudia said, *Oh, that first one. Can't we leave him out of it?*

Love to, Evan said. Yet a moment later, starkly, heart flopping, he thought, It was supposed to be us that had the baby.

Claudia looked at him. *What is it, Ev?* she asked. *You went kind of blank there.*

Evan buried his face against her neck and inhaled. He felt her hand on his shoulder blade, rubbing slowly.

After a minute she said, *Actually, Sadie thought you were a very nice young man at first. We all did.*

Chicago

EVAN WATCHES MAUREEN and Ned climbing the staircase, single file. A few seconds later, he follows.

In her room, Ned draws up the camisole and stoops to suck the small perfect breast. Maureen's arms remain at her sides, but her head is tipped back so her neck gives a dull white glow. The evening light washes through the dormer window, burnishing the floorboards, tangling with the dowels of her drying rack.

She says something neither man can hear.

Ned murmurs, *Hmmm?*

Gentle, she says.

Then they're down on her bed, almost floor level. Ned is kneeling, his own shirt half off, still suckling at her. The fingers of her free hand are curled, dragging absently across the other breast, turning it to gooseflesh. Ned bumps his way down her ribs, kisses the flat belly. Evan can see the white sole of her foot, the toes clenching and unclenching. So here it is, the thing you're not supposed to watch.

But he's seen the others—if anything is Evan's business, everything is. For the Kuhls, it was infrequent, but they were kind with each other. Roberta took the lead—she must've seen what Evan saw, that this was the only time her husband really inhabited his life, and been grateful to know there was such a simple thing she could do to jolly him up. She was the same in bed as she always was—unrushed, incapable of awkward moves. Only her voice changed, going husky, rising into a slow insistent chorus like a gospel song, *Oh now, oh now*—

But there was the night she froze and went, *Shhh, Steve. Someone's here.* Her husband tried to lift up, said, *What*—? She pressed her hand down on his chest. *In the room here,* she said. A small liquid sound as they disengaged, a hesitation, then Stephen swung his feet to the floor, got up, and stood listening. Evan had frozen, too. He waited. *No, there's nobody,* Stephen said finally. *Here, I'm going to turn on the light.* Roberta put a hand in front of her eyes. Stephen's naked body leapt out of the darkness, white shoulders glaring. What an anticlimax, moments later, to discover that what Roberta had sensed was only the son, Greggie—he'd dragged his blanket and pillow down the hall and wedged himself against the door to their bedroom.

After the Kuhls, it was the DiNobilos. Separate beds for them, and no visiting back and forth. Edward with his priggish, self-satisfied way of examining himself in the shaving mirror. And Sheila, disdainful of her shapeless flesh, it seemed to Evan, so tired of being stuck inside it. Then Mack and Ellie Fessenden—three kids, busy as hell, yet they still stole the time for sex. Both were vaguely youthful, athletic in a mild suburban way. Often they instructed each other—*scoot your leg up a little, can you?* Maybe they demystified it too much, maybe it was too close to a healthful session at the gym for Evan's taste, but it was rare that one of them didn't get the giggles—they had such a good time, how could you not be happy for them? And then, one drizzly afternoon, the rest of the family safely out of the picture, the oldest daughter led her boyfriend up to the back bedroom. She was a swimmer and soccer player, a nice-looking medium-sized girl. Very fine chestnut hair, barely long enough for a ponytail, calm brown eyes. She and the boy lay on the bed, kissing and fooling around. He seemed nondescript to Evan at first, one of a thousand boys you'd see jamming the halls of a high school between periods. Curly bangs that needed flicking back constantly, a face still boyishly soft. But then Evan started to see him through *her* eyes. He saw that the boy was decent, smitten, giving her his undivided attention. They stopped and talked every so often, then fell to touching again. At one point, she reached under her jersey and worked her bra off, drew it out a sleeve, and let it drop to the floor. It was pale blue, satiny. More rolling around. Then, suddenly, she leapt from the bed, stripped off her shirt, and threw her arms in the air, as if to say, *Here it is, what do you think?* She had the same brown nipples Frannie Marx had had. Her breasts were still growing; she was only sixteen. Evan stood watching from the doorway. Should he have turned away? But he was as far beyond titillation as he was beyond shame—what he mostly was was *fascinated.* He remembered Claudia removing her top that morning on the boat. Such aplomb, such generosity. The girl stepped back toward the bed. Please let this go well, Evan thought. And maybe it was the spirit of her parents' sex life flowing into her, or just one of the random miracles the world coughs up, but it did go well. Evan was so proud of them.

What a different story tonight is. Maureen and the doctor who won't stay away, whose touch seems so coolly proprietary.

But suddenly Evan hears Maureen ask, *You have a condom?*

Condom? Ned responds, as if it's a word in Martian. *But don't you—?* And Evan understands that formerly it was her job, diaphragm maybe.

She says, *You've got to use a condom, Ned. I mean it.*

Then Ned is back on his elbows, squinting, trying to get a clear look at her through the bands of shadow. *Christ, it never occurred to me,* he says.

Maureen says, *It's not negotiable.*

Ned stares. *Then why'd you get me up here?* he says.

I didn't get you anywhere, Ned.

Nothing for a moment.

Then Maureen's weight shifting. Her voice plainer, she says, *Why don't I suck you off? You like that.*

Ned tells her don't be crude.

Maureen says she wasn't being.

Only expedient, Evan thinks.

She says something else, but it's lost as she rolls her head away.

What? Ned asks.

Maureen says, *I said you're the only man in the history of the world to turn down a blowjob.*

Evan guesses it's exactly the kind of remark that used to make Ned laugh out loud, that would dispel whatever tension had crept between them.

Not tonight, though.

After a few moments, Ned sits up and plants his feet on the floor, only now scanning this room he finds himself in. But he's impatient; his eyes don't settle. Humblest place they've ever been, maybe he's thinking. They've used hotels, Evan imagines, and Maureen's old place, which was surely more decorated and had at least a queen-sized mattress (and now it occurs to Evan that she's ditched it in favor of this austere single). And once in a while a borrowed condo or time-share. But never Ned's own house, Evan thinks, never his own bed, on principle.

And possibly, now, Ned is wondering how far it is to the closest Rite-Aid, to a goddamn Bartell's, maybe asking himself bluntly if she's worth the aggravation, if he can stand any more of her contrariness. But the answer to that is clear enough. Evan understands that her being difficult is one of the very things that's brought Ned here, that accounts for his tenacious craving.

The last of the light creeps up the wall, dimming. Maureen draws herself against Ned's back, cheek to skin. *Is this punishment?* he asks.

She says, *I'm not* punishing *you, Ned. For god's sake—*

You could've fooled me.

Oh, don't talk, Maureen says. *Don't say anything more, just don't, all right?*

For a few moments, he doesn't.

At an impasse, the lovers lie back, side by side. Ned's eyes are open, milky half-moons. He's breathing like a fighter between rounds.

Evan squats by the bed, one hand on the mattress. *Why don't you give her up,* he says. *Don't you see how hard you're making it?* He waits, studying Ned, as if the man's been listening and they're going to engage in an honest debate.

Instead, Ned says, *So why don't you tell me about the new job.*

We're going to talk about my job now? Maureen says.

Humor me, OK?

My job is dandy, she says.

Ned frowns at the ceiling, starts to protest the sound in her voice, but doesn't.

She says, *Who told you where I was? It wasn't Pam?*

He says no, not her loyal friend Pamela.

Who? Marty?

He says, *I'm not getting into that, Maureen.*

You're not, she says. *That's wonderful.*

Ned says, *It's not so easy to just disappear. You'd be surprised.*

You had me tailed, didn't you? Maureen says.

Ned says he's not discussing it.

I'm supposed to sleep with a man who had me tailed? Maureen says.

I didn't have you tailed, *for Christ's sake, Maureen.*

She says she doesn't believe it.

You watch too much TV, he says.

I don't have a TV, she tells him. *I gave it away.*

A deep sigh from Ned. *Why'd you do that? You gave it away?*

She says, *Now we're going to talk about my* television set?

Their words have no carry in this room—they circle like moths, gray on gray.

I was thinking about Chicago, Maureen says then.

Chicago?

That's when I almost disappeared, Maureen says. *While you were at the meeting.*

Ned says, *I thought we had a good time in Chicago. Didn't we?*

Yes, she says. *That's what I mean. That was my point.*

You were going to leave?

She says, *You were off listening to what's-his-name, from Duke.*

Hofner.

Yes. Hofner.

Ned says, *Even Hofner was good. He was talking about spiral CT. I thought you went shopping. I thought you were going to buy a jacket or something.*

Did you see any Marshall Field's bags, Ned?

I was too busy looking at you probably, he answers.

No, she says, *you weren't.*

She tells him she took a cab clear out to O'Hare. *I had my suitcase. That's when I was going to disappear.*

Where were you going to go?

She says, *The next dimension.*

Careful what you wish for, Evan says.

Ned says, *I had no idea you left.*

No, you didn't.

You were in the shower when I got back, he says.

I was cold, she says. *I was cold and I felt like I had this coating of—*

He jumps in and says, *I remember that night, that was the night we walked to Famous Dave's. I remember you combing out your hair, it wasn't all chopped off.*

My concubine hair, she says. Ned tells her he liked it that way and Maureen says, *Of course.*

There's the rustle of fabric on fabric, then Evan sees the white of Ned's hand as it strokes her skull, feeling the nap of the short hair. He says, *So you got to O'Hare but you didn't get on a plane.* She says, *I wasn't ready, I guess.* He says, *But now you are.* Maureen slides out from under him without answering. He says, *But now you've finally had enough of Ned.* She says, *Yes.* Ned says, *And this time you're absolutely positive?*

She says, *Don't play with me.*

Is that what I'm doing?

She tells him yes, that's how it feels. He says, *It's just I'm trying to get a handle on what you're thinking.* She says, *You know what I'm thinking, you just don't want to know.*

He says, *Maureen.*

But now, at last, the night breeze appears, enough to start clearing the day's heat from the upstairs of this thinly insulated house, sieving it out through the window screens across the room. Evan notices it stealing past his skin and thinks momentarily of Mrs. DiNobilo's sister and her little shivers.

It's Ned who turns his face to the air. *Wait,* he says, *feel that?* He pulls back farther so it can reach her. Down the hall the change of pressure sucks a door closed, but not hard enough for the latch to grab. A sound Evan remembers well—how it startles you, though you know it's coming.

Wouldn't you like to go on a trip? Ned says in a minute, his voice changed, renewed. *I always thought we'd go somewhere.*

I don't go on trips with you, she answers. *I'm the other one.*

We went to Chicago, he says.

Right, right, she says. *We went to a radiology conference.*

After a minute, Ned says, *But I always saw us, I don't know, going down a narrow street, whitewashed walls, must be one of the Greek islands. You've got a straw sun hat and the brim waffles up and down as you walk. Then there's a stone terrace, we've got drinks.*

Maureen says, *I can't believe you haven't gotten that out of your system.*

What?

She says, *All that. That fantasy stuff. It's poison.* Ned stares. It's hard to see her in this light. He shakes his head. *I'll tell you what's poison,* he says. But the moment stretches out and he says no more about poison.

He sinks onto his back again. Maureen suspends her face above his, staring down. She begins to kiss him, dry hypnotic kisses, about his cheek, along his jaw line. Ned accepts them without moving a muscle.

She stops, straightens, lets out a frustrated breath.

She says, *I'm sorry, Ned. I still can't let you. Not without—* But she balks at saying it again. How exactly did her life *get* like this?

Barely two feet away, Evan watches the thin light skimming down her ribs. He remembers how she was that day with Pamela, so adamant that Ned could never find out he'd made her pregnant, so resolved to take control, to hold herself back. She's not the same tonight. She sounds tough, but it's a smoke screen—really, she's exhausted, starting to slip. She could say almost anything.

But, all at once, Ned seems to reach his saturation point. He swings his legs to the floor, and says, *You know what? I think what I'm going to do is go now.*

I'm *not standing in your way,* Maureen says. But the instant the words are out she wants them back. *Look, Ned,* she says. *I didn't mean that.*

He's already on his feet, though, already working his shirt tails into his slacks and re-securing his belt.

She says, *Ned?* Staring up, lips parted, waiting to see if he'll answer. She begins to say something else, but her face collapses into a look of raw supplication. Jesus, Evan thinks, don't let him see that. His instinct is to jump up and shield her from Ned's eyes.

But Ned's not looking, he's scanning for his other shoe, then working his foot into it without bothering to bend down. He leaves it untied, says nothing further, and makes his way into the darkened hallway, hesitates at the landing to get a sense of how the stairs turn, then starts down, one hand against the plaster. Evan follows, sees him out the front door, then across the brittle grass.

The car's lock chirrups; the door makes an expensive *chuff* as it shuts. Evan stares in at the man and says, *I hope to god I never see you again.* But he might as well be talking through two miles of rock. Ned flings his arm over the passenger seat and backs out. Evan hears the shift into second, listens to the rising pitch until it's swallowed by the terrain, the grid of dark houses.

After that, there's only the jostling of the bamboo chimes.

When He Was Home

W‌HEN HE WAS HOME, Evan made a stringent effort to be at home and not at Frannie's. Even the simplest actions required a new concentration. Was this how an innocent man stood at his wife's shoulder brushing his teeth? Is this how a man with a clean heart looked as he stripped off his shirt and hung it on the dresser knob?

He considered his position on bald-faced lying. Would he stonewall? *I don't know what you're talking about, Claudia.* Or not deny it so much as say she'd apparently gotten the wrong idea. *It was just this stupid thing I got wrapped up in.* Which was to deny Frannie. Where did he stand on that? He heard his voice engaged in these evasions. It sounded pinched and boyish.

One evening, Claudia asked point-blank if he was sorry he married her. She'd stopped in the midst of unwinding the film in her Pentax. Her arms hung. Oh, Christ, here it is, Evan thought, his stomach clenching. The old animal response, protect your middle.

Half an hour earlier they'd been on the roof of the building, gazing through a telephoto lens her old boss had lent her. Another cloudless summer night, the day's stored-up heat coming off the sooty bricks of the chimney stacks. They'd been checking out the trim work high up on other buildings—moldings, stone cornices with scrolls, roundels and walrus heads. Everything through the glass looked watery and hypothetical.

Do I act sorry? Evan asked.

Claudia paused for a second, seemed to actually be thinking about it. *No,* she said, *not exactly.*

But I'm happy with you, Evan said. *I love you. What did you mean? You must've meant something.*

She was out in the center of the floor. The Healey Avenue apartment, tall white walls, carpet with mangelike patches of jute showing. She wore shoes with no heels, black cotton flats from Taiwan; she had a way of standing, toes out, balanced on both feet. To this day he can see it.

It was now she'd break down and accuse him: *Anybody can see how distracted you are, Evan. God knows where you are, but you're sure not here with me.*

Instead, Claudia finished unloading the camera, dropped the film roll into her breast pocket, methodically cranked in its replacement. That ratcheting sound he can still hear, too. She looked up again, leveled her glasses with her index finger. *Tell me this whole operation's going to fly,* she said. *This life of ours.*

Of course, Evan answered at once.

Claudia screwed up her face. She said, *Sometimes I don't feel competent to be a grownup. I'm sorry, I don't even know how to put this.*

He said of all the people he knew, she had the *least* reason to feel incompetent or overwhelmed or whatever it was. As long as he'd known her (and years earlier, according to Sadie), Claudia had radiated an aura of self-confidence. She knew her mind; she *trusted* it. Evan had fallen for this quality during his first ten minutes with her. He'd wanted in on it; he'd wanted it to radiate onto him.

But now she stared back mercilessly. *You could be giving me too much credit,* she said finally. *I have my moments of doubt, like anyone.*

Evan nodded.

She said, *I don't want to disappoint you, Ev.*

Evan said, *You're* not.

But this exchange had left him out of whack. At bedtime that night, he watched her scuffle from the bathroom wearing the man's ribbed white undershirt with the skinny straps that made him crazy. He moved into her path and told her, *I meant what I said before.*

And what was that?

That I'm not sorry I married you, Evan said.

Claudia rested her head on his shoulder, and he ran his hands up and down her back. What a powerful urge, to reassure. And how weird, too, that in the midst of all this, Evan should have a nearly irresistible desire to tell her about Frannie, about the miraculous new angles his life had acquired. But then, maybe not so weird. They'd always spoken freely, told each other what was on their minds. He was new to this, sifting through his thoughts for the safe thing to say aloud.

In the meantime, Dimond & Associates was scrambling to get out a series of proposals for major clients. Everyone seemed testy and preoccupied for several weeks. Evan and Frannie saw little of each other—Frannie staying late to check proofs; Evan leaving at the usual hour but bringing a sheaf of drafts home with him and hammering away at them in the kitchen after the dishes were done, because they needed to be presentable by nine the next morning, but also, he realized uneasily, so that Claudia could see that he really did need to work late sometimes. Then, suddenly, the crunch was over, and they'd prevailed. The office was awash with euphoria. Evan couldn't wait for this to be translated into sex with Frannie—before they could get to it, though, she was called out of town for an aunt's funeral.

A funeral, really? But he had no reason to think otherwise.

One afternoon the following week, Evan walked her to the car. It was early October now, the sidewalk-buckling old shade trees in the boulevard beginning to drop their dusty leaves. Frannie said, *You know what, Evan, I don't think I can have you come back tonight.*

Evan said, *No?*

She said, *I don't think it would be a good night.* She looked past him up the street as if they were being observed, then squeezed his hand quickly, and unlocked the car. *It's nothing to do with you,* she said.

He started to say, *I'm dying for you,* but held back. Hunger was one thing, neediness another. He braced himself against the Ghia's roof and bent down.

I'll see you tomorrow, Evan, she said, and started the motor.

His time with her was periodic, he understood that. It couldn't be otherwise. He knew that if he pressed her—

But he wasn't going to press.

Even so, the next time they lay in bed Evan watched her closely —he *always* watched her closely, but now it was to find out if anything had changed, if a gap had opened between them.

Frannie wasn't a woman who went away when she made love; she never acted as if his mission was to launch her into oblivion. Just the opposite: She seized him by the upper arms to keep from tumbling away; she said, *Evan, oh babe, look at me,* desperate for eye contact. They were chocolate-brown, her eyes, but out from the pupils shot rays of bronze or wheat-gold that you didn't notice unless you were as close as Evan was during such moments. Just about unbearably lovely eyes.

Then why, tonight, was he so on guard? The unadorned answer was he didn't belong here.

He knew a little about Frannie's girlhood and her brief marriage. He knew a few of her likes and dislikes, how she handled people at work, how her body language softened as soon as she left the office. His ear had begun to pick out expressions of hers, inflections unlike Claudia's, the chummy-but-sexy way she sometimes called him by his last name, and so on. A modest cache of fact and observation. But what did it amount to? They were virtually strangers. Not so uncommon an insight among new lovers, he realized, but still. He tried to visualize actually living with her—sitting down to eat each evening, driving the wet streets to meet some relative of hers, and all the rest of it—being with her *from now on.* No, he couldn't do it; something balked; a chill ran through the middle of him.

He said, *I feel like I'm using you.*

Frannie said, *Do you? I don't feel used.* She asked if he was already sick of coming here. *It's not that, is it?*

Evan said, *God, no.*

She turned her eyes on him again and said, *Don't furrow your brow, Evan. I'll let you know if I have a problem.*

Will you? he asked.

She told him he'd be the first to know.

But I don't want you to have any problems with me, with this, Evan said.

Frannie said, *I won't then,* stretching over to kiss him.

Later, as he was leaving, he said, *You have to know how much I love coming here.*

She could've made him declare himself profusely, *No, I'm not sure, why don't you tell me again?* But that wasn't her way. She said, *Don't buy trouble, Evan. I'm not busting up your marriage, I'm not making demands, am I?*

True enough. But why not?

How little he examined it from her side, hardly at all. Maybe she was hanging back, awaiting further developments. Or maybe she was in it only for fun, to make life somewhat more interesting.

Maybe it was just this stupid thing she got wrapped up in.

You Sleep with Me

THEN IT WAS DECEMBER: short days, early penetrating dark. Evan spent the holidays close to home, nursing Claudia through a cold that had settled in her chest. Claudia, rib-sore from hacking, then loopy on gulps of Robitussin, telling him he was her sweetest sweet prince. Claudia sleeping upright in the stuffed chair, Evan reading chapters of *One Flew Over the Cuckoo's Nest* to her until she dropped off, then crashing on the sofa nearby.

Work acquired a new treacherousness. Acting as if he and Frannie were no more than office mates became untenable, not only hard to pull off but sapping now as well. Whereas in summer he'd carried on with a mighty energy.

He'd always hated endings—he had a nearly supernatural dread of them. The most ordinary leave-taking could suddenly bare its teeth at him. Tucking him in on the eve of his birthday, Patricia might say, *Well, kiddo, you're almost done being a ten-year-old.* She'd kiss him and go off to check on Gayle, who was a notoriously fussy sleeper. Later, he'd hear her feet on the staircase. But one of those February nights, the implication of what she'd said stayed behind to keep him company. *When you stop being ten,* it told him, *you'll never be ten again, no matter how long the world lasts.* He tried to think of something else. When he couldn't, he had to go into the lighted bathroom and sit for a few minutes (out of the heating duct floated saxophone and drums). But when he got back in bed, it was still there. Sometime between now and the year 2048 or so, it said, would come his *last* birthday. *No matter what.* It was completely straightforward, just numbers. And as his father often said, *Numbers don't lie.*

Amazingly, though, he'd wake and find a bright gray light at the windows and understand that he'd slept, after all. Then he'd slip on his mukluks, go downstairs, and have pancakes with blackberry syrup, and later Patricia would send him off, saying, *Enjoy your special day.* And the thing was, for the most, he *would* enjoy the day. He didn't drag his chin on the ground. He kidded around like other people; he got into things; he wasn't all grim and depressed. It was just that even as a grown man he sometimes couldn't bear the ending of anything. Even individual days—one o'clock in the morning, and he'd still be up, half-comatose but trying to squeeze out a few more pages of reading, or a few more minutes of TV, instead of undressing and calling it a night. Sometimes calling it a night horrified him.

In any case, he had to put an end to seeing Frannie.

How would she react? Fight for him, blow up? Or would it just be, *Been nice doing business with you, Evan?*

It was a blustery night, the pavement slick with black leaves. They climbed the stairs to her apartment. Frannie hung up her purse and went around switching on lights, talking back over her shoulder. But when she turned, Evan still had his jacket on.

Evan, what—?

Doggedly, he delivered the message he'd come to deliver. Frannie kept her cool. Her face assumed a look he knew from work, consternation kept in check. She put on water for tea, motioned toward the kitchen chair. *You think it's irrevocable?* she said. *This decision?*

Irrevocable, he thought, what a word.

She said, *I mean, Evan, is there any chance you'll see it differently in a few days?*

Evan said, honestly, he didn't think so.

Frannie set the tea before him and handed him the plastic honey bear. She told him it made her sad, that was all. Just very, very sad.

I'm no good at this, he said—as if even now it was her job to bolster him, as if she was supposed to say, *Oh no, Evan, you're doing a fine job, as always.*

Instead, she came up behind him and touched his head and began to stroke his hair. She said, *I can't tell you how to live your life. I just want to say you don't have to do this.*

Evan said no, he did. He thought his throat would close.

A week passed, two. Crappy, dispiriting days. Evenings with Claudia, the dishes, the TV news, her friend Holly stopping by with a taciturn new boyfriend who worked on a fishing boat, another night seeing *Shampoo* in Wallingford and arguing all the way home about the Warren Beatty character, whether he was or wasn't totally pathetic. Twice they made love. The first time was right after breaking off with Frannie, and though it had been Claudia's idea, Evan had asked too much of the act, maybe hoping it would purify him or cauterize his double-mindedness. Whatever he'd expected, the occasion was less than cathartic, and later Claudia asked, *What was up with you, hon? You seemed a little frantic there for a minute.* Evan had no constructive reply. The other time Claudia actually cut it short—she'd *never* done that before. When he tried to get at what the trouble was, she said she wasn't in the right head space. Evan took her tone to mean, *Why don't you leave it alone, OK?* For a half-hour he listened to the radiator, and the window frame jittering in its sash. He didn't know if he could stay in bed beside her, or if he'd have to go to the other room until he settled down, and was not optimistic, but then, after all, he slept.

Late one afternoon at work, breaking protocol, he took Frannie's wrist in a secluded turn of the stairwell. *How are you?*

You better not, Evan.

He said, sorry, but it wasn't going so well on his end. He needed a few minutes with her. She said they couldn't go back to the apartment, not the way things were now, he understood that, didn't he? *Let's drive,* he said. *Just anywhere.* She hesitated, then nodded. It was early to leave work, but they slipped away. Out on the street, there was just enough rain to wet Evan's hair. They walked side by side, saying nothing until they were in her car where it sat in the lot. One kiss that rewarded neither of them, then Evan found himself staring through the streaky windshield at a wall of leafless ivy, hands in his lap. The rain started to come down harder.

Later that evening, Evan would hear about Claudia's day.

Early afternoon, she'd been to the gynecologist. The cough was gone, but she had a wicked yeast infection now—for a week it had simmered, then she and Evan made love and it exploded. The doctor's waiting room was backed up with women—it seemed airless, rancid-smelling. She *hated* being there. She stood up to leave at one point, then sat again. At long last, she was called in but had to wait another half-hour in the exam room with the stirrups looming. Then the doctor came and looked her over—in fairness, he had a light touch, an aura of calm. He sounded surprised she'd never had this before, said she was lucky. He wrote on his prescription pad, then dug out a handful of cream samples, dropped them in a small brown sack, and said the medicine would knock it out in no time. Claudia finally brought herself to ask how long before she and Evan could resume *relations*—she hated having to talk about it, having people know about her needs. He told her, *Soon. You'll know.*

All this she explained to Evan. She told him she'd left the gynecologist's feeling as if something dreadful had been forestalled. Suddenly, she was ravenous—for food, and for him, her *husband.* That was why she'd driven to Dimond & Associates, not to surprise him, but to see if he could leave early with her.

She circled, looking for a parking spot. It was raining now. She finally parked illegally, got out, and stood waiting to cross the street, when she noticed the small turquoise car with the ragtop—it was bumping out of a gravelly lot, and in the passenger seat was Evan, talking away, gesturing avidly with both hands. She yelled his name, waved. But already the light had changed and they were gone. She thought, Well, damn.

Hours later, she told Evan, *But then I thought, OK, he's getting a ride, he'll be home in a few minutes. So I drove back here, and on the way I stopped and got a six-pack, and it was the goddamn good stuff, Evan, and then I came upstairs and I opened one and put on a record and I sat here for a while trying to figure out whether I'd tell you about the doctor or not. And then the record got over, and I got out another beer, and then I just sat here and it got fucking dark.*

When Evan arrived, Claudia was in the chair by the front window, three long-necked bottles at her side. The place was cold and stank of unemptied ashtrays, and the only light was spilling in from the entryway where he stood trying to get a sense of what was happening. Immediately, she was on her feet. And so it was that the affair with Frannie Marx came out only after it had ended, and only because Claudia—stir-crazy from the day she'd had, too much sitting and waiting, too much reflection, then the beer—said, *What took you so long, Evan? I saw you in that car hours ago,* and Evan, disarmed by the rawness of her face, found he was unwilling to cough up one more small lie.

Claudia said, *But you sleep with* me.

Evan had never seen her this righteous and affronted. It shocked him—shouldn't have but it did. She wanted to know exactly what she was dealing with, precisely which evenings he'd been with Frannie, and so on. Her memory of the past six months seemed impeccable. His own was a blur—already those hours in the cornflower light felt irretrievably distant.

She kept pushing. She asked what Frannie was like.

What do you mean? he answered.

Claudia said, *You know what I mean, what's she like?*

I don't know what you want to know, Evan said. By now, he'd put on the lights and cranked open the radiator—it knocked intermittently and steam hissed from the valve, but the apartment seemed no warmer. Claudia stood hugging her arms. Through the lenses of her glasses her eyes looked twice their normal size.

So she's a pretty hot ticket, huh? she said.

Evan told her he wasn't getting into that.

Oh, you're not, she said. *That's excellent.*

Evan stared back.

She said, *I didn't realize that this wasn't doing it for you, Evan.*

You've got to understand it wasn't about you, he said.

How could it not be about me? she said. *For god's sake, Evan, get real.*

Coils and coils of talk looping back on themselves like razor wire.

And then it was late, Evan exhausted but buzzing. Claudia finally said, *I can't be around you,* thrusting her arms in her jacket and snatching the car keys from the blue bowl.

Look, don't go anywhere, he told her. *It's a bad idea.*

Claudia spun away, her black bangs flying out from her face.

What was he supposed to do, bar the door, act like a thug? Before he could say anything else, she was out in the glaring hallway. He took a couple of steps after her as if sucked along in her wake. He saw her stop at the head of the stairs and turn abruptly. His heart was thudding.

I'll get the car back to you, she said.

Evan stared, not sure he'd heard right. *The car?* he said. *I don't care about the goddamn car.*

But then she was down the stairs and gone.

After an hour, he put on a hooded sweatshirt and sat outside on the stoop listening to the white noise of tires on wet pavement. The rain came in spattering gusts. There'd been times when Patricia had had enough of Donovan and removed herself— two or three days at most. *Your mother's up in Vancouver.* Code words. Had the old man pulled stunts like this, was that what lay behind the absences? He didn't know what to think, and sure as hell wasn't about to ask him now. He watched the windows go black in the building across the street. *You sleep with* me, Evan kept hearing. He thought, *That* flesh and *that* flesh. God, but it was cold out here. Another twenty minutes and he went inside, hiked up the stairs, wearily undressed. He wondered if he should call someone, and who it would be. Not Frannie— it was amazing how little he wanted to talk with her now. He sank onto the bed. The idea of involving *anybody* was horrifying. He dozed atop the bedspread, woke chilly, eventually dozed again.

In the morning, he ran a needling shower on his skin, staying until the hot water was depleted. He filled a Thermos with instant coffee, rode the bus to work, and tried to lose himself in minutiae—for short spells, he could actually manage this. He took a long lunch and spent it walking. Low overhead the sky was sullen, but the rain had given way to mist. He found a slab of dry concrete in a tiny park and sat. As soon as he'd gotten into the Karmann Ghia the day before, the clouds had let loose. Frannie's wipers were so anemic you couldn't see past the sheets of water—she'd had to pull over beside an industrial park, and the whole time they talked drips fell from small punctures in the ragtop. It was agony to be six inches from her and not touch, not kiss. Three more hours of going back over it all, Evan apologizing for his weakness, telling her he'd never before given up someone he loved, Frannie saying, *Evan, do you really think I'm in a position to comfort you?* and Evan responding fiercely, *It's not that, I'm not asking you for anything more, I just want you to—* But he was lost, he couldn't say what he wanted. Everything, he wanted everything. Outside, trucks banged over a lip in the pavement and spray slapped the side of the car. And so it went, back and forth in that tight space, fogged in by their breath, Frannie's patience eventually giving out, a stiff weary look overtaking her mouth and eyes, which he was now seeing in the light of the dials—somehow it had gotten dark. All he knew was he couldn't have it end on this note of exhaustion and dismissal. So more talk, more talk, climbing back toward a place where they could separate.

Now he stood. The cold seemed to have gone up his spine. He glanced at the soggy flower beds lining the cement path, at the matted pockets of litter. *Walk,* he told himself. He returned to the office, and the rest of the day made an effort not to cross paths with Frannie. He had no desire to tell her about Claudia, and at the same time the prospect of making innocuous chat with her seemed altogether beyond him. It was only when he was leaving for the day that he learned she hadn't come in that morning. He was just beginning to wonder about that when one of the older men passed him in the corridor, did a double take, and asked if he was all right. Evan blanked. He had to *answer,* but for a long moment he was vacant, completely stripped of thought. Then he came back into himself and was able to produce a smilelike expression and wave off the concern. *Just a crappy night, not much sleep,* he said. *We all have them,* he was told.

The apartment seemed exactly as he'd left it. He stood in a dumb stare, stiff-necked, his eyes hot and scratchy in their sockets. He was pretty sure nothing terrible had happened to Claudia overnight, beyond what he'd done. But his thoughts started to get away from him. He wondered if she'd shown up for work. Was she a *missing person,* would he have the *authorities* here? He could already hear their voices boring in on him: *Nine times out of ten it's the spouse*— But, Jesus, no, that was irrational. He had to focus. She'd be with one of two friends, he was almost certain. Or else, less likely, back at Sadie's. Then he saw that she *had* been here. On the back of a chair was the flannel shirt she'd fled in, and on the hook behind the bathroom door a damp towel. For a second, he thought maybe she was there *now,* somewhere he hadn't yet looked. But that couldn't be true, it was just the three rooms. A wave of chagrin then, his cheeks burning—how readily he clutched at straws. He took a slow breath and went back through the apartment. There was nothing else to see, no message, no clue to her intentions. So, he realized, she was missing only to *him.*

The second night she was gone, he finished the beer in the fridge, then discovered there was nothing stronger than cranberry juice on hand—not that he meant to get drunk, but he was having trouble settling down. Three blocks up Healey was the neighborhood store he and Claudia used for emergencies: sunflower seeds, Creamsicles, Lucky Lager or Burgy on special for ninety-nine cents. But he couldn't stand the thought of being gone if the phone happened to ring. He didn't think it would—still, leaving seemed like a mistake. It was as if one of them needed to hold down the fort or everything would start disintegrating. He switched on the clock radio and let it play in the background as he picked up the apartment, but the apartment didn't need much picking up. Nothing held his interest. Finally, despite what he'd decided earlier, he threw on his jacket and went out. But when he was opposite the store, he couldn't make himself enter—the place was too empty, too starkly lit, and suddenly the image of him trotting home with a sackful of beer seemed woefully predictable. He turned away.

The third afternoon, Evan saw their car, the venerable two-toned Mercury, wedged into its customary spot. He bounded up the two flights of stairs, not letting himself rehearse any speech. He unlocked the door of the apartment and thrust it open. But still no Claudia. The two worn car keys had been removed from their ring and lay side by side on the table. Ignition, trunk. Then he discovered that the small tan suitcase was gone, along with the rest of her things from the bathroom cupboard. That evening, he loitered at the kitchen sink, chugging milk from the carton, half a sandwich in his other hand. He pictured himself dialing one of the friends' numbers and being warned off with a growl, *You leave her alone.* Evan as pariah. Later, he sat and wrote her a note, folded it, taped it to the doorjamb outside the bedroom. Two days later it was still there, taunting him. He took it down, crumpled it, kicked it under the radiator.

But in the morning he tried again. *I understand that you'd rather be incognito, but I'm afraid of what will happen if we don't keep talking. This is our chance, right now. Can you give me half an hour?*

On the outside, he printed PLEASE READ THIS.

After work the next day, Claudia was waiting for him in the kitchen. But her back was much too straight, her jacket was still on, her wristwatch was conspicuously out on the table. Already she looked as if she didn't live here.

Coffee? he asked.

She shook her head.

Evan eyed the teakettle on the range but sat instead, brushing away crumbs. *I hate to see this all go to pieces,* he said.

Me too, she answered, but there was nothing comforting in how she said it.

If she'd been crying, it didn't show. Her jaw was set; her hair was pulled into a tight ponytail. Her fury seemed to have burned down to a coal giving off steady heat.

He suddenly knew he was no match for it. *I can keep telling you how sorry I am,* he said.

Claudia nodded. She said it didn't matter. She got that he was sorry, but it changed nothing.

Evan looked away. He still believed he loved her and knew he should say it aloud, should *insist* on it. But she'd fling it right back at him, *No, you can't love me and do what you did.* Only now did he start to understand that the two of them must mean different things when they used the word.

Is there anything I can do? Evan asked finally.

I don't think so, Evan.

He said, *You're not sure, though.*

No, I'm sure, she said.

There it was, a moment he'd pick at for the rest of his life. But how much clearer it all is now. He'd wanted to show how *reasonable* he was, wanted desperately not to be a bigger asshole than he'd already been. He didn't try to break her down, didn't plead for fear of sounding pathetic. He failed to see that there were more important things than saving face—or even being *nice,* being a good boy. He was up against an absolute. The only thing to counter an absolute was another absolute. But he'd offered Claudia nothing grander than her own hurt to hang onto, no vision of their future, no reconstituted vow so ablaze with confidence she couldn't turn her back on it. Absent that, he let her be dazzled by the wrong done to her, let her believe that being intractable was the only virtue in the world.

The Human Touch

WHEN NED IS SAFELY GONE, Evan comes inside, returns to the upstairs bedroom.

Maureen hasn't budged, except now she's facing away from the door, on her side, a low ridge under a thin sheet, hip jutting, ribs barely rising as she breathes. He'd love to believe she's conned herself into sleep, but after a couple of minutes, she scrambles to her feet and strides off to the bathroom, closes the door, latches it. Only a filament of yellow light shows along the threshold.

Evan stands by the bed, waiting.

He used to wake in this room—muted early mornings, the silence making him wonder if Claudia had already left for work. Amazing sometimes, the sweetness of being alone, spared the duties of relating to another human. But equally amazing, five minutes, ten minutes later, the relief that gushed in when he heard a makeup bottle tick on the glass shelf or the wincing floor plank in the hall. *Hey, you awake, Ev? Oh, look at you—nope, don't even think about it, I'm late.*

To have been someone's sweetheart.

Maureen emerges at last, barefoot, in her kimono, the sashes trailing down. She's showered, her legs are wet, her hair is combed back in tight furrows. She stares about the room with its bands of thick shadow and makes her way to the dormer window. Earlier, she too must've heard Ned's car leave, but there's no substitute for seeing the bare driveway with her own eyes. Forearms against the sill, she looks out, the breeze grazing her on its way in.

Evan comes alongside. For the first time, he lets himself put his hand on her, just the backs of his fingers, on her neck where a trickle of water rolls down, not quite body temperature. His presence has no noticeable effect. After a minute, satisfied, or only restless, Maureen turns from the window. She lowers herself to the bed, squints at the clock radio, picks up the phone, but leaves it in her lap. It's late. There's no one she's willing to disturb at this hour, after all.

She rises again and, not bothering with her sandals, hurries downstairs. Evan follows, a few steps behind. Rude surprise, the front of the house is still wide open—even the screen door is unlatched, from when Ned walked out and let it slap behind him. Quickly, with her bare foot, Maureen shoves aside the brick stopping the inner door, then closes it firmly, and snaps the deadbolt into place. She turns and heads to the kitchen to check the back door, and it too is open to the night. When she has it shut and locked, she pivots, but before she can take a step, Evan sees her shoulders give a single involuntary shiver, as if seized from behind.

Then she's standing flatfooted, gazing into the icebox, and finally pulls out beer in a green bottle and unscrews the cap. She returns to what used to be Evan's dining room, clicks on the overhead lamp, but immediately, appalled by the torrent of light, clicks it off. Now it occurs to her to flip down the louvers on the window shade nearest the computer table, and only then sits, takes a long drink, blots her bottom lip with the back of her hand, and pokes on the monitor.

She reads from the screen, round-shouldered, a graceless posture, but endearing in its way, Evan thinks. He watches her eyes going back and forth over the headlines of the day. When you don't know what to do with yourself, there's always the news. He looks along with her. There's a band of coal miners streaming with mud, lifted one by one from a hastily bored shaft no wider than their shoulders. Then the Middle East, West Bank, Gaza, still so bleak—it could be two hundred years from now and he'd still be reading the same stuff. So he backs off finally, preferring the sight of her face in the electronic light.

He hears himself say: *With me it was the radio. Late at night? It was different from playing a record—there was a live person at the other end.*

The human touch, you know?

He starts to mention Claudia, but stops—Maureen knows none of that story. Then again, what does it matter? So he goes ahead, *When my wife and I were getting back together, she asked if I still kept the radio on, teasing me a little—she was entitled, I guess. I'd forgotten, but before we slept together I had to play the radio or I couldn't fall asleep. I'd done it since junior high. I either listened to the night guy on KJR or slowly worked my way up and down the dial, seeing what else was out there.*

Remembering more clearly, he adds, *It was the moment of going to sleep that was the problem. If I thought about it, I couldn't do it. I couldn't give myself over. I had to have a diversion. But then Claudia couldn't sleep with it on, so I phased it out. Anyway, I didn't need it anymore.*

The house gives one of its periodic cracks, the old plaster shrinking as it cools. Maureen's head shoots up. She listens acutely, stands, angling her head.

It's OK, he's gone, Evan says. But he decides to duck outside and make sure. It's true, all is calm. Just that breath of night wind, the weeds rasping against each other, a pinecone ticking down through branches and bouncing in the dry duff.

When Evan returns to Maureen, she's writing, not an e-mail but an ordinary letter to her father. Evan recalls her shift of voice when they talk on the phone; there's something heart-grabbing about the sound of *Daddy—?* on a grown woman's lips. Only now is she replying to his request for company later in the summer, reminding him she hasn't been at the new job long enough to accrue vacation. If she came, it would need to be brief. *I'm so sorry,* she types, pauses, stares, deletes these last words, says, *Stop apologizing.*

How much does her father know about Ned? Not all of it. Maybe, responding to questions, she admitted she's been seeing someone, a doctor actually, a man she's very fond of, but left it at that, deflecting further inquiry with quiet evasions, even at her age afraid of his judgment, or maybe at pains not to parcel out more disappointment. It's too late to level with him now, even if she wanted to. And maybe she does, maybe she'd love to unpack that baggage, and even as she's saying she can't come she's giving the picture of being at home with her father a trial run. Evan's never been near upstate New York, but in his mind's eye he sees Maureen on the seat of her father's stalwart Ford, or maybe it's a truck with the orchard's name on the door in faded scroll, Maureen at Janey's age, riding with her father the doctor, staring at the dense green understory of the hardwoods as it smears by, bored, daydreamy, yet safe with him in a way she'll never be again.

Twice now, oblivious, Maureen lifts the bottle to her lips, but it's already empty, and then she stares at it, *Do I want another?* but doesn't rise.

He watches as she rereads the letter, sees her disgust. It's all wrong, what she's written, flat and phony; who is this woman she's become? He can tell she wanted the break with Ned to be clean, purgative, a prelude to a new siege of life, but it hasn't worked out that way. He sees her asking herself which character flaw to blame it on. She brings her fist to her mouth, her eyes close, she doesn't move for so long Evan thinks she's asleep, and maybe she does drift into a state between here and not here, but, returning, she rids the screen of what she's written, pushes back from the table, stands, and looks as though she's *this close* to upending it, sending it flying.

Deep breath, sweetheart, Evan says.

Oddly, it does seem as if Maureen goes slack a moment and locates her composure. *Yes, better,* Evan says.

This is the hour she'd put on the TV, maybe. If she had one. Maybe an old movie, *Roman Holiday* or *Separate Tables,* something she hasn't seen in years, to remind her of who she once was.

Finally, options dwindled, she tries bed again. It can be such an ally some nights. She unsashes the kimono but keeps it on, lies outside the sheets, closes her eyes, one hand fallen open at her side, the other curled on the freckled skin of her chest.

The Five-Hundred-Pound Gorilla

IT SEEMED LIKE EVERYBODY knew someone who'd married the same person twice. Even Liz. And she was more than happy to share the gory details. She'd dropped out of college to au pair for an American family on sabbatical in Brittany, then stayed on, she explained. The landlady of her building had a younger sister who'd twice married the same man. *Her name was Geneviève—the sister, I mean. My landlady I called Madame Tussaud in honor of my fellow lodgers. I was so clever in those days.*

Donovan was out of town on an installation, and Evan had asked Liz to lunch. They were at a slatted wrought-iron table outside a gyro and hummus place. Early June, hazy bright.

Anyway, she said, *Geneviève was barely eighteen the first go-round. The husband was a little older, maybe twenty-five, and he drove a taxicab. She discovered she didn't like him being out all hours of the night—he was supposed to be home with her, his young wife. They argued. He said people needed rides, and besides he had to work, didn't he? She didn't approve of the men he associated with or the coarse ideas they planted in his head. And then other things crept in—he wouldn't go to church with her anymore, for instance. He wasn't the man she'd been led to believe he was, that was all. She shouldn't have lost her head and married him so fast, was Madame Tussaud's opinion. She thought her sister was kind of an airhead.*

During the occupation, the ex-husband more or less disappeared. It wasn't until the end of the forties that they ran into each other again, in Cherbourg—Geneviève was waiting to pick someone up at the ferry from England. It turned out he'd been active in the underground, the ex-husband. In fact, he'd been known for his resourcefulness and bravery, and he'd recently been appointed to some post in the local government. He seemed like a new man. Not boyish, more handsome than she recalled. He had a new solid-ness of character. It turned out he'd married during the war, but his second wife had been killed just after D-Day—she'd been caught in a mortar shelling and a roof timber had broken her neck. So they began to see each other again, Geneviève and her ex. There was still some heat there apparently. Inside of six months they had remarried. I imagine he was glad for the chance to have her see who he really was, not the early draft, so to speak. That would be very powerful, don't you think? Like a vindication? And maybe af-ter all he'd been through, he wanted to live more normally now. And as for her—

Evan stopped her to ask if she'd ever laid eyes on this Genev-iève.

Oh, yes, Liz said. *She was in her fifties by then.* She made a jog-gling gesture with two cupped palms. *Très zaftig. Too much heavy cream. But she was only in her mid-thirties when she married this man again, and maybe she was thinking, you know, she'd jumped ship too soon, should've given him the benefit of the doubt.*

Evan asked what had gone wrong the second time.

Now what makes you think something went wrong?

Evan said it sounded like that kind of story.

I guess it is, she went on. *Madame Tussaud said her sister was always flying off half-cocked, too* impulsif, *this was just one more example. In English she told me,* I wash my hands of her. *She was probably a little jealous, Madame Tussaud—she'd always cast herself as the responsible one, the family rock, but she was something of a killjoy, if you want my opinion. I think it was reasonable enough, them trying it again, Geneviève and her old love. They had to be open to the possibility. It's just that the heat turned out not to be enough. It didn't last. I guess they saw that they'd been fooled. They were pretty much strangers, after all. More's the pity.*

She reached over and gave Evan's hand a friendly pat, and added, *None of which necessarily applies to you, dear boy.*

Thanks for the clarification, he said.

Just then, a motorcycle tore by, spitting a huge blat of noise that caromed between the storefronts. Evan stared after it until there was enough quiet to talk again. Then a few moments longer.

Evan? Liz said.

He said, *It's the five-hundred-pound gorilla. Marrying again.*

Liz smiled softly. *I can't tell you what to do, Evan.*

I'm not asking.

She said, *Liar.*

Evan shook his head.

Liz said, *The only thing I'd say is if you're not sure, that probably means you shouldn't.*

No, I'm sure, Evan said. *We both are.*

Then why does it matter what I think?

Evan gave her a look.

Well, really, she said.

Evan said, *I guess I'm just sort of superstitious. I mean, are we tempting fate?*

You don't believe in fate, Liz reminded him.

Evan inspected his coffee cup, but it was still empty. He said, *Fate doesn't care whether I believe in it or not, that's the thing.*

I give up, Liz said.

Evan smiled a little. *You want some baklava?* he asked.

Of course, she said. *But I'm going to abstain. I can't look too blown out for the wedding. Too zaftig.*

Evan said, *You know, we haven't really decided about having a formal* —

I'm not giving you my opinion on that, either, Liz said.

Evan nodded.

Though fate might have something to say about you two slinking off to City Hall.

Evan propped his chin in his palm and let out a slow breath.

Liz said, *I'm teasing you, sweetie. I just want you to be happy.*

I am, he said.

Really?

Would you like it in writing?

She said, *I don't think that'll be necessary.*

Dry Land

EVEN BEFORE THE EARTHQUAKE, Claudia hadn't been wild about the apartment she and Janey shared—faded gentility masking code violations. Now, as an added reminder, plywood blotted out half the skylight above the stairwell. She'd planned on moving when the lease ran out, anyway. Should they all live at Madrona Street? In principle, uprooting Janey seemed like a mistake, but the school year was almost over, and less than a mile from Evan's house was a private academy they might be able to get her into for the fall—definitely a leg up on her current school, which she loathed anyway. For Claudia, relocating to Evan's meant a nastier commute, but she told him she could stagger her workday and avoid the worst of it—and, anyway, the drive gave her time to think.

Evan's house was a good size for the three of them, big enough without being a monster to care for. It stood at the end of a quiet street. It had the cedars. You could see the water below the hill, and farther off, the ragged skyline of the Olympics. He was a little worried that Claudia and Janey might continue to feel like visitors there, or that he'd somehow act too proprietary, or, despite himself, give them the idea that he resented surrendering his peace and quiet. But he put all that aside and they came. Janey took the back bedroom upstairs — it had the morning light, the clearest view of the sky — and Claudia joined Evan in the big front bedroom with the dormers.

Next was the question of the wedding. Evan had always considered it hypocritical to marry in a church if you weren't a believer and, if possible, Claudia was even less swayed by religion than he was. But shortly after his lunch with Liz, he found himself making the offer.

It was early evening. Janey was inside, prostrate with her Walkman. Claudia was on the back steps having a leisurely smoke. Evan had just returned from checking on the raspberry canes and was standing in front of her now, sneakers damp from the long grass. In reply, she cast him a look, as if to say, *What's gotten to* you?

Evan dug his hands into his pockets. He said, *I thought maybe you felt slighted the first time. It was kind of bare bones.*

Claudia said, *I thought the first time was nice. I loved you. We had our friends there. It was elegant in its way, unusual. Besides, if you want to know, Lucas and I went for the whole dress-with-a-train, gathered-together-in-the-sight-of-you-know-who. I got it out of my system.*

You're sure? Evan asked.

Completely and totally, she said. Then added, *But we probably ought to stick to dry land this time.*

Evan nodded. *Terra firma,* he said. Then he said, *For that matter, we don't need to* have *a ceremony. We could always —*

But Claudia stopped him. *No, I want to,* she said. *Don't you think? But something manageable, just a party. Maybe outside?*

Evan stood mulling that. After a while, he said, *What about rings?*

Rings, definitely, Claudia answered.

I meant should we get new ones?

She said, *You still have yours?*

You don't?

God, Evan, she said, *I threw it off the Bay Bridge. You didn't really expect me to save it, did you? What a dreamer.*

OK, that made him feel a little naive; that stung a little. He said, *Right. New rings.*

You really kept yours? Claudia asked. *Where'd you keep it?*

You want to know where I kept it? Evan said, staring.

Claudia nodded.

He rubbed his face. *Sock drawer,* he said.

Ah, she replied, *The Trove of Secret Treasure.*

Evan tried to suppress his grin.

Later, upstairs, he felt her hands slipping around his midsection, her cheek on the back of his neck.

She said, *Evan, I kept my ring, but I don't want to reuse it. If it's all right with you.*

Absolutely, he said.

So that's how it went as they made their plans: *Evan & Claudia II* floated atop *Evan & Claudia I*, semitransparent, their former selves hazily visible below, going about their outmoded business. Nonetheless, they ordered a cake (not carrot this time, but white on white), a packet of invitations went out, and on the fifth of August, 1989, Claudia and Evan were remarried in a dappled corner of the Japanese Garden.

Sadie had no one to conspire with about the groom now (Claudia's grandmother Frieda was bedridden, non compos mentis). A few others were missing—Harry Weinstock, Claudia's one-time boss (it seemed a lifetime ago she'd worked for him), the couple across the alley from her growing up (husband dead, wife living near a grown daughter in Walla Walla, according to Sadie), and one of the girlfriends who'd stood up with her (they'd had a falling out, Claudia said—it was complicated). And the same on his side of the aisle, changed circumstance, attrition. Worst by far was Patricia's absence (but Liz had quietly given Claudia a bride's bouquet of Gerber daisies from the terraced beds Patricia had established long ago—the perfect Liz gesture, Evan thought). He was loath to plant words in the mouth of the dead, but he believed Patricia would've liked seeing them reunite. As he collected himself before the proceedings began, it almost seemed as if he sensed her presence there. (You live a charmed life, Evan.)

He looked up in time to see Liz guiding Janey toward the wooden chairs. Janey wore a long lilac dress with a high waist and streamers of lace. Her hair had been braided and the braids pinned to the sides of her head, Princess Leia fashion. He'd never seen her dolled up—she looked nice, he thought (and she was making an effort to hold herself straighter), yet it occurred to him she was one of those girls who would never feel quite at ease in party clothes.

Then it was four o'clock. Unaccompanied, Evan coming from the left, Claudia from the right, they met on the granite slab where Sonny Nicolette—Evan's friend from Ballard High days, concertina player turned magistrate—awaited them. Claudia was in pearly silk that clung to her, moving as she moved. Evan had planned to tease her about not reprising the white mini-dress, but all thought of that went out of his head. He leaned toward her and whispered, *Wow.*

Within minutes, they were circulating among the guests, holding hands, thanking everyone, accepting hugs and good wishes. The champagne came around. Donovan raised his glass and suddenly there was no sound but the wash of air through leaves and the far-off buzz of a speedboat. *What a goddamn fine day,* he announced. He gazed out the tops of his half-lenses to see if anyone had a contrary opinion. *I promised Evan no embarrassing anecdotes,* he went on. Not true, Evan thought, his guard going up. Here Donovan hesitated, as if teetering on a fulcrum. Then he said, *And since I seem to recall that he offered some charitable remarks about Liz and myself a while ago, I believe I'll return the favor.* The part about Evan's little speech was true—and, boy, hadn't he sweated bullets over it. So Donovan orated a bit, finally saying, *In any case, I just want to point out the obvious: Anybody can marry a person once—doing it again's reserved for the hard cases. So, Ev, Claudia*—he looked each in the eye—*here's to love's hard cases.*

Love's hard cases, people said.

When the music started, Donovan stripped off his jacket and danced with Liz, still a powerful man at sixty-nine, in his red suspenders, the white dress shirt gradually dampening across his back. Patricia used to love when Donovan waltzed her across the kitchen, spur-of-the-moment—premeditated dancing she'd never really cared for, couldn't see its point, quite. But Liz was in her element, clearly a dancer from way back. She'd lost ten pounds since that day they talked about her landlady's sister. She was full of bounce, her hair rising off her neck in a great wiry mass, its slash of white not so prominent now amid the gray.

Evan saw her beckoning him over Donovan's shoulder. *Go on,* Claudia said. So he went to cut in on his father, and then his arms were full of Donovan's *bosom friend,* the bosom squashing pleasantly against his own chest.

How're you bearing up? Liz asked up toward his ear.

Evan said, *You know what, I'm good.*

I can tell, she answered.

Slowly, they spun through the leaf shadow quavering on the makeshift dance floor, squares of portable parquet laid atop the grass. By now, Donovan had grabbed up Claudia. How strange, in a way, to see your father dancing with your wife—between Donovan and *any* woman there was sexual energy. But what really struck Evan was how, from behind, Claudia could be Patricia: slender, black-haired, the top of her head a couple of inches above Donovan's. Evan abandoned himself to this illusion momentarily, feeling nothing so definite as jealousy or melancholy, only the curious sense of floating in time. He was brought back by Liz saying, *Did I mention we'd gotten up a pool? How long the happy couple will last this go-round.* His feet still shuffling, Evan pulled away far enough to check her face. *Just seeing if you were paying attention,* Liz said. Evan smiled—you had to expect a little hazing. *I'm here, I'm here,* he said.

A little later, he noticed his father box-stepping Janey among the dancers. Donovan's big hand dwarfed hers, but he had a solid grip on her and his lips were going, *One-two-three, one-two-three,* and when Janey rotated, Evan could see that Donovan had managed to more or less neutralize her jitters. Bless your heart, Evan thought.

He located Claudia and they danced again.

Then he danced with his sister. *Wasn't sure you'd put in an appearance,* Evan whispered, his cheek by hers.

She gave him a look as if to ask, *Why's that?*

Too boo-jwah, Evan said.

Oh, lay off, Gayle answered. *As if you didn't have some funny ideas.*

Gayle had recently suffered through the collapse of a long-term affair and she'd come without a date today. She and Evan would never be best buddies, but it seemed less mandatory for them to nettle each other now. Evan let the teasing die.

Later still, he looked up and noticed his mother-in-law at loose ends. Sadie had never been the type to have men buzzing around, but age had given her a certain sinew and the gaze of a woman who'd quietly outlasted the fluttery and the nubile. He made his way to her and held out his hand. She nodded, placed hers in it (dry, cool), and off they went, Evan trying not to relive their encounter outside the movie theater, disdain oozing from her as she said, *Oh, it's you.* Evan's other hand pressed the slippery fabric at the small of her back. The mild flowery scent of bath splash rose from her neck. Evan struggled for a pleasantly benign remark, but settled for giving her a dignified few minutes on the dance floor.

Before long, the number came to an end and they disengaged. Evan was all set to say, *Thanks, Sadie, that was nice*—already parched, taking a first step toward the table with the punch bowl—but the band lit into a feverish swing tune and suddenly Sadie was tugging him back, and the look she aimed at him said, *You're not bailing out on me now, are you?* An awkward little moment. Evan recovered, made a show of mock-horror *(Bail? Not me!),* then he was fast-dancing with his mother-in-law, attempting a rudimentary jitterbug, and—why should this come as any surprise?—Sadie was a whiz. It was as if a switch had been thrown in her. Pretty soon, everyone had stopped to watch and whoop out encouragement, especially Claudia and Liz, side by side. The hem of Sadie's dress was flared, and as her hips moved it switched back and forth—for the first time in years, Evan thought of the absent man, Claudia's father, caught a glimmer of his one-time attraction to Sadie. Dancing away, Evan smiled across at her and she smiled back. What a funny thing, life.

Anyway, it *was* a goddamn fine day. A day with nothing wrong in it—no reversal of weather, no allergic reaction to the crab dip, no blown fuses—a day as bereft of omens as you were likely to find. At one point, looking out at friends and family, Evan found himself simply engulfed by relief—almost a physical pleasure, like blood rushing back into a sleeping limb.

The earlier wedding had brought relief, too, but this was different. By the day they'd stepped onto the boat to be married, Evan wasn't so worried that Claudia would suddenly see into him a little deeper and flinch. More than he'd ever managed before, or since, he'd simply laid out the goods and taken his chances. He was willing to trust the idea that they really *were* meant for each other—it wasn't just run-of-the-mill lovers' talk, it had currency in the real world. Donovan and Patricia were there, Sadie, Frieda, and the rest. Everyone was convened in its honor; everyone was acting as if they were buying into this new entity, Evan-and-Claudia. So, *yes,* Evan had been relieved.

And now today: He didn't believe that marrying Claudia again would undo the past or set anything right. The past was what it was. But he *did* feel that people were willing to let him consign old sins to the back burner. Willing to hear him proclaim that he'd been right the first time, after all.

So, he was relieved all over again. Relief was good; who didn't like relief?

And yet, now that he's relieved himself of living, Evan can't help asking why he'd always measured happiness that way—in terms of relief, of being rid of something awful. Pretty damn odd for a boy born healthy, born loved, born to a family whose bills got paid on time.

Laissez les Bon Temps Roulez

A MONTH AFTER THE WEDDING, the last weekend of summer, they drove to a hot spring in the mountains. Evan, Claudia, Janey—a replica of a family, close enough to fool the naked eye.

A dozen or so cabins around a flagpole. A bar and café, an outdoor pool painted blue, two canopied hot plunges flanked by a pine-sided bathhouse. The first night, they had a quick soak, ate, turned in before ten. Evan toppled into a blank sleep and woke early, deliciously empty. Claudia was already up, out on the cabin steps in her nightgown, sipping coffee. He loitered at the screen door, barefoot, watching the back of her head, remembering that long-ago morning on Toshi's boat. *I hear you back there,* Claudia said. Evan came and sat by her. *Woman with White Mug,* he said. Claudia smiled drowsily and wrapped her free arm around his knee.

Later that morning, the three of them followed a trail winding back into old-growth forest. Hemlock and cedar, saplings poking from mossed-over deadwood. A dry summer in town, but still wet here. There were seeping outcrops, fiddlehead ferns, lush shoots of skunk cabbage where the ground was marshy. The sunlight came obliquely, high overhead. Evan had anticipated resistance from Janey. He remembered himself at that age, when hiking was like a forced march—and with Janey you never knew when she'd balk. But for now she loped along between himself and Claudia, uncomplaining, her hair under a blue bandanna, her face turning side to side with a look approaching awe.

They crested a low ridge where the view opened out, the valley green-black with fir, juts of exposed rock higher up. Evan stopped and unslung the daypack. *Doing OK?* he asked Janey.

She nodded.

He tossed her a packet of gorp, which she caught two-handed, clutching it to her chest. *And how about you?* he said to Claudia.

Well, I'm very fine, she said.

Evan passed her the water bottle. She drank, staring off at the bands of blue haze. *I don't believe we're here,* she said.

We are, Evan answered.

It's like I'm always indoors, she said, as if it were only now occurring to her.

Evan smiled.

No one spoke for a while. Evan remembered an architectural truism of Donovan's: Low ceilings cramp your thoughts, whereas vaulted ceilings, especially if they were circular and open to natural light like the one in the old Christian Science Church on First Hill, tended to release your thoughts, to let them rise. This had sounded like typical Donovan hocus-pocus to Evan at fifteen, but was of course palpably true, he later saw. And being in the mountains, no roof at all—even if you were a thoroughgoing atheist like Evan, even if you shrugged and turned away when people talked about their *spirits,* their *souls,* and so on, you nonetheless felt something rising in you, expanding into the un-limited space above.

After lunch, he lazed in one of the hot pools amid steam smell-ing of sulfur and bicarbonate.

Janey lay out on the concrete apron in a modest two-piece. She was dark like Lucas, able to soak up sun. Long, knobby-kneed legs, prescription shades, a flapping copy of *The Left Hand of Darkness*. Evan had taken in a bag of hardbacks for credit at the used bookstore and told her she could get whatever she wanted—Le Guin was too old for her probably, but she seemed totally absorbed.

And there was Claudia, black tank suit, floppy-brimmed hat, stretched out in a cone of shadow, slowly working on a Coke, and paging through a stack of glossy mags.

Evan smiled at the world's largesse and let his eyes droop shut.

When he looked up again, the shadow had moved on and Clau-dia was gone. He straightened, scanning. He couldn't spot her among the swimmers and was thinking about climbing out of the water when she reappeared with her camera bag and tripod. The morning of the wedding Evan had given her a vintage Has-selblad, a reconditioned 500C with an 80mm Zeiss Planar lens and prism viewfinder, the camera she'd coveted when they were first together and couldn't begin to afford it—actually, he wor-ried the gift might strike her as too steeped in nostalgia, but she seemed genuinely touched. Now he watched as she fixed it to the tripod and screwed on the long cable release.

One of the best shots from that afternoon became the black-and-white blowup that hung (too briefly) in the house at Ma-drona Street. A razor-sharp silver gelatin print in a black frame: three sets of bare shoulders, three dead-on faces, three pairs of sunglasses.

At the last minute, for no obvious reason, Janey had refused to take her sunglasses off. Claudia waffled momentarily—make a federal case of this?—but then said, *OK, no, I like it. Ev, put yours on,* digging out her own. Janey could've fought back, ripped the glasses off and flung them, or else flounced away, but chose instead to act as if the cool design of the picture had originated with her.

Anyway, Evan frankly loved this picture. It *was* cool.

On the right, Evan, stubble-cheeked, smile unfeigned. His eyes didn't show through the smoky glass (they belonged to Patricia's line of watchers and cogitators) but the part of him you could see was obviously, despite their differences, Donovan's. A grown man's face. When exactly had *that* happened?

On the other side, Claudia. She'd been in the big pool earlier; her hair had dried, and the ringlets had sprung back and were every which way, but that seemed to be the style now. She was giving her looks more attention these days, tweezing the black brows into submission, drawing on lip color before she went out. She had the start of crow's feet, deeper on the left side where she squinted. But, all in all (Evan used to think, admiring this triptych en route from the foot of the stairs to the kitchen), a keener, handsomer face than she'd possessed at nineteen.

And there was Janey, sandwiched by the adults. The thrust-out chin, the cockiness, as if to say she was really one of *them,* don't blame her for being stranded in this gangling girl's body. How tempted he always was to be encouraged by this expression—except he knew it was deceptive, only a minor triumph concerning the sunglasses. And he remembered, too, that Claudia had been trying without success to interest Janey in photography; by Janey's age, Claudia had been prowling her neighborhood with a Kodak of Sadie's. Whether Janey honestly didn't care for it, or because it was her mother's thing and therefore off-limits, Evan hadn't yet determined.

That night, after supper, the three of them played backgammon, round robin. Janey had learned enough that Evan could play her straight, not talking her through every move. But she was throwing lousy dice tonight, while Claudia's rolls were uncanny—six-two, double fours, whatever she needed, that's what tumbled from her cup. Evan saw Janey's frustration building. He said, *I think your old mom's resorting to psychokinesis.* Janey shot him a questioning look. Evan pointed at the dice, touched his forehead, and made a *Twilight Zone* noise.

You two, Claudia said. *Sorry if you can't keep up with my brilliance.*

Janey finally announced she'd had enough, then drifted to the back bedroom with her novel. Evan and Claudia finished their game, and a little later Claudia stuck her head around Janey's door and told her they were going up to have a beer.

The bar was a low, timber-sided addition to the hot spring's lodge. Surely dead much of the time but cranked up tonight with end-of-season revelry. Chuck Berry blared from the sound system—those ringing triplets on the high strings that instantly stirred Evan's bones. People were dancing on the plank flooring, some of the girls in flip-flops, filmy shirts over their swimsuits.

Way too much commotion for a quiet chat. But what the hell, Evan thought. He went off to get drinks. By the time he was back, Claudia had snagged a pair of shots from partyers at the next table. It came out that another couple had also just married, so there was toasting all around, more shots, and pretty soon Evan and Claudia were out among the pack of dancers. They'd never danced much in the old days—when they went to hear a band, it was to hear the band. Later, on his own, Evan mostly avoided the clubs (sweaty public foreplay, in his opinion). Tonight, though—maybe it was the Cuervo, maybe the fact they'd danced fairly successfully at the wedding weeks earlier—Evan felt expansive, wanted his body out there amid the action.

Privately, he'd never considered Claudia much of a dancer. She lacked the slinkiness some women had—she was a little too forthright or self-contained or something. But he was starting to revise this opinion. The black ringlets were moving *very nicely* tonight. In fact, the more Evan observed her, the smarter Claudia's dancing seemed. Since they were virtually the same height, she sometimes cupped her hands over his shoulder bones and danced straight-armed, her gaze on him, as if to say, *Whatcha thinking in there, bud?* And what Evan had been thinking, off and on all day, was that as satisfactory as the ceremony in the Japanese Garden had been, it was for everyone else's sake. An announcement, a promise. Whereas tonight's joyous chaos was *theirs*—not a honeymoon exactly, considering Janey, but close enough. Right after *Chuck Berry's Greatest Hits* came an infectious blast of zydeco, Clifton Chenier and friends. Evan twirled Claudia in and kissed her salty neck. They didn't sit down the rest of the night.

Later, they made their way toward the cabin, arms about each other, Claudia still kind of sashaying. She said, *Oh, look at you. Steam's coming off your head.*

I'm a hot guy, Evan replied.

Among the campsites a portable generator quit for the night. The wind sounded huge all of a sudden, raking through the canyon, thrashing the fir-tops. The last few cabins were dark, including their own, except for the glow of Janey's window shade. Evan unlocked the door quietly, underhanded the key onto the saggy couch, and Claudia tiptoed in to switch off Janey's light. But she was back right away, saying, *She's not in there, Ev.*

They both looked toward the bathroom, but its door was open, the light off.

Claudia called out, *Janey—?*

She can't be far, Evan said.

Claudia was already headed back outside. For a second, their eyes met. *Make me believe you,* she was asking, but Evan was just starting to wonder if something was actually wrong here. He trailed her down the porch steps, heard her casting her daughter's name into the shadows.

He circled around the opposite way. He hadn't gone ten steps when he heard Janey's voice, miserable-sounding. *I'm right* here— He shielded his eyes against the pole light. Her shoulder blades were back against the board and batten, the flannel nightshirt a thin swath of gray.

What's up? he asked.

She said nothing. A moment later, Claudia arrived at his side.

Janey stared at them, fidgeting, crossing one leg over the other. She said, *The wind blew the door shut and you had the key.*

But why were you outside? Claudia asked.

Janey looked from her mother to Evan and back again as if the two of them were ganging up on her. *You were taking too long,* she said.

Oh, honey, Claudia said, *we were just dancing a little. I'm sorry, I thought you'd be sound asleep.*

Well, I wasn't, Janey said, her voice suddenly venomous.

Nobody knew what to do for a second. Finally Evan said, *Look, I'm sorry, too.* He stuck a hand out. *Let's go in, huh?*

He figured Janey would snub him. But with only a minor hesitation, she straightened and, with an air of ceremony, draped her own hand atop his as if they were about to promenade down a long red carpet.

Back inside, Claudia made hot chocolate on the cabin's hot plate. Janey sat watching the steam rise off her cup, stirring mechanically. After a minute, Claudia bent and kissed the top of her head.

Later, when Janey was squared away, Evan and Claudia undressed and crawled between the chilly sheets and pulled the blanket to their chins.

What do you suppose that was about? Claudia asked.

Evan said, *I was going to ask you.*

I'm not convinced she was telling the truth, Claudia said.

Don't you think she was just a little freaked to be in the cabin alone? Evan asked.

Maybe, she said, rearranging herself in the bed. *But I don't like the idea of her wandering around in the night. What if she'd gone down by the creek?*

Evan said, *Well, it's not like she's a toddler who's going to fall in and be swept away.*

I still don't like it, Claudia said.

Evan extended his arm so she'd move in against him, and after a moment, she did.

Your feet still cold? he asked.

Icy.

Then don't get them near mine, Evan said.

Claudia immediately put her feet on his.

Whooo, jeez, he said. *Where's your blood?*

I've got plenty of blood, Claudia said. *It's just a distribution problem.*

Evan reached down and took one of her feet in his hands and started rubbing it. He said, *I really ought to be using gloves for this operation. Here, give me the other one.*

God, that feels good, Claudia said.

Gradually the bed warmed. Evan whispered into her hair, *So what should we do tomorrow?*

Let's have another day like today, Claudia said.

Absolutely, he answered. He held her, listening to the wind, the slap of the flagpole's rope. Then he said, *What should we do with the rest of this one?*

We can't, Evan, she's still up, Claudia whispered. *She's in there reading with the flashlight, I know it.*

Evan massaged her hipbone under the covers, then the smooth skin of her belly. He felt the start of a giggle. She said, *Shhhh, Ev. Oh, stop, oh, honey, come on, it's gonna squeak!*

Evan lay smiling. Softly, he hummed a couple bars of "Jambalaya."

Janey

T HEY COULD STILL have a baby of their own. Claudia was thirty-eight and in good health—it wasn't a sure thing, but they could certainly try. They'd begun to talk around the edges of the subject, sounding each other out. It was daunting for Evan to picture himself in his fifties with a child in grade school, to be taken for a grandfather, to know he'd likely die before the child was far into adulthood; he'd been only thirty-one when he'd lost Patricia. And so on, all the drawbacks. But then he thought, So what? Reuniting with Claudia had begun to seem like a miracle, and the prospect of having a baby seemed to have the same light shining on it. He thought: If Claudia's game, I'm game.

But before they'd made any decision, Janey's situation began to eclipse everything.

Evan and Claudia were both wrong about her, as it turned out. She *was* somewhat morbid, and the owlish moods were *not* entirely a result of the divorce.

She liked her new school even less than the old one. She hated the uniform—white blouse, dorky tartan skirt, knee socks that itched and peppered the skin of her calves with red bumps. To her mother, she complained of the other girls' cliques, but when Claudia investigated she was told that typically it was Janey who held herself apart, acting above it all sometimes, but at other times oddly diffident.

After an abundance of horsing around over arrangements, Claudia flew Janey down to her father's for Thanksgiving. The following week, Lucas called to say he thought they should have her checked out. If Claudia didn't cooperate, he'd see to it himself. *What are you implying?* she said. Evan usually made himself scarce when they conferred, but now Claudia was motioning emphatically for him to stay, so he came and sat on the arm of the sofa. To Lucas she said, *You're honestly telling me—no, I mean it, Luc, on the basis of three days with her? Did she do something?* Claudia listened a moment, lips parted. She said, *OK, well, I'm sorry, I just don't trust your impressions, Luc.*

She insisted, afterward, that this was simply more payback from Lucas. *That man doesn't miss a beat. He can't stand it that we moved up here. Janey's vulnerable enough at this age without him putting ideas in her head.*

I get that, Evan said. He wished he could step in with a remedy, or at least be as solid a physical presence as Donovan had been for Patricia. Nonetheless, he went ahead, gingerly, *I don't want to seem like a turncoat, but it's possible what she's going through is more than the usual. She hasn't even gotten the big load of hormones yet. I think you should—*

Claudia stared back as if he *were* being a little disloyal. *I should what?* she asked.

Keep an eye on her.

Claudia said, *I've got my eye on her.*

Moments later, she said, *She has moods, Evan.*

Yeah, well, we've all got our moods, Evan answered. *But hers—I mean, one minute she's incredibly caustic, the next she's like a creature that's been pried from its shell.*

Claudia looked stung. He wished he'd been less blunt, though what he said was true. Clearly, she wasn't ready to entertain any diminished visions of her daughter's future.

Then, one Thursday late in January, Janey failed to return from school. Most days either Claudia or Evan would've been home minutes after the bus dropped her, and the days neither could be there, she stayed late at school. But today, when Claudia arrived home about six, she found the house dark. By the time Evan arrived, close to seven, she'd made a dozen phone calls and learned that no one had a clue where Janey was. *Evan, she wasn't even at school today,* she said. His coat still on, Evan said he'd seen her leave for the bus stop. *You're sure that was today?* Claudia asked him. *Nobody remembers seeing her on the bus.* Evan said he was sure. *I thought she was checking in with you,* Claudia said. *This was the afternoon I had to go up to Everett,* he said. *I thought we were clear on that.*

Claudia said, *Jesus, Evan.*

When the police arrived they wanted to know if Janey might've gone to her father's. Claudia said she doubted it, Lucas was in California, after all. They asked about the custody arrangement, could the father have taken her?

No, Claudia said, that didn't seem like the most likely thing. *He's not—*

They waited.

She said, *OK, he's not incapable of it, but I think I'd have seen it coming.*

They asked if Claudia had contacted him.

No, she said, vehemently. Evan saw how much she hated to give Lucas ammunition against her.

The officer moved on. *You said you recently relocated. Could she've gone back to her old house?*

Claudia said, *That doesn't seem very likely, either—I mean, she wasn't happy there. It wasn't like she had friends in the building.*

And so on. Was there anything out of the ordinary in her demeanor, anything about her room? What about drugs? *She's in the sixth grade,* Claudia said. *And she isn't like that.*

A steady sleeting rain ticked at the window. Evan kept thinking, Just another few minutes and she'll show up. Not even his flesh and blood, but suddenly the floor seemed to come out from under him, that sudden etherized plummeting, then he was locked in the bathroom, his entire insides liquefied and roaring out of him. He hung onto the towel bar with one hand, panting, feeling the sweat in his scalp beginning to cool. His heart was whanging. *Please, please slow down,* he said. In a few minutes, he cleaned himself up, rooted around in the cupboard, and found a plastic bottle with broken bits of Xanax and let a couple dissolve bitterly on his tongue, not enough to actually do much, but he was able to talk himself back out with Claudia where he belonged.

Nothing had changed, though. No one had a blessed clue about Janey.

Claudia's style of worry was to be hyperrational. But when the sensible questions led nowhere, she became not only terrified for Janey, but also frustrated to the point of anger. Why couldn't she figure it out? She kept saying, *But where is she, Evan?* Evan tried to hold her but she couldn't sit still. As the night progressed, more scenarios occurred to them, variants of the two stories: Janey had been abducted or she'd run off. It didn't help that before Christmas, the national news had been saturated with the case of the thirteen-year-old daughter of a Pepperdine University professor—snatched from her suburban bedroom and still unaccounted for.

That was the trouble with being glued to the news. But Evan felt the chances of Janey being grabbed off the street, lured into a car, were pretty remote. Which meant she'd intended to inflict her absence on them, or else had given no thought to how they'd react. And he wasn't so sure they could eliminate the possibility that she'd lit out for her father's. Finally, hours after midnight, in the brutal light of the kitchen, he brought it up again. *I realize you don't want to call Luc,* he said, *but you really need to.*

Claudia shook her head, more weary than resistant.

Evan said, *I don't think you have a choice.*

Claudia said, *I know. But I'm not going to call now and wake him up. Let's say if we don't hear anything by noon, then I'll call.*

Evan nodded. It would have to do.

He came and stood by her chair and tipped her face up. *You've got to get your contacts out,* he said. *Your eyes look raw.* He smoothed the hair back from her temple and kept stroking it for a moment.

But they didn't have to call Luc. A little after nine the next morning, with no fanfare, Janey came through the back door. Shoulders hunched, face averted, still in her school clothes, minus the knee socks. It turned out, she *had* gone back to her former neighborhood. Claudia and Evan never did receive a satisfying account of what she'd done all day, but she did admit she'd spent the night holed up in a storage room off their old building's laundry area. When it was finally morning, light enough not to arouse suspicion, she walked to a bakery and bought a sweet roll, then took the bus home. Actually, three buses. Evan had seen the bus books in her drawer as he and Claudia had searched for clues—

but they were out-of-date Seattle Metro books, and he hadn't put things together. He didn't say it aloud, but in a way he was proud of her, how she'd figured out the routes.

What were you thinking? Claudia said, once it was clear that Janey was in one piece. *Don't you know what you put us through?*

Janey wouldn't answer. Or couldn't, Evan thought.

No, that's not good enough, Claudia persisted. *You have to tell me. Why do you just one day not show up at school? I mean if I can't trust you now—*

Janey stood motionless, her long bare legs blue-looking. Evan asked her to have a seat at the kitchen table and fixed her a mug of milky coffee. He watched her wet her finger, then bring it to her lips.

After a moment, Claudia started in again, *I want to know the thought process here, because, really, if it's to the point where—*

Abruptly, Janey stood, her hip banging the table and knocking over the coffee, which ran onto the floor. *I just wanted to go somewhere,* she shrieked, her face stiffened into the same snarl she'd given them outside the cabin that night.

But Evan saw something else: The trouble she was in with them was incidental. The sad truth, for her, was that she hadn't come up with anything very novel to do. She'd bailed out on her adventure; already she was foreseeing a future plagued by failures of imagination, or nerve. Evan sensed this instantly, and knew that Claudia didn't. His gut reaction was to jump in and comfort Janey: *Sweetie, look, don't do this, don't give up on yourself. You won't necessarily be the same later, people grow—* But his allegiance to Claudia seemed to forbid it. Looking back, he reads this as a failure of nerve, or imagination, on his part.

Not long after that night, they received a call from Janey's school, asking them to come in for a conference. Here they were told that she'd done some good work in social studies—even given an oral report on a book she'd read about Egyptian burial practices. She was capable of *very original* ideas, said the teacher, who seemed to be picking her words judiciously. *But she skips certain assignments altogether. Math worksheets, and some of our daily things, the journal entries, for instance. She only does the work when it suits her.*

Claudia frowned at this news.

We need her to focus on consistency, the teacher said. She drew out a manila folder and let it sit unopened in front of her. *I'd like to give you a checklist of the assignments each week. And then, if you'd go over it with her—?*

We can certainly do that, Claudia answered. Then she said, *But what about improvements in how she, you know, gets along with the other girls, and the staff?*

The teacher looked genuinely sorry she couldn't give a better report. *Actually,* she said, *that's the other thing I wanted to discuss. One day last week, Janey wouldn't come out of a stall in the girl's room after lunch. For quite a long time, most of two periods. We had the nurse come and talk to her. Mrs. Androes? She's very good with the girls.*

She offered a brief smile of concern.

At first, she continued, *Janey refused to say anything, except that she wanted to be left alone. That in itself isn't so uncommon.*

Evan pictured the school nurse on the other side of a steel partition from Janey, perched on a lidless institutional toilet. *Bless me, father, for I have sinned.*

The teacher said, *But Mrs. Androes didn't have a good feeling about leaving her there. She felt we needed to see what had set this off. Janey can be very stubborn, of course. She finally told Mrs. Androes that she had a nosebleed. Mrs. Androes asked her if it had started on its own, or if she'd bumped into something, or maybe been pushed? Janey wouldn't answer. Then Mrs. Androes asked her if it had stopped. Janey indicated that it was still bleeding.*

She'd been in there well over an hour by this time, so Mrs. Androes was naturally concerned that this wasn't an ordinary nosebleed. She explained that she needed to have a look. Janey said she didn't want anybody seeing it. They were at something of a standoff. You can imagine that Mrs. Androes didn't want to be put in the position of climbing up and looking into the stall, not if she could help it.

The teacher stopped, eyed them both again, and said, *I'm sorry to drag this out. Eventually, Janey agreed to open the door, and there did seem to be blood on her face and her shirt, so Mrs. Androes walked her down to the nurse's office and packed her nose with cotton and had her lie down and then sponged her off a bit.*

Claudia started to respond, perhaps to ask if they were maybe overreacting, but the teacher put her hand up and went on, *Mrs. Androes seemed to feel that Janey had caused the nosebleed herself.* She paused to let this sink in. *Apparently,* she said, *a pen was found.*

Claudia said, *A pen?*

I apologize, the teacher said. *I don't mean to be too graphic about this, but there seemed to be little doubt that it had been up her nose.*

Claudia said, *You're kidding. That's so—*

Nobody knew what to say for a second. Then the teacher said, *I don't imagine she mentioned any of this.*

No, nothing, Claudia answered. She turned abruptly to Evan. He shook his head. Then he remembered that he *had* seen her come home in her sweats one afternoon recently—of course, at the time, he'd thought nothing of it.

It's hard to know what to make of it, the teacher said. *But even beyond an incident like this, she seems ill at ease. New girls often act that way at first, but with Janey it seems to be hanging on. We're never quite sure how she's going to react to anything. I don't think she knows, frankly. The other girls have started leaving a little space around her. Some of the girls. They don't much like people to be unpredictable at that age, I'm afraid.*

Or any age, Evan thought.

He watched the teacher slip a page of photocopying from the folder and hand it to Claudia. *Before I forget,* she said, *here's next week's assignment sheet. I'll send one of these home with her every Monday.* Claudia took it, folded it away without glancing at it.

Later, they walked back to the car in a misting rain. Evan sat with his hands in his lap a moment before reaching for the ignition.

Claudia said, *I just wonder where this is coming from, Evan.*

I'm not sure what to tell you, he said.

She turned toward him on the seat. She said, *I mean, I grew up with no father and a mother who worked constantly and I never felt all this estrangement, or whatever it is.*

Maybe it doesn't have anything to do with that, Evan said.

And the schoolwork, she said. *I never got away with skipping math assignments, either. Honestly, I don't get it.*

You liked *math,* Evan said.

Claudia said, *Come on, Evan. I'm serious.*

He stared out the spattered windshield a moment, then said, *I know. I'm with you. I'm just saying, she's not you, that's all.*

Claudia gave a frustrated sigh. She said, *Well, what should I— Should I confront her?*

Evan said, *Well, maybe not confront. But find a way to, you know, let her talk about it as if it were her idea.*

But it turned out that Claudia *wasn't* able to coax out Janey's side of the nosebleed story. She didn't deny it, she didn't admit it—she just acted as if Claudia was a little twisted, a little prurient for being interested in such a thing. The upshot was that Claudia began to consider the subject of counseling for Janey, and soon she located a therapist, said to be excellent, a woman of about fifty named Nancy Klaas. Janey submitted to a preliminary interview, then the therapist wrote up a short report, and agreed to see her twice a week on a trial basis. Evan had expected Janey to put up more of a fight. Instead, she went off to those first sessions in a state of dull-eyed obedience. Was it pure fatalism? Or had she succumbed to Claudia's cover story: that these dialogues weren't needed because she was damaged, but because, as is so often the case with bright or talented girls, her nature was full of twists and turns a third party could help her navigate? Or maybe she had reasons of her own.

One sodden afternoon, six weeks into the new regimen, Evan and Claudia met the therapist alone. The office was up a flight of stairs, a softly lit room with hanging textiles and the smell of cloves. *There's a problem we sometimes call the Basic Fault,* Nancy Klaas told them. She was unadorned—hair tucked behind her ears, plain blouse, cardigan buttoned only at the neck. But her eyes were intense and lucid, blue-gray, unsettling in their calm. *You see it often in midlife adults, this sense that there's something wrong at their core. You hear it described as a gnawing absence—they feel they've been let down or abandoned or failed by someone, but it's so embedded in their histories it seems to be a defect in themselves.*

Now in Janey's case —

Evan caught the slight stiffening of Claudia's spine, the beginnings of an objection. She said, *But you have to understand, she's been loved every step of the way.*

I don't doubt that, Nancy Klaas replied. Evan couldn't tell if she was only being diplomatic, or, he guessed, the term would be *nonjudgmental.*

Nancy went on, addressing them equally, *Perhaps you've had the dream in which you believe you've murdered someone. Of course, it's terrible. No matter what happens in the dream after that, this knowledge keeps caving in on you like a wall of sand. You're consumed by nausea. You keep thinking, But I never meant to kill anyone, how could this have happened? By now the event itself seems quite murky — you can't seem to grasp it at all. Maybe you're guilty, or maybe you've been framed. Oddly, though, it doesn't seem to matter which. You just feel a pervasive wrongness.*

Evan nodded. The therapist laced her white fingers together, focusing her gaze on him. He was convinced she saw straight through his poker face and knew how her words were resonating in him. He said, *It's like original sin.*

Nancy Klaas offered him her quiet smile. She said, *I've often thought the church drew on a very basic human fear.*

But here Claudia broke in, *And you think Janey's this way?*

I mention the dream by way of analogy, Nancy Klaas said. *The strength of what it invokes, and how cause and effect become tangled. As I said, this ordinarily comes to light in adults, but sometimes even children can —*

I'm sorry, Claudia said, *but I need to know if she's* ill.

Nancy Klaas said it wasn't up to her to make a clinical diagnosis. She repeated what she'd put in the report, that Janey should have a physical and be evaluated by an adolescent psychiatrist.

Claudia had already seen to the first part—except for a slight anemia, perhaps owing to her growth spurt, Janey's labs were fine. But the other remained to be done. *I mean, is this a case of her needing to be* on *something?* Claudia persisted.

Evan figured Nancy Klaas for the type to shun pill-pushing, but after a moment she said, *Sometimes it makes all the difference. We need to keep an open mind. For now, what we know is that Janey's troubled, and I think our sessions will be a good help. Already she seems less reluctant to take part. Perhaps you've noticed this?*

Yes, Claudia said.

It did seem that Janey had been coming here without any foot-dragging. At least, Evan thought, it didn't require the floppy white judo outfit and repeated falls to a dusty mat. As to what was talked about, he knew Claudia wanted to hang back and award Janey some privacy. She asked only in general terms how the appointments were going. Janey always said, blandly, they were going all right, but showed no interest in sharing the details. Later, when Claudia asked more pointedly, Janey simply stared back, then raised her fingers in front of her face and made a cryptic riffling motion (words floating downstream?) before turning and exiting. Evan saw how this refusal ate at Claudia, how it even seemed like another symptom, because, as she told him, Janey hadn't been one of those painfully secretive little girls. Evan had never had any luck keeping secrets from his own parents, but *wanting to* didn't strike him as deviant. What bothered him were these gestures of hers. If she was only being spontaneous and creative, then great. Unfortunately, they reminded him of the disconnected souls he sometimes saw riding the bus, hands signing away inscrutably.

A few weeks passed.

Now that daylight savings was finally back, Evan and Claudia often walked after supper. On one of those evenings, she stopped abruptly and grabbed up Evan's wrist and said, *If she were to really hurt herself, Evan. You know what I mean?*

They'd drawn alongside the pebbly retaining wall where they would watch the traffic on the sound—tugs, barges heaped with sawdust, flat-hulled container ships red-gold in the low sun. She said, *I can't believe I'm even* saying *these things.* Evan helped to boost her up and then they sat looking out. She said, *How crazy would it make me to know I hadn't been given all the information?*

Evan assured her that the therapist would warn them if there was the remotest chance of that.

She's not infallible, Claudia said.

Evan was still wondering how to respond when Claudia went on, *I feel like she's judging me. Nancy.*

I don't think she is, he said.

You don't see it, Claudia said, *but I feel like behind that serenity she has these scathing opinions of me.*

Evan nodded. There was no point in arguing with Claudia when she was like this. Even so, he said, *I'm telling you, I think you're inventing it. It's not her business to have scathing opinions. She must bend over backwards not to.*

Claudia said nothing. When she spoke again, she said, *I'm beginning to feel cut out of things, Evan. Excluded.*

You're just a little jealous, Evan answered, then regretted it.

Claudia glared at him. Sometimes he forgot her need not to possess unattractive qualities. *Whose side are you on?* she asked.

Everyone's, Evan said. How lame it sounded.

Claudia slid down from the wall and brushed off the seat of her slacks. She said, *You really think I'm jealous? Of the therapist? I don't* believe *that.* She opened her mouth to say more, but instead turned and started walking back toward the house, briskly. Evan let her go.

Later that night, getting ready for bed, Claudia said, *Things are getting away from me.*

The argument had gone out of her voice. Her eyes were red-rimmed, tired-looking. *That's not a great feeling,* Evan said. He meant it as a peace offering.

Claudia only nodded and went into the bathroom. Evan heard the water run. He waited, sitting on the bed. When she didn't come out right away, he kicked off his shoes and lay atop the spread. Usually, it was work that tired her, he thought. She went full bore, then collapsed. But that fatigue came with a shine of accomplishment. This was different—low-grade, constant. And, worse for someone with a mind like hers, it offered no reliable markers to tell her how well she was doing.

Evan woke suddenly. It seemed only a minute or two later, but the room was dark, and though the covers were disturbed on Claudia's half of the bed, she didn't seem to be in it. He propped himself on his elbows and called out in a scratchy whisper, cleared his throat and tried again. He poked the button that illuminated the face of his watch. Quarter to two. He thought, Now what?

He found her asleep on the sofa downstairs, a steno pad clasped to her chest, and a small mound of fresh butts in the ashtray. He studied her, then lowered himself onto the coffee table, leaned over, and lifted the hair away from her mouth. He wished he knew what she'd been writing, but the pad was face-down. He left it alone. Her face went so slack when she slept, he thought—it was as if she could detach whatever made her *her* and slip away with it. Just an illusion, but eerie. He looked around at the downstairs a moment. The house seemed intensely still. That too felt a little eerie, as if he were, somehow, seeing into a sealed, unoccupied room. He stretched up and switched off the floor lamp, then covered her loosely with the afghan, and went back upstairs.

Janey's custody arrangement called for her to spend eight weeks with her father over the summer. As the time drew closer, calls flew back and forth. Evan heard Claudia offering up various reasons why they might want to reconsider the plan. Was uprooting Janey again such a good idea? What about the counseling? But it became clear that Lucas had no intention of surrendering his rights. In fact, he'd thrown together a twenty-day father-daughter road trip. He'd rent an RV, pick up Janey, then head south through Oregon into the desert. Indian caves, stargazing, jet skis, and the like. When he returned to work, his parents would look after her, and she'd have a pack of cousins her age to hang out with.

Jet skis? Evan thought. Janey?

Going out of his way not to provoke Claudia seemed like an excellent idea at this point, Evan thought. But a few nights before Lucas was due, she took Evan aside and said, *Look, when he gets here, I can't have any pissing matches. OK?*

Evan and Lucas had yet to meet—it was inevitable, but Evan was dreading it. *Tell him,* he answered, *I don't have anything to prove.* Then regretted the flippant tone. Claudia was in no mood.

She gave him a look. *I'm telling you,* she said.

Luc's original plan had been to pick up Janey and head out immediately. But when he called again, Claudia told him she didn't like the sound of that—too much driving for one day. Furthermore, she wanted the four of them to eat a civilized supper together. That wasn't too much to ask, was it? He and Janey could leave first thing the next morning. Apparently, then, Lucas offered to take them out to dinner, but Claudia said, no, she was going to cook, they'd barbecue.

The afternoon Lucas was due, Evan watched Claudia fussing around the house, checking supplies she'd already checked, cutting more flowers. He finally told her to go for a walk.

No, I'm good, she said.

Evan said, *I know, but go for a walk anyway. I can hold down the fort.* She looked ready to keep insisting that she was perfectly calm. *Besides,* he went on, *I'm making a new rule: If you have cigarettes going in more than one room, you have to go outside for a while.*

When she returned, half an hour later, she had color in her cheeks. But the first thing she said was, *Watch, he'll be late. He'll make us all stand here and wait for him to make his appearance.* Evan pretended to turn her around and shoo her back outdoors. Then he held her for a few seconds and she relaxed against him. *I have to shower again,* she said finally.

Then shower, Evan told her.

As it turned out, Lucas appeared right on the stroke of six o'clock, as scheduled.

Evan strode down the walkway and shook his hand and welcomed him. *Evan,* Lucas said evenly. Not quite Evan's height, but trim and poised, ceding nothing. Seeing him, Evan wondered for a second how Claudia had ever broken free. As the two men stood figuring out who'd speak next, Janey came galloping toward them, keeping her face in check until it was pasted to her father's chest. *There's my girl,* he said, smoothing her hair.

Claudia waited on the steps, arms folded.

Earlier, thunderclouds had swept across the sound, and now there were swirls of grit in the air, and a second band of blue-black cloud was looming. The plan to eat outside was scrapped. Claudia asked Janey to set the table in the dining room while the grownups had a beer.

As Claudia and Luc made cheerless small talk, Evan studied his counterpart. Shirt with palm fronds and toucans, slacks, loafers with tassels. Sportswear, Evan thought. He tipped back his beer bottle and was surprised to find he'd already drained it. He was forced to admit the situation was somewhat odder than he'd anticipated, sitting opposite a man who'd slept with (not to mention impregnated) his wife. Evan had never been the insanely jealous type, but he couldn't shake the image of Claudia's white legs locked around Luc's. Actually, it was a more disturbing image than that: Evan was *present,* watching from beside the bed like a young boy, being told to get out, to *go,* he didn't belong there. But now Claudia was asking why the RV had to be such a big one. It looked top-heavy; how would it handle at highway speed? Lucas made no condescending comeback, simply shifted his weight in the chair and said it was a very stable unit, according to *Consumer Reports,* plus he'd driven one just like it before. The occasion called for composure so he was composed, that's what Evan saw. He, too, had decided not to rankle Claudia. He wouldn't refer to events from their marriage, or make Janey testify in front of her about the fun they'd have without her. Skillful performance, Evan thought.

Finally, Claudia excused herself and went to check on things in the kitchen.

Evan pointed his chin at Luc's beer, said, *Another?* Lucas said he was fine. In fear of silence, Evan asked if Lucas went to any ball games. Luc said now and then, when he could get away. *Giants or A's?* Evan asked. Lucas said he was more of an American League guy. Evan said, *A's are sure on a roll.* Luc nodded. He kept expecting Lucas to flash him a malignant smile and say, *Why don't you cut the bullshit, Evan.* But of course he didn't. He was a salesman, he could do this kind of work indefinitely, never breaking a sweat.

Luc spent the night in the motor home, parked in the turn-around. Evan heard the whir of its exhaust fan as he lay upstairs. The wind had finally died and the house was stuffy. The bathroom light clicked off, then Claudia crossed through the shadows—white tank top, thin cotton bottoms. She stood at the dormer window, looking down, one hand on the plaster.

Evan said, *Come to bed, huh?*

In a minute, she said. Evan waited a while but eventually dozed off.

In the morning, dressing, he heard Claudia going into her daughter's room—doling out last-minute instructions, he imagined. A little later, Janey thumped into the kitchen with her bags. Evan caught her eye and said, *Send me the silliest postcard you can find, OK?*

She produced a modest smile. Nancy Klaas had given her a journal to write in and the number of her answering service. *We'll be around if you need us,* Evan reminded her, but added, *Not that you will.* Janey stretched up and touched her cheek to his. Then they all went outside. Janey stowed her duffel and neon-pink backpack, pulled herself up into the RV's shotgun seat, and put on a game face. Lucas gave the tires and tie-downs a quick check (for his ex-wife's benefit, Evan assumed). Claudia watched, but said no more about the rig's roadworthiness. She waited until Luc was behind the wheel, went to his side of the vehicle, and said, *Make sure she calls me.* She circled back to Janey. *Well, you got a lovely day,* she said, and squeezed her daughter's hand where it curled over the rolled-down window.

She'll be fine, Evan said when they'd done waving and turned to go inside.

You believe that? Claudia asked him.

I wouldn't say it if I didn't, Evan lied.

Sleep on Beach

SHORTLY AFTER JANEY rode off with her father, the weather turned hot, and the rest of the summer no rain fell. Evan didn't say it aloud, but having time to themselves felt like a reprieve. They grilled most nights—burgers, salmon, teriyaki chicken on wooden skewers. They ate outside on the brick terrace he'd laid down along the row of cedars, as barn swallows looped and plummeted above the blackberries, feeding on the glitter of insects. Such sweet evenings. One night, he and Claudia met friends at a neighborhood pub called Varney's. Another, they carried lawn chairs to a grassy bowl where the city band played. A memory: Evan picking his way between the spread-out blankets, a lime Sno-Kone in either hand, *Fascinatin' Rhythm* segueing into *The Theme from Star Wars*. And Claudia, returning from a moment's reverie, scanning the audience—her hair like it used to be, black and straight, with bangs, her long white legs in culottes—catching sight of him, brightening.

One weekend they drove to the coast and slept on the beach up past Kalaloch. A moonless night, the stars like needle pricks, enough wind to keep the flies off and raise a roaring surf. They let the fire burn down, stretched out on the slippery nylon, and watched for satellites. Claudia finally put her head on his chest. She started to say something but broke off.

Evan waited a second, then muttered, *Hmmm?*

She said, *This is just very powerful, Ev, looking out into all that. You know? I'm sort of tongue-tied.*

Evan said it was that type of night. Later, when they'd zipped the bags together and slid inside, he told her about the Perseid meteor shower. *It's usually the first week of August,* he said. *We should come back. It needs to be good and dark like this.*

Claudia said, *God, that sounds lovely. Beyond lovely.*

Home again, Evan went so far as to double-check the date of the Perseid in an almanac, circled the days on the wall calendar, and wrote, *Sleep on Beach.* But then Claudia's work life changed dramatically. Suddenly, she was frantically busy.

Acropolis was launching a new product and it had to be presentable in time for the Las Vegas COMDEX trade show in November. The original delivery date had turned out to be overly optimistic. There'd been setbacks. The managing partners were now having fits. The testers were going round-the-clock, and everyone else was scrambling as if the fate of the company hinged on this one product (it wasn't precisely true but that didn't help much). By the start of August, Claudia wasn't getting home until nine or ten o'clock and Evan needed to help her decompress. He had a beer and a Cobb salad waiting for her; he listened to her reports from the war zone. They stayed up insanely late those nights, woke bleary the next morning, bumped around the kitchen as if it were exam week at college. Claudia seemed to be living on caffeine, power bars, and the execrable low-tar cigarettes she'd switched to. Evan plied her with vitamins and slices of orange, located missing shoes and car keys. As she blew through the kitchen, he slowed her down long enough for a kiss. After she was out the door, he stood rubbing his lips together, feeling the gloss she'd left on them, thinking that crazy as things were, he was happy. It was an adventure, this life of theirs — even if the meteor shower was out of the question now.

But as August deepened, the mood in the house began to turn. Lack of sleep was part of it, also the prospect of Janey's return, still a few weeks off. They were less patient with each other, less likely to overlook tiny screw-ups. When Evan pressed her, Claudia finally admitted it wasn't just that Acropolis was getting to her, she was worried also that Lucas would try to have the terms of Janey's custody reversed.

They were in the kitchen. Claudia leaned over and put her cigarette out under the faucet, a habit Evan found strangely disgusting. *What makes you think that?* he asked. *What's he said?*

It's nothing specific, she answered. *But I* know *him.*

Evan nodded. He said, *They don't just overturn these things without good cause.*

Claudia gave him back a flat stare.

What?

She said, *It's just, I'm sorry, Evan, but I don't think you really know a lot about this stuff.*

Even so, he answered.

You don't understand how things get used against you, she said. *His lawyer could make me out to be a workaholic. They could say I'm never home.*

Evan said. *You're* home. *It's just this push, it's temporary. Anyway, I'm here when you're not.*

Claudia shook her head. *It's not the same, Evan. There's a double standard about the mother. Everything can get twisted. And the other thing is you really don't know how Luc can be.*

I don't care, Evan told her. *The guy's not above reproach himself, I know that much.*

Claudia said, *He'll argue that Janey was a wreck when he got hold of her. Miserable, isolated, all the rest. That this isn't a good environment for her. I mean, it's ridiculous, but he can be very convincing when he needs to be.*

It was true, Evan thought—he wasn't experienced in these matters and didn't really know how justified her fears were.

Again, I know it's crazy, Claudia went on, *but he might try to implicate you in some way, Evan. He could claim you have an unhealthy influence on her. Or something worse.*

This stopped Evan cold. *Like sexual—?* he said. *You don't think that, do you?*

That Luc might accuse you?

No, Evan said sharply. *That I could ever do something like that.*

Claudia said of course not.

Evan stood mute. After a moment, he said, *Because not in a million years—*

Claudia said, *I know, Evan. Don't get weird on me.*

OK, all right, he said.

The thing is, she said, *it doesn't have to be true. He can just dirty the water with it.*

He wouldn't do that, Evan said.

She said, *You can't say whether he would or not.*

He'd be dirtying her, too, Evan said.

They looked at each other.

Claudia finally crossed the kitchen to the drawer that held the carton of Merits and pulled out a fresh pack and picked at the plastic with her thumbnail. *I don't think he'd stoop to that,* she said then. *I just don't want to have to go through it.*

Evan said, *You probably won't have to.*

But there was the flat stare again.

It troubled him that he couldn't comfort her any better than this. And he *did* see the odd position Claudia was in: If Janey came home in better shape, she'd be relieved, naturally. But if Lucas could take credit for it, Claudia could wind up with more reason to fear losing her.

Whenever Janey checked in by phone that summer, Evan heard Claudia's restraint, how she tried to listen patiently and not ask pointed questions. He heard how willful her cheery tone was. Janey must have, too. When Evan talked to Janey himself, he always signed off with something like: *OK, sweetheart, I'm not going to say have fun, I wouldn't want to pressure you or anything—* This gave her license to tease him back if she was in the mood, to say, for instance, that she knew how excellent a summer he and Claudia were having with her out of the picture. *Absolutely right,* Evan replied. *We're having the time of our lives.* He took this back-and-forth as a good sign—that she wasn't fiercely homesick or overwhelmed by the cousins or something less easily named. For her part, Claudia wasn't convinced they were getting the real story. *For all we know,* she complained to Evan, *Luc's hovering over her, monitoring every word.*

When Janey did arrive, only days before school began, she seemed no worse for wear. She'd gotten some sun and looked a little hardier, in Evan's opinion, less like a head growing on a long stem. Maybe it was the change of venue, maybe just the opening salvo of puberty. Claudia helped her unpack, and later, when Evan came up to see how they were doing, he noticed the new thicket of Plexiglas photo holders on her bedside table. The adoration of the father, he thought. He reminded himself not to take it personally. Janey was sprawled on the floor. Evan got her attention and said, *We were wondering if you'd like your room painted. You can pick the color. What do you say?* She shot a look up at the nearest wall, as if there were something wrong with it that she'd never noticed. Evan said, *It's completely up to you. But, you know, if you'd like it brighter or whatever.* Janey said she'd think about it. Evan let two weeks go by, then asked again. This time she just shrugged and said they could paint her room if they wanted to. Evan said, *Honey, it's not about pleasing us, that wasn't it at all.* Janey shrugged again. That was the end of it.

In truth, the summer had resolved nothing. They looked at Janey and didn't trust what they saw. She could act utterly normal, but at other times seem as if she had a permanent case of the spooks. Was the next episode a day away, or a month—or would she, as most people eventually did, acquire the knack of turning away from thoughts she couldn't bear? In any case, another school year was beginning. Claudia held her breath. Evan, too.

The rain started, the first frost came; they made the switch to Pacific Standard Time. By four-thirty, the afternoons were as dark as a root cellar. Acropolis had weathered the crisis of late summer, but already the make-or-break feeling had given way to anticlimax, and they were on to the next project. Janey continued to see Nancy Klaas that fall, every Thursday, or every second Thursday, and Claudia seemed to accept that the appointments would continue for the foreseeable future. Then, in October, Janey announced that the school was having a night of one-act plays, and that she'd already tried out and gotten a part. In fact, she was going to be in the upper-school production of *The Gallagher Girls*—someone Janey's age was needed for the part of Rosemary, the youngest of five sisters. Evan was astonished that she'd even *consider* acting, putting herself in front of people so blatantly. He was dying to know, as Claudia called it, her thought process, but knew enough not to ask. (His own acting career had come to an abrupt halt during his junior year, when he learned that no matter how religiously he worked on his lines, they could simply vanish when he stepped on stage.)

As rehearsals progressed, Evan prayed nothing would come along to mess things up, no bullying from the upper-school girls, no failure of nerve or act of God. The night of the show, Janey refused to eat but otherwise seemed composed. Evan and Claudia took seats far enough back in the theater that Janey wouldn't see them. Her costume consisted of black leggings, a T-shirt so oversized she could draw her arms inside it, and a thick application of black eyeliner, which gave her a somewhat haunted, wise-beyond-her-years look. Evan watched—more nervous than Claudia, if possible—but then found himself getting into the play as he realized that Janey was actually doing a good job. Backstage afterward, they avoided the mistake of praising her too lavishly—exactly the kind of thing that could set her off, phony parent talk. *All I could see was Rosemary,* Evan told her. *You were completely inside her.* Janey nodded, giving him a sly smile, as if, yes, he got it. This, too, seemed a cause for optimism.

Because of the rehearsal schedule, they'd agreed to switch the arrangement for the holidays—Janey would stay with Claudia and Evan for Thanksgiving, then have Christmas with Lucas. So, three weeks after the night of plays, they drove her to SeaTac and put her on the plane for San Francisco.

Claudia took a few vacation days before New Year's and then it was just the two of them again. A raw fog rolled in off the Sound, swallowing up headlights, adhering to exposed skin like wet plaster. He and Claudia had planned just to kick back and enjoy themselves as they had in early summer, but now the house began to feel kind of hollow, kind of cheerless.

Don't Be a Stranger

That winter, Evan gradually realized he wasn't feeling well again. He'd been denying the evidence for weeks. People often got sluggish in the off-season, he reasoned: less light, less activity, more starch in the diet. Except, paradoxically, his own sluggishness came with disconcerting spurts of electricity up the cords of the neck and a wandering mind. Actually, his thoughts didn't so much wander as behave like BBs in a wooden box.

You've got an awful short fuse these days, Claudia said. *I never know what's going to set you off.* Evan hated to admit it, but he *did* seem to be taking offense a lot, letting himself get worked up. Hurling commentary at the TV screen, for instance—not his usual brand of sarcasm but something less bemused, blacker, personally affronted. *That's the exact same moronic laugh track they used on the last show,* he said one night. *Can't you hear it?* Claudia said, *Ev, it's just television. Let it go.* Evan said, *No, c'mon, there's that same guy, that snorting? And then those two women with the high-pitched—*

But then there was the news on cable, the Gulf War. Evan found himself watching the coverage for hours at a time: Wolf Blitzer hunkered on a hotel balcony, the night sky erupting at his back, intercut with the grainy images coming from cameras mounted in the noses of missiles—streaking through the ether, a roof rushing up to meet it, the picture winking out. He knew he was being manipulated, shielded from the human carnage, yet here he was letting the spectacle suck him in, rooting for his side as if it were the Olympics. What had become of the peacenik part of himself? And why was it so hard to pin down what he really felt about this so-called war? *Evan, come to bed,* Claudia kept saying. *No, I need to see this,* he told her. If she'd forced him to say why, he might've answered: *You have to pay attention. It's history.* But she didn't ask. She went to bed without him—she had to get up early and go to work. A small thing, their different bedtimes. But how revealing it seems now: He was already wary of trying to sleep, already stalling longer each night. Eventually, he crawled in beside Claudia, ran his hand down her flank, and listened for the long pulls of breath that soothed him whenever he woke and wondered where he was (hearing her was like hearing a ship's engine far below decks). But he knew something had changed. Already a degree of intimacy had been sacrificed.

And later, in February, the war coverage *did* make him legitimately gut-sick. The Kuwaiti oil fields were on fire, as many as seven hundred wells. Immense roiling fireballs rising into opaque carbon-black clouds, easily witnessed by orbiting satellites. A vision of hell on earth. He didn't need to be there to smell the smell—it was millions of burning truck tires, the very antithesis of air. In the middle of the night, Evan found himself sobbing in front of the TV, feeling a desolation he couldn't begin to describe.

More and more, he seemed to take his ill humor out on Claudia. Finding fault, accusing her of treating him coldly, of giving him funny looks. He'd go back over these episodes afterward and not be able to figure out why he'd taken such umbrage. He remembered saying things like, *You wouldn't talk to me that way if you loved me — that tone of voice is inconsistent with love.* He thought: Inconsistent with love? Where was he getting this stuff? He *knew* she loved him; he *knew* he was being unfair. After the pleasure of the past summer, it was all hugely disorientating. Contrite, pissed at himself, yet trying to appear good-natured and low-key, he'd go and find her and say he was sorry. She accepted the apologies, but with a look that seemed to say: *If you're sorry, just don't do it anymore. This isn't rocket science, Ev.*

He knew he had to go back to the doctor. Every day, he told himself to call and every day he didn't. More weeks passed.

What finally got him to take action had nothing to do with self-discipline — it was the three obituary photos of men his own age, side by side in one morning's *Tribune*. He didn't believe in signs and portents, of course — nonetheless, a few days later, he was back in Dr. Bonney's exam room.

In the four years since Evan had seen him, the doctor had shed twenty or thirty pounds. His head was shaved and the jowls had shrunk. He looked more formidable, like a rock climber. Evan ran through the list of symptoms. The doctor listened, nodding as if he found none of this surprising. He said to be on the safe side they'd have Evan get another blood work-up, but in light of what he called *the recurrence*, Evan was probably going to need an antidepressant. Since Evan's last set of visits, he explained, a new generation of these drugs had come into being.

Evan said, *But I'm not depressed.*

Dr. Bonney was ready for him. *Well, two things, Evan,* he said. *First, that remains to be seen. And second, these drugs seem to work on both ends of the spectrum, the black hole kind of depression, as well as for people like you who are more, let's say, stirred up.*

Evan was no less leery of being medicated than he'd been the last time. He kept flashing on a drawing from an old *Psychology Today:* a man with the top of his skull hinged open, a second man, in a lab coat, cheerily scrambling the gray matter with a wire whisk. Not that Evan was a purist, exactly. Heart medicine he'd have been OK with, ulcer medicine, thyroid medicine. But this was his *brain.* He had *reservations.* He'd never taken LSD or mescaline for the same reason. It used to stun him, the abandon with which some of his peers ingested hits of whatever was making the rounds. *No, thank you.* In fact, a year before the party where Evan and Claudia had met, Evan had been at the same apartment one night when a kid came unglued from an unidentified psychedelic. Never before or since has Evan seen anyone so terrified. A tall, pale boy with girlish features. It turned out that nobody actually knew him; he'd just floated in from another apartment, or the street. They'd heard his monkey-like keening from inside the locked bathroom and finally had to splinter the doorjamb to get at him. They all worked at calming him, but each time he seemed close to the point of carrying on a rudimentary conversation, another gust of weirdness took him away. In the end, someone drove him to the emergency room. Evan never saw him again, but he didn't forget his eyes: grossly dilated, not caroming around like cartoon eyeballs, but fixed in a watery stare. You could sense, Evan thought, the exact second when he broke his connection with the room around him. It was like watching someone die.

On the other hand, Evan really did feel crappy. Barring a miracle, he'd need to keep coming back here, and it wouldn't take the doctor long to burn out on his resistance to medical advice.

I want you to think about this, Dr. Bonney said. He wrote out a new tranquilizer prescription, passed it across to Evan, and added, *Don't wait until it's completely cranked up before you take one of these. Let's see if we can keep it from getting to that point.*

You may do better if you take a small amount around the clock.

Evan nodded and tucked the paper away.

The doctor went on, *Go and have the lab work done, and when you come back we can make a plan.* He stood, moved a step closer to Evan. He said, *And the other thing is I'd really like you to hook up with a therapist. I could suggest a few people.*

Evan started to say he didn't put a lot of stock in that sort of thing, but it occurred to him that he hadn't felt like that about Janey's counseling. For a second, he pictured himself opposite Nancy Klaas in that room smelling of cloves. Talking and talking and talking. It gave him a dismal, trapped feeling.

Dr. Bonney filled out an appointment card for Evan, then plucked a second one from his shirt pocket and scratched a number on the back. *Here's the line that rings through to my office,* he said. *Use it if you need to. Leave a message and I'll call you. OK?*

Evan nodded again, heart racing.

Not long after this doctor visit, Lucas called to inform Claudia that—exactly as she'd feared—he was, quote unquote, revisiting the custody issue. That prick, Evan thought. The last thing Janey needed was to be whipsawed between parents. Evan told Claudia again what he'd said months earlier: They'd block any legal stunts her ex-husband tried. But this time he wasn't sure he believed it himself. The whole business with Janey had been unsettling. Trying to be proactive (one of Claudia's words), he asked around and got the name of an attorney who specialized in custody cases. Claudia sent off copies of the documentation, then she and Evan met him at his office.

The lawyer asked if there were new circumstances that might warrant a change in the agreement.

Here Evan was forced to watch Claudia's discomfort at having to characterize Janey's situation. *We've had her visiting a psychologist,* she said. *She seems to be having trouble adjusting to—*

Evan gave her a look of solidarity.

—growing up, I guess. The facts of life. A split-second later Claudia realized what she'd said, and blushed; she never blushed, even with the pale skin. *I don't mean those facts,* she said. *But it's like she hasn't accepted the basic—what it takes to be a capable person. I don't know if it's immaturity or something more sinister that's only beginning to come out.*

She consulted her lap, where she was slowly rotating her wedding ring, then added, *But I don't see how uprooting her again would help.*

The lawyer listened, jotting notes. He was in his fifties, Evan guessed. He had a blunt bald head, an air of scrappiness tempered by a patient gaze. *Your ex-husband's aware of this counseling?* he asked.

Claudia nodded. He waited for her to go on. She said, *He's in favor of it. But I'm sure he believes none of this would've happened if I hadn't ripped her away from him.*

The lawyer took this down. They talked a while longer, Evan adding his two cents' worth, and in the end, the lawyer promised to do the necessary follow-up, then assured them that based on what he could see now, they had no real cause for worry. But undercut this by adding, *Though you can always get a bum judge, if it comes to that. Which is why it's good to be prepared.*

Evan had hoped that tackling this business jointly would bolster their ailing sense of togetherness.

It didn't seem to.

In the meantime, Evan had made an effort to talk to Janey more candidly. Why not drop the façade, he'd thought, why not level with her? From the start, he'd wanted to avoid the sin of pretending to be a second father. Earlier, joking, he'd referred to himself as *an interested third party*, but Nancy Klaas had since taken over that role. In any case, what he had to say now was more intimate and came from a genuine bond between them.

As he and Janey drove across town one evening, Evan said, *I just wanted to tell you that you're not the only one facing some tough sledding.* He waited a second, checking the traffic. *You get what that means, tough sledding?*

Her response was too minimal to read, so he kept going, *Picture kids going downhill on sleds, whizzing along, good slippery snow under the runners. But one or two are going down the hill where patches of bare ground are showing through. Every time they hit one, they come to a dead stop. They have to pick up the sled and carry it to where the snow starts again.*

Evan stole a peek at her. *Ever been on a sled?* he asked. She shook her head. He said, *But it's not hard to picture, right?* She nodded. Evan went on, *Anyway, it's hard work carrying the sled and everybody gets ahead of you and you keep wondering why there isn't more snow where* you *happen to be.* It occurred to him now that Janey might actually *like* having bare ground slow her down, but that was too much to factor in.

He concentrated on his driving for a minute, then he said, *I was just thinking maybe you felt like you didn't have good snow sometimes. And I wanted to tell you that I've been hitting my own patches of dirt. I'm sure you must've noticed. That I haven't been my usual sweet-tempered self?* He heard the arch tone invading his voice; he wasn't deaf to it, just not good at shushing it. He looked over at Janey again. She seemed to say something. Evan went, *Hmm?*

A fraction louder, she said, *Yes, I noticed.*

Evan nodded. He cornered into the dry cleaner's lot and parked. *I'm not trying to scare you or anything,* he said. *Actually, just the opposite. I wanted you not to feel singled out.*

It looked as though she was about to say, *I don't,* but it would've been so nakedly untrue she only sucked the corner of her lip in, bit at it, and, abruptly, got out of the car.

OK, enough for now, Evan thought. He wasn't sure how much of it got through. She'd paid attention, more or less. She hadn't produced the furtive smirk that sometimes commandeered her face. Or the stricken look.

Soon, despite his apologies and good intentions, Evan was badgering Claudia again. He didn't recognize it as badgering—he thought he was only reacting to incidents Claudia had started, only setting the record straight. By now, he'd acquired an unquenchable thirst for defending himself—even against nonexistent threats. Sometimes, as if dodging desperation punches, she let his accusations fly past without landing. Other times, she faced him down. *You make me feel like I'm beside the point,* Evan heard himself complain one night. He'd trailed her upstairs after an earlier skirmish in the kitchen. Now she was trying to undress and stood by the closet door in a black slip. She turned sharply and said, *What's that supposed to* mean, *Evan? Tell me how I do that.*

Being reasonable, using her logic against him, he thought. *It's like you're not with me,* he said. *You're distancing your—*

No, she said, *you've got to give me an example.*

I don't know, he answered. *I mean, everything I say just bounces off. I can see you just waiting until I'm done talking so you can get on with your business. You're so* impervious.

She stared back. After a second she slid up the one strap she'd already lowered.

He said, *Unless it's Luc pushing your buttons. Boy, that you respond to.*

Claudia said, *But I have to take his threats seriously, Evan. You want me not to?*

It's not that, Evan said.

She said, *Well?*

How easily he lost his way in these sessions. Yet it's so plain in hindsight: He was scared of being sick and scared of losing Claudia a second time. She seemed to be building a safe room in herself where he wasn't allowed. In other words, *cutting him off, excluding him* — the exact thing she'd complained of herself with regard to Janey and her counselor. Unfortunately, neither of them quite saw this at the time.

Spring came early that year, followed by an early summer. Evan realized that, subconsciously, at least, he'd been counting on the hot weather to bring his cure with it. The days would lengthen, the rains would quit, he'd get out more. Whatever ailed him would begin to lose its grip. Hadn't it before? Thus, he was kind of shocked to look up and discover that the school year had dwindled away and it was June already. The season had turned, but he was no better. If anything, he felt lousier. He'd been deluding himself, hanging on for cavalry that wasn't coming.

Now his *medical situation* (how clumsily he referred to it) took center stage. If, earlier, he'd occasionally told Claudia that he felt out of it, rummy and jittery simultaneously (there were many ways of describing it, none quite accurate), now he gave it as the source of his crankiness, his altered behavior — for instance, the last-minute refusal to accompany her to a couple of work-related social gigs, or, just recently, to meet friends for drinks and pizza (the place was too damn bright, and pounding with techno-pop).

Claudia said, *Ev, if you don't feel well, maybe you should go to the doctor.*

I've been to the doctor, Evan said.

Claudia looked surprised, not happily. *Really? You didn't mention it.*

Evan shrugged as if it was nothing. Actually, by now he'd been several times.

Claudia said, *So what did he tell you?*

You know, he did a blood work-up and all that.

And?

The numbers were OK, basically, Evan said. *There was a possibility that my thyroid—* Why was he making this so difficult?

Claudia waited for him to keep going.

Evan said, *I think he thinks I'm becoming a nutcase.*

He's not the only one, she answered.

Evan checked her eyes to see what percentage of this was friendly banter. Not enough, he decided.

They were left staring back and forth.

If Claudia had said, gently, like his fondest ally in the world, *Don't hide things from me, Evan. We were going to put everything out there this time.* If she'd said, *Whatever it is, we'll cope with it, but you need to look at things straight on, you can't bullshit yourself,* who knows, the dam might've broken right then, the last sticks of his resistance might've snapped and washed away, he'd have wept and felt the vacancy that follows weeping and the calm resolve that follows that.

But even Claudia retreated from this moment. For all her scientific outlook, she wasn't keen on doctors herself. She had blind spots of her own. She dropped the last of the silverware into the dishwasher, thumped it shut, rinsed her fingers under the tap, and patted them against her jeans. Only then did she say, *He want you to take anything?*

Evan said, *I guess.*

Are you going to? she asked.

He gave her a tiny sideways nod, indicating that the jury was still out.

Over the following months he did try the drugs. *I feel like I'm being played at the wrong speed,* he reported to the doctor, marginally capable of humor. But he was horridly dry-mouthed—he could barely speak, the walls of his throat seemed to be sticking to each other. Not to mention logy, blunted. Was the idea to be *utterly incapable* of panic? He was told the side effects would moderate. They didn't. He was told a certain amount of trial and error was inevitable. He was switched to another drug, said to have a wonderful track record in Europe. He tried to be patient as the dosage was ramped up over three weeks, five weeks. This one he tolerated—but only because it didn't do much of anything. Dr. Bonney told him to take heart. The arsenal was full of other drugs. Evan failed to be reassured.

There was one piece of good news that spring: Since Lucas was scheming to have Janey live with him, he'd dropped his demand that she come for the whole summer this year, which raised the question of how they'd fill Janey's time while they were working. For once, a solution fell into their laps. Her school was offering a special summer session in language arts and theater. Technically, she was too young, but since she'd already performed once with the older girls, the Powers That Be agreed to waive the age rule.

Thank god for small favors, Evan thought.

Then June, July, August.

Just a mush of days to him now. Confusion, weariness with an edge, one minor disagreement blurring into the next, explanations and apologies going wrong. Doctor visits, long distracted afternoons at work, more and more nights of busted sleep and the frazzle of endlessly recycling thoughts.

Finally, toward the end of summer, Claudia approached him one evening after work and said, *Evan, I realize this is going to sound kind of abrupt—* He knew for a fact he was going to hate any statement beginning like that. Already his insides were clenching. She asked if he remembered Sue Sebastian. Evan tried to come up with a face, but she went on, *It's not important. The thing is, she's over in Hokkaido this year. She's had a college girl housesitting, but it's not working. This girl let the cat out and it got run over. She hasn't kept up with the watering and things are burnt to a crisp. Someone wrote her and now she's all in a flap. So I said I'd step in and see if I couldn't get things straightened out for her.*

Evan listened, nodding in the right spots, he thought.

And then it occurred to me that one solution would be for Janey and me to stay at the house. You have to believe me when I say this wasn't premeditated, Ev, but I started to think about it and it seemed to make a certain sense.

Evan stood expressionless, unsure exactly what she was telling him. All he could manage by way of a reply was to say he still loved her.

She stared back, finally giving her head a subdued shake, as if pitying him for playing his one card so brazenly. *Oh, Evan,* she said, *it's not that I don't love you.*

What then? he said.

I know you'll think I'm being heartless, Claudia answered, arms folded at her waist now. *But the thing is, I can't keep on like this, not under these conditions. You do see that? That I have to focus on Janey?*

A good plea could be made on his behalf, that he'd tame the outbursts and be an upstanding citizen of the house again. He also heard how damaged and supplicating he'd sound making it.

What he did instead was give in.

Once she saw that he wasn't going to put up a fight—at least just then—she softened a little. She said, *I'm not turning my back on you, Ev. Look at me.* She waited a moment, but he wouldn't look; the gesture of a petulant child, he later thought. She went on, *You understand? It's temporary, a trial—or not even a trial, more just a time-out.*

Yet she didn't say what would signal its end.

Only in the aftermath of this lopsided conversation did Evan understand what else she was saying—that she couldn't bear to be the only stable one among them, that there was only so much of her to go around, that she had her own fears.

Evan tried to smile. He wished he could simply cup his hands on the rise of her hips and draw her to him. Instead, he said, *You know, I'm not contagious, if that's what you're worried about.*

Claudia's look sharpened again immediately. *Evan,* she said, *I can't have her watching you unravel, OK? I didn't want to have to say this, but I mean it's too much. And, please, I wish you wouldn't commiserate with her. She's confused, she doesn't need your theories, your—*

Evan said, *My what?* She waved him off. He said, *No, finish it.*

She said, *Well, I mean you act like the two of you are in this exclusive club together. I just find that very* disturbing.

What did she tell you? he asked.

Claudia hesitated, then said, *No, I'm not dragging all that out.*

C'mon, Claudia, he said, *I need to know if I'm being misrepresented. All I was trying to do was let her know that—*

But Claudia's look stopped him. He was only digging himself in deeper. He shook his head and looked away.

After a second, he said, *No good deed goes unfuckingpunished.*

Evan, don't, please, Claudia said. *I can't stand it when you're this way.*

He sucked in a breath and began to say something in his defense, but instead excused himself and went outside and sat on the back steps and did nothing for a while. The air felt stagnant. The leaves stirred listlessly—it was like watching the last bit of motion before the whole yard became encased in amber.

Claudia finally spoke to him through the screen door, asking if he wanted anything to eat. Evan said to go ahead, he'd be in later. She said, *C'mon, honey. I've got sandwiches.*

Without turning around, Evan said, *Not hungry.*

There's a Rolling Rock, she said.

Evan closed his eyes. In a little while, he heard her foot on the floorboard as she turned to go.

The following Saturday, she accepted his offer to drive a couple of loads the eight miles to Sue's. She wasn't taking all that much. The place was fully stocked, after all—how would it look, she must've thought, if she fled with everything she owned? No, it was just clothes, essentials, things of Janey's.

When they were done carrying in, Evan lingered a moment. Claudia asked if he'd like coffee before he left.

Evan said he'd better go.

You're sure? she asked.

And here was his temper spiking again, here he was saying, *Don't suddenly act like you want me around.*

She said, *Evan, I was just trying to be —*

Evan said, *What,* pleasant? *Why do you keep making me feel like I'm misreading every situation?*

She looked at him across this new divide. She seemed ready to say she honestly couldn't be responsible for how he felt, and maybe, too, that his anger was truly scaring her now. But she only stared, her fingers against her cheek. Finally she called Janey in from the other room where she'd been peering at Sue Sebastian's miniature TV.

Honey, Evan's leaving now, she said.

Janey stood with one long leg crossed in front of the other. She and Evan regarded each other. Evan assumed the occasion had bludgeoned her into silence, but she burst out, *Don't be a stranger,* in a John Wayne voice — so goofy an utterance that her own face went dead-blank for an instant, then she sputtered out a single astonished *Hah.*

Evan looked back and forth between them. He said he'd do his best, turned and fled toward the car, keeping his pace steady and not looking back.

There was still plenty of daylight left. He drove, radio off, taking the long way. The Lombardy poplars riffled in the evening breeze. Already a few of the leaves had yellowed and come down and been turned to powder under tires.

Don't be a stranger, he thought.

That first night he disconnected the telephone. He stayed up watching TV, one thing after another. Cop movies, *The Honeymooners* in black and white, General Burgoyne's surrender at Saratoga. Toward morning, he woke in his clothes, roused himself enough to take a leak and undress and make it to the daybed in the other room. When he came to again, a dog was barking and a custardy light was seeping through the blinds. He'd been dreaming—he couldn't remember what about, except there'd been spoiled fruit or vegetables, or maybe meat, and he'd been trying to cover his nose and mouth against the smell. And now, for a second, it felt like his lungs had stopped working on their own, and if he didn't gulp air this instant, he'd lose consciousness. So he took in a gaping breath as if he'd been trapped underwater, then got to his feet, went through the kitchen and out onto the back porch where the air seemed fresh and abundant, and only then did the last layer of sleep fall away. No more of this, he thought. He had to keep it together; he had to take care of himself.

He plugged in the phone but resisted calling Claudia—to show he wasn't desperate, to see how long it would take *her* to call. Then it occurred to him that the answering machine still had the old message, in her voice: *Hi, you've reached Evan, Claudia, and Janey—* He couldn't face the task of looking for the instructions and trying to replace it, so he shut the thing off.

The third night the phone rang. He didn't pick up. Passivity had settled over him like a strange pollen. Eight or ten rings, then silence. He found himself tingling with the pleasure of being unreachable. Maybe twenty minutes passed before he thought, That's perverse. If she calls again, you answer. An hour and a half later, she did. He reminded himself how crucial it was to sound like his old self. And he tried, he honestly did, but immediately they were off on the wrong foot, Claudia saying, *Were you just sitting in there not answering before?* And Evan bristling, having to defend himself, asking why she always had to *accuse* him of something right off the bat. And so on, all downhill from there.

A few more days went by. This time Evan did the calling. He asked if she'd thought of anything they'd forgotten at the house. He said he'd noticed several jackets in the front closet and since it was getting colder he wondered. A pretty thin pretext, but it would have to do. *One of those is Janey's and she's outgrown it,* Claudia said neutrally. Evan said, *Well, I was just checking.* And here Claudia might have told him, *You don't need to be worrying about us, Evan, you've got enough on your plate as it is.* But instead she said, *I'm sure I'll think of things. I can just buzz over some night.*

Evan said, *OK, great.* Then added, *Why don't you call first if you're going to come?*

Claudia said, *So you can get the girls out.*

He had to remind himself that she didn't really think there'd be girls here. He said, *That's right.* But what he'd meant was he didn't want to be surprised, even by a good surprise. He said, *If I'm not here, leave a message.*

She said, *I thought you had the machine turned off.*

I'll get it working, Evan said.

So they'd started talking again. Over time this became less awkward. They checked in with each other, not as a daily ritual, but often. And, in a way, it was simpler not being in the same room, not having to figure out what to do with their bodies.

Even before the separation (though they weren't calling it that), Evan had begun to take work home. And sometimes he could actually work on it—in fact, working sometimes stabilized him.

But more and more the beleaguered observer in his mind stole away from the task at hand. *Don't mean to be alarmist,* it said, *but what if this never stops? What if this is the rest of your life?*

You hush, Evan whispered.

Some of the meetings he used to conduct face-to-face he now conducted via telephone. Others he set up for early afternoon. By midday, the morning's wallop of adrenaline had begun to abate. The toxic feeling was always worse in the morning—it was as if it had rested and could attack again fresh at daybreak. Sparks shot from a site in his groin and radiated to his extremities. His tissue felt like it was sizzling, down in the cells. *It's like being thrilled without the thrill,* he told the doctor once. There followed a few hours when he was alert and able to focus. But, later, the fatigue set in. And what a demanding fatigue it was, like driving a quavery ribbon of interstate in the baking sun, nodding off, recovering, nodding off. He'd wake with papers strewn at his feet, coffee soaking his lap, and even then sleep would come again for him. He shook himself, stood forcibly, fighting it as if it were something more—anesthesia, coma.

He was always behind now, needing to reschedule, to call in chits, go in the hole. Notes gathered on his desktop:

Sorry we missed you—

I have to report back to the Northstar guy, Ev, gimme a buzz.

Evan, I left a message for you on Tuesday, I'm wondering if you got it??

Last time, he'd made a valiant effort to keep anyone at work from knowing he was sick. He hated making excuses, another legacy from Donovan (and Patricia, for that matter), but he was starting to realize that flying under the radar wasn't an option now. In the back of his mind was the woman in the office who'd

tried to keep working through two rounds of noxious chemo-
therapy but couldn't in the end. They'd all donated sick days to
her, then she'd died anyway. Thirty-nine years old, as crappy a
situation as you'd ever want to see.

Evan wouldn't put himself in her league, he wasn't mortally ill
like that—but he wasn't right and was becoming less right by
the week. So why did it surprise him when Harry Glover called
him into his office one morning in October and the HR person
was already seated there, folder in her lap?

Go get better was the gist of this conversation. By this time, Evan
went back almost nine years with Harry, and if they weren't
chummy outside work, they got on well there; they'd had their
triumphs together. Harry was trying to do this without strong-
arming, trying to make it seem humane and mutual. Still, it
amounted to this: *Turn in your badge and pistol.*

So Evan went on leave.

He had almost forty days of sick time coming, and after that,
vacation. As a gesture of goodwill, the firm offered a token salary
to take effect once the benefits were exhausted, plus he could
stay on the health plan (no small thing). Don't sweat the money,
he told himself. True, the escrow for house payment and property tax and insurance was significant. But he'd live more simply now, his other expenses would drop, he'd skate by. The last
thing he needed was to roil himself up over bills.

He no longer routinely dropped by the house in Ballard or the
smithy and had begged off on enough recent invitations to
arouse Liz's suspicions. He hadn't discussed Claudia's reloca-
tion with them, but Liz had found out anyway. Evan tried to
make light of the new arrangement, to suggest it was only a matter of temporary logistics. He knew that wouldn't fly. He sensed
Liz's disappointment at the other end of the line. She said, *Don't
shut me out, Ev.* Evan said no, he wouldn't do that, it was just

a confusing time. Liz said to phone her, whenever. Evan said of course. But after he stopped working, more than two weeks passed before he felt up to having that conversation with her, and when he did call, he managed to reach his father instead. Perfect, he thought. Before Donovan could get onto the subject of Claudia—surely Liz had told him *something* was afoot—Evan went ahead and said he was taking some time off work.

Over the course of forty years, Donovan had lost maybe two dozen workdays to illness (and most of these had to do with passing kidney stones). The man didn't get sick. Needless to say, he attributed this to strength of character. All in all, Evan would've just as soon not have gotten into this stuff with his father, but since it seemed to be unavoidable, he said, *They're telling me I need to rest up for a little while.*

Donovan did him the courtesy of not saying, *From what?* After a slight hesitation, he simply asked if Evan was getting bona fide medical attention.

Evan said he was. In lieu of making his father pry, he added, *It's kind of a stress-related deal.*

Donovan made a little sound of assessment. *Well, stay on top of it,* he said.

I will, Evan said.

And look, his father said, *don't be a stranger, OK?*

And here Evan had to croak out a laugh.

What's funny? Donovan asked.

Evan said he'd explain it someday.

I mean it, Donovan went on, *I don't like to think of you turning into a hermit over there.*

Evan said he wasn't.

What about finances? Donovan asked then. *You set OK?*

Evan said he was doing all right; he'd let him know.

Mornings now, Evan walked, trying to burn off excess fuel. He couldn't *not* walk. Exercise blunted the discomfort some-what—while he was doing it and for an hour or two afterward. If he felt up to it, he detoured into the branch library or a café on Lomax Avenue, where he scanned the papers, losing himself in a crossword when he could summon the concentration, but often (unobtrusively, he hoped) just studied the other coffee drinkers before setting out again. It was amazing, he thought, how they treated the day as if it were a standard-issue Tuesday or Thursday, as if their supply of them were unlimited. Other mornings, he changed into sweats and ran along Madrona at a brisk trudge, then up Fenton to 206th and into a wooded park laced with running trails. Rhododendrons, evergreens dripping blue-gray moss. He went along through the shadows, counting his strides, a thousand left feet to the mile.

At home, he was tempted to flick on CNN but refused to be a man who had the TV on during the day. And, increasingly, he found himself needing to fend off the voices of the newscast-ers—they seemed too insistent, too stimulating, plus he was hav-ing a hard time deciding what concerned him and what didn't. He hauled a dresser out to the shed and sanded it painstakingly by hand, stained it, applied six coats of sealer. One day Liz came by with the Squeezo and a sack of Jonathans and they made applesauce. She asked if he was cooking for himself, if he was eating. Evan shrugged. His appetite had grown iffy. Unsweet-ened breakfast cereal was OK. Also black beans, raw carrots, dried fruits, dry bagels. Anything buttery or oily, though, and his stomach recoiled. Sometimes he got away with a potpie, but no canned soup—the beads of fat dotting the cold broth sickened him. Sometimes, on his walks, he'd pass downwind from the vent of a restaurant fan and have to veer away. It was unnerving—he'd always *loved* food, always eaten with gusto. Never had he faced the fact that appetite was an entity made by his brain and could therefore be unmade. Disturbing as this thought was, it led to worse ones. If the desire for food could be removed, so could the desire for sex. Desire *itself* could go by the wayside, that's what he came to see. It could just dribble away.

Ten units yesterday, seven today, five tomorrow.

He went nowhere without the plastic bottle of Xanax in his pocket now. It rattled like a noisemaker full of dried beans as he scampered up and down stairs. When he couldn't bear the turmoil in his body, the poisoned, rushing sensation, painlike but different, he'd snap off half a tablet and take it, then wait— it was never enough—take another half, and another if he had to, and so on. Xanax worked quickly: It wrapped him in gauze, slowed the inner whizzing, turned the ringing in his ears to the faint rustle of weeds. But it wore off quickly. He worried he was taking too much, he worried that his system would get used to it and it would stop working (*then* what?), he worried that he'd fly completely apart if he had to go without. Nor could he duck the horror stories people were eager to share—for example, some-body's first wife racked with convulsions when she tried to get off the stuff. But at least the irony wasn't entirely lost on him, how the tranquilizer made him anxious.

On better days, he tried connecting with friends. Of course, they still had jobs, and since he couldn't tolerate going out af-ter dark, he met them over lunch. In hindsight, he sees what a high-wire act those lunches were—his not wanting to look like a goldbrick, but at the same time not wanting to seem so dam-aged, so palpably loony that he scared these friends. Couldn't have been any picnic for them, either, he realizes. They were people he'd known for years, people he'd have gone to the mat for had the tables been turned. Still, he saw it in their faces, heard it in their overcautious words. They wanted to know, but didn't, or *couldn't,* maybe that was closer. *It's not like I'm worried about anything in particular,* he tried to explain. *I just feel* sick. *If I'm anxious, that's what I'm anxious about. When I start feeling better, then I'll feel better. And don't think I don't know how that sounds.*

Tactfully, they asked about Claudia, about his living arrangement, said this had to be an added strain. He tried to downplay it. If they persisted, he simply nodded and said Claudia had a situation going with Janey and left it at that. They asked what they could do. He knew they were sincere, but he didn't have a good answer. *Just stay in touch,* he said. He meant it. At the same time, he craved isolation; he wanted desperately not to be seen by anyone. They said of course, and, as Liz had, made him promise to call if he needed to, day or night. Then lunch would be over. They'd want to pick up the tab, but Evan couldn't stand to be the charity case—besides, he'd have barely touched his food.

Tiles

In her thin sleep, Maureen's fingers flex and twitch. It's as if she's still trying to type, Evan thinks. He'd will her into deeper water if he could, but all he can do is watch from the wicker-bottomed chair opposite the bed, thinking his thoughts.

Ten years he's been picking through the strewn tiles of his mosaic, trying to finger them into a semblance of order, wishing more of them had landed face up, and it's only now, in this dead time after Ned's departure, that he's at last able to place himself in the cellar. He's known all along that he went down there, known it logically. But this is different. Suddenly, tonight, he can *see* it.

He'd been trying to read in his office at home. After the holidays, a new year, 1992. Claudia had left behind a slew of magazines — he'd been paging through a two-year-old *Scientific American* but kept getting distracted by a sound coming from the cellar. Intermittent, like a bridge cable straining and relaxing. When he went down to check, it seemed to quit. He crept around in his moccasins, angling his head. He came upstairs, but before he could sit he heard it again. This time he walked outside and stared up at the roof where the power line hooked onto its brown insulator, then eyed the other two, telephone and cable. It was a dank day, not enough wind to make the wires sway and stretch, and though the trees around the house needed trimming, he now saw, none of their branches was scratching the shakes. He went back to the cellar and listened again. Was he making this up? Waiting, wondering what next, he found himself beside a rack of storage shelves with sealed boxes of Claudia's. OLD SWEATERS, one said. He let out a long breath, went and located a utility knife, then slit through the packing tape. Here was a raveling blue button-up she'd worn before they were married. He lifted it to his nose. The wool smelled tired, currylike, unless it was a remnant of patchouli.

Now, immediately, the next tile: The small steel box, lifted down from its high shelf, open on the workbench now, and next to it, the straggle of picture-frame wire that had secured the hasp. It's not the day of the gunshot, he understands, but a day or a week before.

He'd known about this box—where it was kept, what it held. Gluing the broken parts of something at the bench, he'd often glanced up, noticed it, looked away. He and Claudia had talked about disposing of it not long after she'd moved in, but nothing had been decided. So here, smoothed flat under the fluorescent tubes, is the blue T-shirt that reads MENLO PARK, 10K RUN, 1982, and, resting on it, the Ruger nine-millimeter. Brushed nickel with a walnut grip, slightly sweat-darkened from Claudia's palm.

He remembers bringing the barrel to his nose and sniffing (as he'd sniffed the sweater) and thinking the gun oil had a sweetish earthen smell, like wet shale.

What had he done after that?

Maybe lowered the muzzle to his mouth in harmless pantomime. *Click.* Or just turned the weapon over and over in his hand, feeling its heft, examining it in the detached but antsy way he examined everything then. Had a long look, re-swaddled it in its cloth, snapped the lid down, went upstairs to make coffee.

Not that he was supposed to drink coffee anymore.

Thinking of the coffee prohibition flips another tile: one of the last trips to Dr. Bonney's, Evan again perched on the paper-lined exam table, legs dangling, the doctor asking outright if he'd been having thoughts of suicide. Then a moment's staring contest between the two men.

You understand I have to ask this, Evan.

Evan replied, *No more than ever.* Not a good answer. He tried again. *Everybody thinks about it,* he said. *I don't see how you can avoid it, if you're at all aware.* Ruby Harker stuck her nose in again, Ruby and her thirst for natural gas. Evan told her to bug off. *But are they active thoughts?* he went on. *Is this something I crave myself? I don't think so. I've never been that way.*

The room had one strip of window along the ceiling—all Evan could see was the birch branches, shaking soundlessly in the slanting rain outside.

I've always been the opposite, he added. *Pretty scared of it.*

The doctor laid aside his clipboard and studied him. *Actually,* he said after a moment, *being afraid of it isn't as good a protection as you might think. People have been known to kill themselves to get rid of the fear, odd as it sounds.*

Evan stared back.

The doctor said, *This thing's a sonofabitch, Evan. I know I've told you all this before, but there's a very real mortality rate in cases not so different from yours. I know you don't want to hear it. And I know you're frustrated with the meds—to be honest, I thought we'd have more luck by now. I can't force you to keep working at it, but I don't know what more I can do otherwise.*

For the umpteenth time, Evan sees the defunct version of himself shaking his head at Dr. Bonney in futility. *I'm so worn down,* he said finally, barely audible.

The doctor nodded. *Can you try one more?* he asked.

Evan let his eyes close. He did that often now, the equivalent of pulling a blanket over his head. He had to remember how it looked to people on the outside.

He hauled himself back and said, *All right.*

And so he left the office with another slip of paper for the pharmacist, another barrage of instruction: *One capsule at breakfast for five days, then two capsules at breakfast for five days, then, if tolerated, add one capsule at supper for five days, then add one more capsule at supper.*

Not that he was eating breakfast.

Did he stop and have the scrip filled on the way home? Probably had momentum enough for that, he guesses. But the trips to the pharmacy run together; he can't be sure. And uncapping the bottle in the morning, tapping out a capsule, letting it slither down his throat—he can't quite remember that, either. Maybe he'd scraped together the bare minimum of positive thinking and begun again, then failed to carry through—exhausted, out of patience, concentration shot.

Maureen stirs, rolls a quarter-turn, brings her knees toward her chest. Half-smothered sounds come from her throat, dream talk Evan can't decipher.

When she's still again, he gets to his feet, stretches, takes a brief look out one of the dormers, then the other, then returns to Maureen. He foregoes the chair, folds himself down onto the strip of rug by the mattress, sitting cross-legged, a posture he could never manage in the old days but now finds effortless.

He thinks: Ten years of waiting out the disorder of memory, and the rest is about to come. It's all right there, everything previously held back, the tiles that finish the picture. All it needs is a little more quiet persistence.

Prophylaxis

NOW THAT TIME'S immaterial, now that sleep's unnecessary, Evan has acquired intimate knowledge of how a night passes. He knows without checking that it's just past one, still a period of comings and goings, of manmade noises and restive dogs. Ned's vehicle glides down the last section of roadway again and brakes in the gravel. Evan watches him walk to the front door and try the handle and jiggle it brusquely when it doesn't yield. Did the man honestly think she'd leave the house open? Ned hurries around and gives the back door a shake, stands blankly in the grass, finally casts a look at the neighbor's place, at the swaying fir limbs, as if tugging himself back into the here and now. He returns to the car, rests against the driver's door — he's like a teenage boy, Evan thinks, lounging beside his fresh wax job where the girls can see him.

Moments later, he flips out his cell phone. Inside, Maureen's phone trills. Evan has to shake his head — this new technology, signals zipping into space and back again, when Ned's close enough to the house to be using a juice can and waxed string.

He asks where she is.

Where do you think? she answers.

Upstairs?

She doesn't reply.

Go to the window, he says.

I'm not going to the window, Ned.

But then she's wrapping her body in the thin robe and carrying the phone to the dormer, hanging back from the screen enough to be invisible.

He says, *Maureen?*

She rests the handset against her chest, and when she lifts it again, her shoulder's wedged against the plaster and Evan hears no more of Ned's side of the conversation.

But all she has to do is not let him in.

Evan tries out the picture of Ned rushing the bolted door with a stone planter held aloft, something massive. Splintering wood, glass chips raining down, a film clip he half-remembers, was it *Body Heat?* The grand impassioned gesture that changes everything. Except brute force isn't Ned's weapon of choice.

All Maureen has to do is hang up. Evan's seen her do it, too. That first night Ned called, she cut him off straightaway. But she's worn down a little since then—no matter how she sounds on the surface, Ned's presence works on her whether she wants it to or not.

Maybe she's thinking, Not like this. I can't have it end like this.

She tosses the phone onto the bed, goes down the staircase barefoot. Soundlessly, she undoes the deadbolt, then returns to the second floor, and watches out the dormer again.

The cul-de-sac's last streetlight shoots Ned's shadow across the dried-out lawn, the knob of his head just reaching the barberry. She says nothing, only listens as Ned says, *Maureen? I know you're hearing me. I'm going to tell you something, I'm not going away.* In the short-term, he means. *Tonight* he's not going away, not until she lets him in.

She says, *It's open, Ned.*

Then Evan hears the man's weight on the porch boards and imagines the slight hesitation as Ned's fingers go for the handle again. A trick? But no, it's true, she's unlocked it.

Maureen turns away from the window, goes back to the bed, and sits on the edge of it, her legs crossed in front of her, her eyes fixed on the doorway. Then the footsteps in the upstairs hall where there's no longer a strip of Persian rug, no wall hanging to dampen the echo, and Ned reenters the bedroom with a hint of a swagger, hands crammed in the pockets of his pleated trousers.

Lord, you've got it dark in here, he says. Before stopping to touch her, he finds his way to her reading light, kneels, angles its tin shade up toward the wallpaper, and twists the switch.

Needs to see her, Evan thinks, needs the visual stimulation.

Wordlessly, deadpan, Ned reaches into the breast pocket of his shirt and plucks out three or four square foil packets and drops them onto the bedspread. But before Maureen can re-act, he fishes around and locates another couple in the same pocket, lets them fall. He tries a pants pocket and comes up with a pretty fair handful, then the other side, and darn if there aren't a few more. He dumps these onto the pile, pats himself down. OK, that's it, that's the last of them. But then he raises a finger in the air, *No, wait,* removes his billfold, digs out one final packet and flips it to the bed. Evan can't help but think of clowns pouring from a clown car.

Ned kneels again, rummages his hand among them as if they're gold doubloons. *You like the kind with ribs?* he asks. *Designed for mutual pleasure, special reservoir tip for extra security. And if I'm not mistaken, individually tested.*

Maureen says, *Jesus Christ, Ned,* trying to look anywhere else. But she's not immune to his tomfoolery, Evan can see. This cornucopia is so frankly sexual—she'd like to ignore it, but it seems to be getting to her.

For the second time tonight, Ned unbuttons his shirt, and this time it comes all the way off and drops noiselessly to the floor. He kneels and buries his face against Maureen's neck, breathes the shampoo smell, the gingery residue of scent that never entirely leaves her skin. He slides the kimono off one shoulder, then the other, and eases her onto her back.

Later, in the aftermath, Maureen says, *Don't fall asleep, Ned.* She waits a moment, pokes with her elbow.

Ned says, *I get so—*

I know you do, Maureen says. *But don't, OK?*

He rolls onto his side in order to see her, or let himself be seen, but Maureen is still on her back, gazing at the angled plaster. Her breasts pool and nearly vanish when she lies like this—a look the living Evan found ferociously erotic.

Well, I've got all night, he says.

No, you don't, Maureen answers.

C'mon, he says, *there's all these,* his fingers dallying with the foil packets again. *Give me ten minutes. I'll be good as new.*

No, she says.

Five then.

Maureen's a beat slow to respond. She says, *I'm done, Ned. You have to go.* Whatever trace of banter was in her voice, it's gone.

Ned says, *I've heard that kind of talk before.*

No answer.

You got a lease on this place? he asks after a while. *You planning on staying here?*

I was.

But now?

She says, *No, I am, Ned.* And here's that same irritation a similar question of Pamela's drew from her. *Nobody likes you to start a new life,* she says quietly.

What's that? Ned asks.

But she doesn't repeat it. Another little dead space.

You know, I wasn't kidding, Ned says. *I don't have to be any-where.*

By anywhere, of course, he means home. Ned puts a hand on her belly. *It's too hot,* she says.

Ned starts to say, *They're all up at—*

Maureen jerks out from under the hand. She says, *Don't tell me where they all are, for Christ's sake. I can't bear it.*

Ned offers a tiny shrug. This is all just postcoital petulance to him, it seems, par for the course. After a second, he swings his feet to the floor and goes off toward the bathroom, takes a long noisy leak—Evan can hear him clear over in the dormer. Then he comes back rubbing his upper body with a hand towel he's run under the tap. He stands gazing down at Maureen. She's made an X of her arms, blocking her chest.

Here, he says.

I don't want it, she answers.

He moves to wipe the skin of her belly, but she bats at the cloth. *Don't you listen?* she says.

You'll feel better, he says.

Nothing from Maureen.

You know what your trouble is, he says, sitting.

Maureen says, *The mystery is why I'm still having it.*

How you suffer.

He lifts the towel, squeezes out a few drops onto her legs, then lets it fall with a little thump to the carpet runner. He reaches for her free hand and brings it to his lips, to his cheek, where a light bristle has grown by now—it's another day, almost.

When he bends over her she averts her face. *Don't,* he says. *Let me see you.* He tries to straighten her jaw but those are strong muscles. He could apply more pressure, whatever it takes. Instead, he kisses the slope of her neck, then down along the collarbone, his weight sinking onto her again.

He says, *Your trouble is you make everything difficult. Everything's a fight. You waste so much time and energy.*

Maureen squirms, begins to shuck her way out from under him, but he keeps her there. She says, *I told you I'm too hot.*

Ned's hips move, a little bump, a little tease, so she can feel that he's restored. *Pretty decent stuff for a guy of fifty,* he doesn't have to say aloud.

Downstairs, earlier, she didn't want to hear about his missing her, didn't want to know how barren the time without her was, how he couldn't stand having his life reduced to ordinary circumstances. But here's the evidence of his body—she can't ignore it, can't refuse it. How could she think he'd give that up without a fight?

He cups a hand under her and lifts. A shudder rattles through Evan, a bolt of sick loathing.

There's the underside of Maureen's forearm where the skin is unfreckled, bone white in the semidark. It's up against Ned's throat, against his Adam's apple. He works it away, twisting, getting purchase on her.

Ned, she says. *I don't want it.*

But *he* does.

He lifts again, bears down, grinds his way in. And this time he won't be so boyishly trigger-happy; he'll show her his goddamn staying power.

And no condom this time, Evan thinks. He hears the caught breath and skin slap, sees the white of Maureen's leg as it lolls to one side like bleached wood jostled by the surf.

He flies at Ned.

Balls his hand, bangs the knuckles onto the bony ridge where skull meets neck, grabs at the slick musky-smelling shoulders, and heaves, balancing his weight in order to drive his shoe into the solar plexus or groin when he gets the man rolled off her, a fury that comes out of nowhere, the last thing in the world Ned would expect, an ungodly rush of noise, as if the air were ripping at a seam.

But no. Evan finds himself face-down on the floorboards, inert, varnish dust in his nostrils, his breathing confused, labored. It's all he can do to lift his head, to scrabble back on his haunches and get his bearings.

The only sound is coming from Ned, urgent and showy: *Uh, uh, uh, uhhhh, Christ*—

Then it's still again.

Maureen in Tears

S HE'S NOT THE KIND who's seized by passing wistfulness.
Working in health care, flanked by the doomed, the scared,
people waiting for news, she's toughened, or maybe it's how she
was raised in Dr. Keniston's house, to be not indifferent but a
half-step removed in order to keep a professional edge. Anyway,
there's been no sign of weepiness in her, even those nights she's
clearly most beside herself, most distrustful of her resolve. But
after the house has emptied of Ned a second time, she rushes
back through the upstairs hall in the half-dark, and before the
next mood can establish itself, her bare toes stub against the
end of an open door. They give an audible crack. It's the white
shot of pain that sets her off. She collapses to the landing, seizes
the foot, and all at once she's sobbing, moaning, gasping crudely
for air.

A minute later, without warning, she backhands her fist against
the row of white-painted spindles that support the railing. One
comes loose, dangles by a single finishing nail. She wrenches it
free and smacks the plaster wall, leaving a spidery depression.
Then she rights herself, strikes with it again. Two-handed, full-

force. Crumbles of undercoat rattle down behind the lath. Her arm draws back once more. Instinctively, Evan makes a grab for the club, but instead she lowers it—she's done, she casts it away. It bangs end over end down the steps.

Evan could show her the spot where he drove the doorknob through his office wall—it's been spackled over, but you can see the dimple if you know where to look. Or the chipped tiles in the kitchen, or the tight cluster of peen marks on his workbench. Mementos of the final half year. Never did violence to a fellow human but sometimes gave in to frustration and let the energy discharge. A few seconds of feeling cleaned out, beautifully vacant, then he'd see the mess, the jagged slivers of dinner plate, or notice he was still gripping the hammer, and flip it away as if it were contaminating his hand. He'd show Maureen if he could, he'd tell her he's been *right there*.

Now she's sitting on the stairs, a little below the landing, hunched over, the damaged toes gripped in her hand, as if squeezing them hard enough will trap the pain there. But they have to be throbbing to beat the band by now. This stupid body, she must be thinking. This unappeasable goddamn—

If not the avenging angel, Evan thinks, let him be the angel of mercy. One touch, one breath like spring water. But as Rilke said, *Every angel is terrifying*. Even the angel of sudden beauty. Even the angel who releases you from torment.

An Afternoon in Late February

$\mathbb{S}$O IT WAS AN AFTERNOON in late February, 1992, raining.

Or the rain had quit and everything was dripping. The eaves, the tips of the cedar branches, the water collecting in slow motion like clear sap, hanging, letting go. He'd been carrying the gun since morning, in his hand, or tucked in his waistband. He'd come to like its weight, the downward tug. If he laid it aside, he didn't feel right until he grabbed it up again. All day he'd had the sense of waiting for something. In the meantime, the house felt inert, like cold storage, like a meat locker.

He's not as clear about the morning, but it must have been like the other mornings then. Considering the rain, maybe he hadn't taken his walk or run. Unless it was absolutely pelting down, he usually didn't let that stop him—he'd be sweat-soaked any-way, what could it matter? But maybe it had looked too leaden and miserable out, and he couldn't summon the willpower, even knowing he'd feel less toxic later if he went. In any case, the only slice of the morning he'd really like back is the one that shows him in the cellar again: unsnapping the clasps of the metal box and this time bringing the gun upstairs.

Now he remembers sitting on the bed after lunch (not that he'd eaten), dialing Claudia's work number, and being told she'd stepped away from her desk. Would he like to leave a voice message? *Please,* he said. He was transferred and then he said, *Sweetheart, Claudia, this is Evan, I'd like it a lot if you'd call me, I'm here at the house—* He wanted to say more but paused so long he was afraid of how it would sound if he started talking again, so he set the phone back in its cradle.

What had he meant to say?

That he'd slid over a line, that he was having trouble with his thoughts? Did he intend to threaten: *If you don't X, then I'll Y?* If she didn't *what?* Come home this instant and nursemaid him? He didn't want to be nursed exactly; he didn't want to demand that she drop her other troubles in favor of his. But how obvious it is in hindsight that he'd needed help and failed to ask for it plainly. How simple it would've been to call back and insist: *No, you* have *to get her for me. I'm sorry, this can't wait.* How fatalistic he'd become. He'd turned acquiescence into a thing to be proud of. Not calling back showed that he finally understood a fundamental truth: Thinking you were mated to somebody was a delusion, just one more pathetic way of ignoring the fact you were solitary meat. What an insight that had seemed at the time, what a dazzling revelation.

Later he tried Liz. He remembers hearing the rings, picturing them radiating through the Ballard house like the squiggly sound waves in a comic book. *No one to home,* he said to himself. Another old expression of Patricia's. It seemed afflicted with significance.

When Liz didn't answer, he sat and did nothing for another half-hour. Then he rang Donovan at the iron shop and waited while they called him to the phone. The old man's voice eventually came on, the usual gruff but affable tone, as if to say, *Hey, let's do us some business—* Evan found himself unable to respond. Quickly, fumbling, he deadened the line.

I don't know what I planned on telling him, Evan says out loud, addressing Maureen (which is undoubtedly pointless—still, it's just the two of them here in the stairwell, where's the harm?). He goes on, *It's too bad I didn't push myself. Donovan would've been over in a flash. We hadn't talked since January, and I never called him at the forge, so if I'd managed to say anything at all, he'd have reacted.*

He was always grabbing the bull by the horns, Donovan.

Suddenly he wonders why it had been so important to resist Donovan all that time, and just as suddenly he's buffeted by love for his father. He'd always blamed Donovan for setting an impossible example, always taken him for one of those overbearing patriarchal types. But so what if Donovan had stamina to burn, so what if he wasn't crippled by the usual qualms and frailties? He was also gifted, ethical, not stingy with his time, and nowhere near as judgmental of Evan as Evan had given him credit for being. The one wisdom he'd tried to pass on was simple and irrefutable: *Be a stand-up guy.* If Evan had lived up to it, he wouldn't have lost Claudia the first time. No, Evan had given his father a bum rap. Donovan had turned out to be another of the nonexistent threats Evan was always trying to duck.

When Evan's up to talking again, he says, *It's seductive to think there was something special about that day. To try and dig out the one thing everything else hinged on.*

I'd had worse days, I know that much. There were days I felt so rotten I was sure I couldn't stand another half-hour. But then I'd stood it.

So here's what I think: If you're running around on bald tires, it doesn't take a special nail. In other words, the only different thing about that day is I stopped trying for a while.

He remembers pacing through the house, eyeing things, sometimes touching the tip of the gun to a hard surface, *tick, tick,* going room to room, restless, unsatisfied, his feet and hands prickling. Midafternoon, he was in the main bedroom upstairs when the phone rang. Claudia, he thought. Then, instantly, braced himself for it *not* to be her. But he was utterly unprepared to find himself talking to a guy selling auto glass. Did any of Evan's vehicles have cracked windshields? *Auto glass?* Evan said. Just some poor shill making cold calls, but the words seemed an impenetrable code. He was offering to cover the deductible, offering to come out to Evan's and make the repairs on site. All Evan could think to say was, *No, don't come here,* his urgency halting the man in his tracks.

Is this a bad time? he asked Evan.

Evan said, *A bad time?*

Here with Maureen, tugging on the chain of memory, he succumbs to a little gasp. It's perfectly ludicrous, his final conversation on Planet Earth!

He tells her, *Suppose I'd said,* Listen, if you're so incredibly interested, I'm three-quarters of an hour from swallowing my gun? *Except I wouldn't have. Even if I'd been that full of malice, I'd stopped trying to sound funny by then.*

Even the self-lacerating stuff. I was past it.

And I still don't think I knew what I was about to do. Not really. There was a good chance it could've gone the other way.

He sees himself getting off the phone, getting squared away, picking up the gun again, then gazing at the hollow it left in the pillow where he'd briefly rested it.

That was when he heard the crows. He went to the dormer window and saw a big gang of them out on the power line, hurling their *fuck you*s back and forth. With a certain affection, Donovan had always called them the Mafiosi. Evan remembers him skirmishing with Patricia over it once, Patricia recounting how she'd seen crows raid a robin's nest that spring—plucked the hatchlings out one by one, carried them to a flat roof nearby, and pecked them to death while the parents flapped around in abject hysteria. *That's how it is in the world*, would've been Donovan's comeback, to which Patricia probably said, *Don't be a pig, sweetheart.* Anyway, after the telephone call he heard the crows. Such lungs. At night, when he was trying his damnedest to sleep, the crows were off in their black dreams, but there was no shortage of other racket: trains sounding at each crossing, air transports lumbering overhead, downthrottling. The odd siren, the odd voice carrying across the neighborhood. Even the seventy-year-old house was unquiet when he'd have given his left nut for silence.

Gradually, Maureen's breathing has lost its urgency. Evan sees her let go of the stubbed toes and straighten up and look around, blinking, eyes obviously stinging. She swipes at them with the heel of her hand, absently dries it on her thigh, then squeezes the lids shut and tries with the back of her knuckle. Finally, still blinking, she puts her head down again, rests her cheek on her bent knees, but her eyes remain open a crack.

The light's no good in the stairwell. The sconce above the landing hasn't worked since the Fessendens left, and the overhead fixture has too small a bulb, which is furred with gray dust. Across her shoulders and down one arm, the rayon kimono gives a weak blue shine, but the rest of her is in shadow.

I'd love to know if I wrote anything that day, Evan says eventually. *I spent my life filling yellow tablets—I always thought if you wrote a thing down it would stay put long enough to see whether it was true or not. So if I'd decided about using the gun, it seems like I would've written something. An explanation.*

I was always trying to explain myself.

He sees his father and sister touring the scene, fingering his belongings. The flannel shirt on a chair back that Donovan couldn't refrain from lifting to his face and smelling. His wrist-watch. Sometime that afternoon, Evan had unfastened it and laid it on his dresser. No longer needed. Nowhere in their terse comments is there any suggestion of a final statement. Nor in Gayle's return, later, in how she tackled his closets and the deep drawers of his desk, paging through the tablets and date books and stapled-together pages of reading notes, and the marbled composition books, scanning them, but finally growing impatient, and dropping the lot noisily into a carton, as if to say, *No, I can't wade into those waters.*

He says, *Or to switch it around, if it's true I didn't write anything, that's all the more reason to think it was just a moment's—*

Just a failure to remain alive.

A minute or two passes.

He goes on, *For some reason, it seems brutally important that Claudia and I never divorced again.*

It was hard to know if we'd swing out just so far, then start swinging back. Circumstances could change. I could start to feel better, or Claudia could decide that being a single parent was too much for her, or she was sick of sleeping alone. Maybe she'd lose track of why it'd seemed so essential to pull away from me.

When we talked on the phone, a lot of it was devoted to Janey. Things were still up in the air with her. Her father had been making noise about taking Claudia to court to get the custody terms changed then finally went ahead with it, but everything seemed to happen in agonizing slow motion. Endless back and forth between the lawyers, skirmishes over who'd evaluate Janey, one postponement after another. But I think he liked that, her ex-husband, having it hang over Claudia's head indefinitely. Anyway, we talked about that. Then it began to seem like Claudia was screening what she told me. There was a new vagueness. Maybe she wanted to spare me, but it felt more like being taken off the case.

Before I went on leave, we talked about our jobs, and later we concentrated on hers. The Internet was just coming to people's attention, just on the verge of exploding. The company where Claudia worked had started out making software for PCs, but they were quick to see how they could shift their focus to the online culture. We talked about all that. I know it must seem strange—we're in the middle of a crisis and we deviate onto these mundane— But, you see, I'd always been her sounding board, she'd always talked through her work life with me. We were trying to hold on to that.

Then she asked if I'd been going to my doctor's appointments. I wanted to keep her up to speed, but somehow I couldn't. I just told her yes, I'd been going. Then she said, And the therapist?

I said I'd been to the therapist, too. What I didn't say was I'd quit going.

The first couple of sessions I'd thought, OK, this is good, I'm doing something. *Except I didn't like the guy. I knew he wasn't the right person, but I didn't trust my judgment. He was all full of that smooshy* "Let's listen to the Wisdom of the Body" *kind of talk. He didn't get me. He had no idea how silly he sounded to me. No sense of irony at all. If I made a joke, he did this delicate little thing with his lips, out of politeness.*

I should've stopped after the second week and scared up someone different, but instead I kept slogging away, fighting him, trying to prove I was right. And when I did stop, it seemed way too daunting to look for anyone else. I just couldn't face it. Though I really did need a good corner man by then, to keep me putting one foot in front of the other.

Evan checks on Maureen again. She hasn't moved. Still off in no man's land.

After a while, he says, *When Claudia and I had been apart maybe a month, we agreed to have supper together one night a week. It was always the three of us, always at their place, in homage to the proposition that we were still a family unit — and so that Janey could be a buffer between us, and Claudia between Janey and me.*

We had pasta salads or beans and rice, omelets, and peanut dishes, because Janey had recently announced that she no longer ate animal flesh. Claudia probably wanted to be sympathetic, but she'd always been a good carnivore, loved her mushroom burgers, her barbecue. This was going to be a problem. And there was the question of why Janey wasn't eating meat. It could've been a normal adolescent fling. On the other hand, maybe it was some horror about her own body. It could escalate — what if she got into bingeing and purging? She didn't have an ounce of extra weight to begin with. If Claudia had interrogated her on the subject, it happened when I wasn't around. All Janey said in my presence was she found the taste of meat repellent. You need to hear her saying it — meat might be vile, but the word repellent *was delicious.*

Each of these suppers, there came a time when Janey carted off a few of the plates, then escaped to her room. Claudia and I stayed at the table. I desperately wanted those minutes to last, but it was hard to sit still, physically, but also hard knowing that Claudia was there assessing me, even if she was trying to be subtle about it. There always came a point when I read her face, then heard myself say it was getting late, I needed to go, and then we were at the front door, hugging, saying good night.

One weekday morning she called and asked if I'd be home later. We'd given lip service to the idea of a conjugal visit — we even called it that, as if to show we could still laugh at ourselves. That morning hadn't been so good, but by the time Claudia arrived I was in somewhat better shape. She'd come straight from the office and had on her business clothes — she'd undone some buttons on the blouse so I could see there was nothing under it. She was always so direct about sex, never coy or anything, but here she was trying to be a little bad, a woman having a tryst. I was touched.

We didn't say much, we didn't discuss the bigger picture. We just came up the stairs. These stairs.

After we were done, she sat up. This would've been time for a cigarette—she used to take these monstrous, death-defying drags, arching her chest out for my benefit. But she'd quit. It was unbelievable. On top of everything else, she'd decided that when she moved to Sue's she wasn't going to smoke anymore—and apparently she was succeeding. Anyway, now she was quietly sitting up, her shoulders rolled over and her hands between her knees. I ran my thumb down the bumps of her backbone. The skin was already a little cool.

She said, Ev, you can be so much fun when you want to be.

I could've jumped all over that, I could have said, My God, you make it sound like I'm doing this on purpose. But I didn't. I knew if I said anything, we'd be right back in the thick of it. I held my tongue and tried to keep the moment alive.

Claudia said, You mind if I have a quick shower? As if the bathroom had stopped being hers. I said, Don't go yet.

She lay back with me without hesitation, I'll give her that. I knew she couldn't linger and I tried not to hang on too greedily. It was a nice few minutes, but then, quietly, she got up and went into the bathroom and ran the shower. I didn't want to move, I wanted to cover my head with the sheet and disappear. But I had to get up, I could feel the adrenaline surge building again. And I hated the idea of having her leave with me still in bed. So I got dressed, then she came from the bathroom, and I watched her take the missing bra and camisole from her purse and put them on.

We came downstairs, and at the front door I said, Thank you, Mr. Dewey. Next time you're in New York, just call me up, *which was Jane Fonda's line in* Barefoot in the Park. I'd said it to Clau-

dia during our first marriage. She didn't recognize it now. She just looked at me blankly—or worse, as if I couldn't be trusted to make sense anymore. Finally she got it and smiled in relief, even sort of laughed, but the damage had been done. So I just said, I'd love to do this again. Claudia leaned in until our foreheads touched. She said, We will, we will.

Upstairs now, there's another change of air pressure. The same unlatched door suddenly claps against its jamb again. Maureen flinches as if touched by dry ice.

Evan sighs. *I'd close it if I could,* he says.

Now that she's raised her head, she sits up the rest of the way. Her eyes are wider, more alert, but still crimped, fighting pain. She hugs her arms in front of her, and after a moment, begins to rock slightly.

There's so much I haven't told you, Evan says. *The whole question of Janey.*

I'd love to believe she made it through this.

Some kids get into their twenties and it's like they've been spit out of the whirlpool. I sometimes picture her on stage with a mike in her fist, doing a monologue or stand-up. Grown into her height finally, not as rickety-looking. Her father's eyes make her seem a bit exotic, and she's probably had laser surgery and gotten rid of the heavy lenses. She's going on about her childhood—how she outlasted it, how she prevailed. She's turned us into characters— Claudia, Lucas, and me. She has a canniness, a deadpan. People laugh. They've been there.

Then she gets to the part where she says: And on top of all that my stepfather put a bullet through his brain.

There's a collective gasp. Everyone assumes she's kidding. It's comedy, right? It's supposed to be over the top. She stalls a few beats, then goes on: We had the darnedest time getting the wall clean.

Finally had to nail up new sheetrock and everything. *She makes a face as if to say,* What a lot of work!

Then: We had to tidy the place up to sell it. *Another pause.* You didn't expect us to *live* there after that, did you? *Another face.*

People are laughing—it's very dark material, but that's what they think they like. Is there more? they wonder. No, she's ready to move on, but first she looks at them a certain way, just for an instant, and at least some of the audience understands that she was simply stating the facts. A chill scurries up their necks, just what she intended.

Evan stops, waits. It's not comic timing in his case.

The sins of the stepfather, he says finally.

You know, I think of the gross stuff men are capable of. Slipping into the daughter's bedroom at night. The bullying and shame that keeps everybody silent.

So I'm tempted to let myself off the hook—I think, See, much worse things could've happened to a girl her age.

Then I remember the sister of a guy who worked for my father when I was about seventeen. I didn't know her very well, but I probably had the first glimmer of love for her. Then, as my father so elegantly put it: She slit her fucking wrists in the bathtub. *Not a sight I saw with my own eyes, of course, but that didn't stop it from burrowing into me. For years, it was dormant, until there came a time when my immunity was worn down.*

The bottom line is I don't have the faintest idea what happened to Janey, but I do know that the last thing on earth she needed was having my example burrow into her.

How could I?

Evan pauses again, takes a few silent breaths, feeling the air's passage in and out of him. Keep going, he tells himself.

He says, *And there's the whole question of who got to the house first.*

You'd think that would be something I'd need to know right off the bat. All I can say is, I was numb. It was like staring out the car window when you're half asleep—just a blur going by, nothing that involves you. My senses came back first, and later the feeling of having an identity. But only gradually. It was summer before I could really think straight. Four months had passed. I know how strange this sounds, but by the time I was conscious enough to be shocked, I was already kind of used to being here.

Have you ever wakened from a dream and felt that big relief—Whew, just a dream! But then realized you're actually in another dream, only this one's a little less dreamlike? And maybe the same thing happens a few more times, and you keep being sure you're awake but you're not. That's how it was. What I'm trying to say is that the ethics of what I'd done, what it meant for other people—No, it's been a long, slow undertaking.

When I finally asked myself who found me, I thought if it was Liz, she at least had a vein of composure, a strong stomach. It seemed to matter enormously that it wasn't a complete stranger. I mean, the thought of someone standing over me, glaring down with contempt, or indifference— But I had no right to ask for it to be Liz. You forfeit things. Anyway, that's beside the point. It had to have been Claudia.

Maybe she heard my phone message and called back and didn't like the way the machine kept answering. She was too rational to heed her own intuition—even so, I think she knew something was going on. She probably considered getting hold of Liz or Donovan or the neighbor we left a key with, but I know she didn't. She wasn't a buck-passer. And I don't think she wanted anyone else coming in here and seeing the state of affairs and judging me, or us.

So she climbed into the car and tore ass down I-5, running through what she'd say when she got here, stamping down her fears. Still, she had to be scared.

Then she was trying the front door, pounding, scrabbling around in her purse for her own key, hurrying through the downstairs, calling out, peeking into the kitchen and office (this may have been the first time she saw the tinfoil coating its window, Evan thinks, and sees her pausing, gaping at it). He goes on, *Maybe she was trying to dredge up when we last talked—what day it was, what we said. Had she missed something? Had she become a person who didn't listen?*

And then she came upstairs.

Or maybe she didn't get my message until the next morning. So it was the next day and I'd had seventeen or eighteen more hours to—

He was going to say *congeal.* Right word, wrong sentiment.

A moment ago, he thought maybe he could roll through this part of the story if he simply kept talking. Not possible. He tips his head back against the plaster, feels the cold spot where his hair was thin.

He says, *I was spared seeing her walk into the room, but she wasn't spared finding me. There it is, the ultimate injustice. And not a thing I can do about it.*

Four in the Morning

Now it's been an hour since Ned disengaged himself from Maureen's bed the final time, since he stood dressing, tucking in, desire wrung from him, the swagger gone and with it his symptoms of aggravation. An hour since he loomed over the bed and said he'd call her. He had the house number, why didn't she tell him the other, too? The cell? He was back into his doctor's voice.

Close the front door this time, Maureen said by way of reply. *Make sure it locks.*

Ned returned a temperate smile. He'd procured the first number, how hard could the second be? He told her good night, told her, *Sweet dreams,* waiting just long enough to see what she'd give back, which was the smallest dip of her head, then he made for the hall.

As soon as she heard the car, Maureen was up, grabbing the blue robe, flying downstairs to see about the doors.

Then, returning, the toes.

Evan brushes her cheek with the backs of his fingers.

He says, *I remember a woman on the radio saying it was as if something had entered her room when she was only months old and pressed itself onto her like a coating of lead, and after that nothing delighted her, no song of her mother's, no bright toy. She'd already been stolen, she was already working for the enemy.*

Lincoln called it his black dog.

Mine was like poison shot directly into the vein. It came in surges that lasted hours or days, and when I couldn't bear it, I stepped on it with increasingly large amounts of tranquilizer. Not a good remedy, as you're aware. Not a long-term solution.

What I'm trying to say is that I never had that irresistible hunger for oblivion, not the way some people do. Mine was a surmountable despair.

I just didn't. Surmount it.

Maureen looks on without comprehension. Her cheeks are still flushed, damp-looking. A stale heat rises from her scalp. Evan makes a brief attempt to lay down the skewed hair at her temple.

He says, OK, *go up to the bathroom and find some Advil — unless you've got something stronger. Take three, all right? I'd say to use ice, too, but I don't think you'd do it, so at least take the Advil. You need to keep the swelling down. Not that you don't know this perfectly well.*

After that, go downstairs and make coffee. You're not going to sleep anyway, you might as well forge ahead. Now that it's a little cooler, hot coffee will probably taste good. I'd love to see you sitting on the back steps with a cup in your hands. I know a drink's the obvious choice — a few slugs of red wine, or what have you, but I think you should resist. It won't make you feel better, only duller — I know you'd debate this, but what you want is clarity.

It'll be light soon, you'll start hearing the foghorns.

It always struck me as funny: The stars would be out when I went to bed and the air would feel bone-dry—you couldn't walk around without things crackling underfoot. But by dawn, morning after morning, the sky was totally socked in. I'd hear the big army planes, the transports, I'd stand in the yard looking up and there'd be absolutely nothing to see. I'd just be tracking this disembodied roar across the bottom of the fog. And then I'd think of some crewman looking down at the top of it, not being able to see me either.

Anyway, try sitting outside.

It'll be hard not to keep thrashing that business upstairs back and forth, but just for now, don't make declarations about yourself, don't go off into revenge fantasies. I know this sounds vaguely impossible, but it's not. Watch the fog for a while, have your coffee.

Some moments later, crookedly, Maureen stands, extends the already-swollen toes over the stair tread, reaching to the wall for balance, her hand almost striking Evan. Not even glancing toward the upstairs bathroom, she starts down, leading with her heel. The staircase right-angles at the bottom, and there's the white spindle, one end blunted, chalky with plaster dust. She ignores it, but a few steps into the dining room she stops and backtracks, stoops, grabs it up, and carries it with her to the kitchen, not so much a cudgel now as debris retrieved from a crash site.

She flicks on the modest light over the stove, goes to the sink, runs the water, staring down. After a while, she cups her hands, bends and douses her face, kneads her eyes, doubles the hands again and drinks from them, then abruptly sticks her whole head under the faucet, letting the cold water cascade over her skull.

She comes up blinking, wild-eyed.

Then she's trying to dry off with the sleeve of the kimono, feeling about for a dishtowel, holding it to her face, saying quietly, *Jesus—*

When her arms drop, she finds herself looking at the remains of the tea she gave Ned eight hours ago. *It's just a glass,* Evan says. *Just melted ice.*

Maureen stares, adjusts the kimono where it blouses open, finally takes the tumbler between two fingers, hurries it to the trash like a used diaper, clomps the lid down, turns to look around as if someone might have caught her in the act.

Then she's dumping the last inch of the morning's coffee, swishing out the carafe, taking the folded-over bag from the freezer, and succumbing, even now, to her habit of taking a long sniff at its opened mouth.

It's heaven, isn't it? Evan says.

As the coffee maker sputters, Maureen stands, fingers on the chair back, lost in another stare. She shakes it off, scans the room, eventually locates her purse out by the computer, returns to the kitchen, roots around inside, removes the wallet, the oversized plastic comb she doesn't need, a couple of pens, a Blistex, finally upending the rest on the oilcloth, and there, after all, is the little bottle of generic ibuprofen. She tips out the contents, rust-brown oblongs, plucks up two, tucks them into her mouth, swallows dry.

When the coffee is done, the white cup filled, she stands over the strew on the table, eventually fingers out another pill, and washes it down with a tiny too-hot sip.

Evan nods. *Very good,* he says softly.

In a minute, Maureen goes to the window and teases back the twill curtain, peers out, and sees that it's getting to be first light. Sloppy term, Evan thinks. There's a thousand first lights, each with its own power. You stay up all night, you know these things. She can carry the coffee outside if she wants, and so she does, goes onto the porch, tests the air, sits, stretches out the bad foot, frowns at it, puts her freckled knees together, and rests the mug there.

Evan gives her a minute.

Then he comes and stands on the cement slab so they're eye-level again, turns briefly to look where she's looking, sees the crows. He smiles, thinks, Wise guys. Three black shapes on the power line, joined by a fourth, making the others sway and adjust their footing.

He says, *I know you don't have vacation coming, I know that's problematic, but I think you should tell them you're going to need a short leave without pay, if that's how it has to be. They might take a hard line, but I doubt they'll risk losing you.*

You were right not to finish that letter to your father earlier. It's like they say in the law, fruit of the poison tree. But now I think you need to go inside and try again. Tell him you'll fly out immediately, that you'd like to stay a couple of weeks. Tell him you're happy he suggested it because it's been too long. I know that's overstating it, but where's the harm?

So, you'll spend a little time in the ancestral sleeping grounds, then when you come back, the first thing will be to contact Ned. You'll tell him you've seen him for the last time. Regardless of how it was between the two of you in the past—and I don't doubt that he excited you, that it even felt promising for a good while. But you have to try for a better happiness.

Upstairs, I heard you tell him, It's not negotiable. *You sounded like you meant it, but you were still negotiating. When you get back from New York, though, you'll be done with that. You're going to tell him you've seen a lawyer and there's a restraining order with his name on it if he makes any effort to see you. No notes in the mail, no late-night calls, no bumping into you at Starbucks. Nothing. He'll think because he's gotten around you once, he can again and again, but that's not the case. You'll sound calm and resolute. You'll tell him you loved him, but loving him cost you too much. You'll say that period of your life is over. You don't need to go into it further.*

And, this is important, don't let yourself sound combative. He feeds off that.

After you make this call, you're going to feel vulnerable, riddled with misgivings. You'll find yourself wondering just how much venom he's capable of—would he stalk you, or something worse? It's not wrong to ask these things, it's entirely reasonable. But I think he has too much to lose. He's a status-quo guy—he doesn't admire that about himself, but it's true. You'll keep looking over your shoulder a while, but I don't think he'll be there. If he did try to test you again, he'd use what he always uses, the sex appeal, the air of authority, he'd trot out your history together—

He won't, though.

You thought you'd made a clean break when you came here, I know that. And now he comes and wears you down, he gets to you again. But here's what you should bear in mind about tonight: You weren't that far from pulling it off. You were most of the way. Next time you won't falter, understand?

He stops there. Maureen is watching the fog.

It's about this hour, Evan thinks, that his friend the cat used to show up. Riley II. If Evan were sitting where Maureen is now, Riley would join him, parading back and forth with his orange-ringed tail in the air, then flopping down to have his ears stroked, and finally rolling onto his back so Evan can access the lighter-tipped belly fur.

Where've you gotten to? Evan wonders.

It stings, the thought of going on alone. How's he supposed to break himself of checking the bushes or that shady strip along the foundation?

After a moment, Evan turns back to Maureen. He says, *Now here's the last thing. When you come back, find yourself another place to live. You shouldn't have to go to the trouble, I realize that. It's a pain in the ass. But listen to me: Be done with this house.*

He sidles into her line of sight again and says, *Get Pamela and some others to help you, OK? It won't take that long.*

And next time why don't you put something up on the walls, get some plants in the windows. The part of you that you had in storage was still in storage—you get that, don't you?

This was only a way station, a stopover.

He watches her.

A little agitation about her lips, that tapping of the front tooth. She tosses her head, the gesture of the long-haired woman, not as easily abandoned as the hair.

She gets to her feet then, limps inside. Evan follows. She refills the cup and proceeds to the dining room—it's washed with grayish light now, its few furnishings reappearing. She kneels on the computer chair, opens a fresh screen, arranges herself in a proper sitting posture, but more minutes go by. Except for reaching a few times toward the cup, her hands wait in her lap.

Then, all at once, she gives up and springs to her feet. Evan would worry, except it's clear something's given way in her, some barrier has just collapsed into kindling sticks. She goes straightaway to the cradle where her phone charges, then she's poking out a number from memory. In her haste, she gets it wrong and has to start over, her lips narrowed into a slow exhale.

She says, *Daddy? Are you up? Oh, of course. No, no, I'm—* She listens, nodding at the floorboards, free arm about her waist. She says, *Me? Oh, everything's—*

But she stops herself. Then says, *OK, you know what? I broke my fucking toe.*

Her face is shameless—really, it's nothing short of radiant. Evan barely recognizes her. But it tells him he was right earlier: Her true face has been under wraps. It's *this* one Ned can't shake, this amazing array of line and shadow.

She says, *No, no, just now, a little while ago. Oh, right, thank you, that's extremely helpful—*

She says, *No, just some Advil. Six hundred. Uh-huh.*

Evan would love to eavesdrop on this but listens only long enough to hear Maureen say she'd gotten her father's letter, she's been thinking about what he said, she agrees, yes, it's been far too long—

He heads outside.

The crows have flown. He can hear the smaller birds hidden among the cedars now. Finches, warblers. The fog inches past, hunching, breaking up. By eleven it will have burned off, noon at the latest.

Today will be another scorcher. Shimmer hovering above the sidewalks, the blacktop softening, maple leaves wilting and curling under. A general lassitude will take over, broken by the occasional motorcycle, the ice cream wagon's tinny incessant rendition of "The Entertainer," which at one time Evan found impossibly grating but no longer does. And then the slide into evening, the long northern twilight. A contrail or two etched into the Day-Glo sky, then darkness and the blinking wing lights of small planes.

He pictures her mattress bumping down the stairwell, that awkward turn at the bottom. Maureen in a black ball cap, cutoffs, the freckled legs, her toe not so hard to walk on by then. Pamela will have brought a six-pack. Later, as she collects the empties from the windowsills, Maureen will make a last walk-through, double-checking the barely used closets.

Then out the back door and into the rented panel truck.

A night or two later, she'll be back with cleaning supplies. Evan sees her swabbing floors, going after the shower stall with a stiff brush.

Toilets, sinks.

So the last he'll smell of her won't be the ginger lotion, after all, but bleach, antimicrobial cleanser.

But he has no time to dwell on this. A thought that's quietly been arranging itself within him now comes into the open: Maybe he *won't* be here.

If the cat, why not him?

Exactly the kind of question that used to throw his heart into a cataclysm of stutter-beats. Not now. The sick fear's been scoured out of him. What he does feel is a fine tingle up and down his limbs, as if he's all champagne bubbles, as if, suddenly, he's attuned to the network of imaginary particles making up Evan Molloy.

He finds himself remembering the night on the beach with Claudia, explaining an old star-watching trick of Patricia's: *Think of the round Earth, then imagine you're standing at the bottom of it, looking* down *into the field of stars. It takes a little getting used to. But sometimes what happens is, all at once, the sky becomes three-dimensional, it seems to yawn away in front of you.*

They'd gotten up off the sleeping bags and tried it. After a couple of minutes, Claudia told him she sort of got it, yeah. It wasn't an experience you could *sort of* have, though. Evan didn't point that out. He was encouraging; he said, *Don't think, just look, it feels like you're about to fall.* He said she could give it another go when they came back for the meteor shower.

But that's exactly how Evan feels at this moment—as if, with the slightest push off, he'd tumble into the sky, into the abyss of stars. And, strangely, it doesn't seem so terrifying.

He ponders this a moment.

The foghorns have begun sounding—he can make out two at least, different pitches, and possibly a third, farther off in the murk. He looks out over the blackberries. From down the hill comes the wan glow of a yard light on a wooden pole. The suggestion of tile roofs, madronas like pen and ink on a Chinese scroll.

Suddenly, tugged back to Riley again, he thinks: Cats may die of excess curiosity, but it's damn hard to picture one killing itself. So why was Riley here in the first place? Who'd punish a cat?

Maybe, he thinks, he's gotten this all *wrong*.

He has assumed that if he's been brought back by design, then its purpose was to *chasten* him, to rub his nose in the sight of a world going on without him—a milder punishment than, for instance, eternal damnation, but nonetheless, retribution.

The alternative was believing it to be a fluke of physics beyond explanation.

Those were the choices, *a* or *b*.

But it occurs to him there's a whole other viewpoint: That punishment is strictly a *human* construction, that if some intelligence has arranged for him to be here, it would take no delight in his anguish. In fact, how twisted it is to believe it *would*. More of that wrathful parent stuff. No, it strikes Evan as immensely more likely that he's simply been given another taste of the world. Muted, a step removed, but still, another dose of its shine and pungency.

It's as if he were being told: *That first time you left, you were so exhausted, so beaten up by fear and sickness. We thought you'd like to try it again.*

The screen door slaps and Maureen returns to the porch.

Evan breaks from his reverie and approaches, stands in front of her again, and just looks for a while. She's in jeans and a green cotton shirt now (how beautiful with her coloring). A sock on the left foot, the other bare. The glow from the phone call is still upon her, only now fading a little as she rests, scanning the sky.

From her coffee cup, a twist of steam.

Is there anything else he needs to say to her? Evan wonders. He guesses not. He guesses she's past the bad spot.

He lays his hands on the curve of her shoulders, bends, puts his lips against hers with a gentle pressure, holds them there long enough to feel their flicker of life.

ACKNOWLEDGMENTS

My thanks to all who helped with fact, reading, and handholding. Especially:

Hamilton Cain, Claire Davis, Jeffrey Funk (forge artist *extraordinaire*), Ed Harkness, Dennis Held, Rick Hodsdon, Joan Soderland Hommel, Michael Lowenthal, Marshall Noice, David Seal, and Valerie Shuman.

To my wonderful agent, Sally Wofford-Girand, and wonderful editor, Heidi Pitlor.

And to the incomparable Susan Schweinsberg Long, patron of the arts.

Special thanks to the Hawthornden International Retreat for Writers, where a draft of this book was written.